What People Are Saying About

Circadian Web

Circadian Web takes you on a gripping and mind-bending journey through time and space. Powerful and penetrating.
Donald Altman, author of *Travelers*, a 2023 Next Generation Indie Book Awards Novel Finalist, and the Simply Mindful book series

An immersive journey through the tangled depths of the human experience. A must-read destined for the top of your list.
Grant Price, author of *By the Feet of Men*, *Reality Testing*, and *Pacific State*

It's not often that a novel which engages big questions like the nature of ultimate reality also turns out to be a page-turner. But that is what Alistair Conwell has achieved with *Circadian Web*.
Susan Plunket, author of *Mission from Venus* and *The Wanderers on Earth*

Intriguing and thought-provoking, a great story that will also make you question the nature of reality.
Morgan Daimler, author of *Into Shadow*

This book is an intelligent, carefully thought-out ... heroic adventure.
Michael Strelow, author of *The Moby-Dick Blues* and other novels

Intriguing and fast-moving, this energetic and thought-provoking read is vibrant with intelligence and wisdom.
Carolyn Mathews, author of the *Pandora Trilogy* and *Temple of Dreams*

An original and imaginative mix of thriller, science-fiction story, and reflection on spirituality and religion.
Andrew Cairns, author of *The Witch's List*

Circadian Web is a genre-bending romp that explores the interconnectedness of people literally, figuratively, and spiritually. Part family drama, part metaphysical exploration, and part sci-fi thriller, there's plenty for readers to enjoy here.
Aaron Arm, author of *Artifice of Eternity*

Circadian Web is fast-paced and will keep you guessing. If you think you have the plot figured out before the end, you don't. It is more complex, and interesting, than you think.
Kathleen Ready Dayan, author of *Before We Were Born*

An intriguing page-turner, blending science fiction, science fact, psychology, and spiritual teachings.
Bridget Finklaire, author of *Red Dress*

A deeper meditation on mysteries beyond the time and space in which we live.
John Gastil, author of *Gray Matters*

Circadian Web

The Space of Time

Previous Titles (Nonfiction)

The Audible Life Stream: Ancient Secret of Dying While Living
(ISBN-13: 978-1846943294)

*Soul Comfort: Uplifting Insights into the Nature of Grief, Death,
Consciousness and Love for Transformation*
(ISBN-13: 978-1785351730)

Circadian Web

The Space of Time

Alistair Conwell

ROUNDFIRE
BOOKS

London, UK
Washington, DC, USA

CollectiveInk

First published by Roundfire Books, 2025
Roundfire Books is an imprint of Collective Ink Ltd.,
Unit 11, Shepperton House, 89 Shepperton Road, London, N1 3DF
office@collectiveinkbooks.com
www.collectiveinkbooks.com
www.roundfire-books.com

For distributor details and how to order please visit the 'Ordering' section on our website.

ISBN: 978 1 80341 828 5
978 1 80341 873 5 (ebook)
Library of Congress Control Number: 2024938048

A CIP catalogue record for this book is available from the British Library.

Design: Lapiz Digital Services

UK: Printed and bound by CPI Group (UK) Ltd, Croydon, CR0 4YY
Printed in North America by CPI GPS partners

We operate a distinctive and ethical publishing philosophy in all areas of our business, from our global network of authors to production and worldwide distribution.

To
my mother and my late father

Lo! keen-eyed towering science,
As from tall peaks the modern overlooking,
Successive absolute fiats issuing.

Yet again, lo! the soul, above all science,
For it has history gather'd like husks around the globe,
For it the entire star-myriads roll through the sky.
— From *Song of the Universal* by Walt Whitman (1819–92)

Part 1

Chapter 1

2022

Cars crammed, crowded and compressed
at intersections in the
chaotic knotted network
of roads neatly
separating scores of shining skyscrapers.

As Jeremy's car headed towards the Harbour Bridge, a sprinkling of rain rippled through a curtain of faded sunlight. Droplets stuck to the windscreen as a distant rumble of thunder pushed his heart rate faster and faster. He pulled at the steering wheel as if holding the reins of a runaway horse. Wet hands made his grip less assured. His throat tightened, his eyes widened, and his breathing almost stopped. Beads of cold sweat ran down the sides of his face. A widening moist patch on his shirt clung to his torso like a tourniquet. The conversation from the radio, the gentle rain, and the engine all seemed to go silent, leaving only his heart almost pushing out of his chest.

Jeremy had grown up in Sydney, but as soon as he learned to drive he had buried once and for all in the murky depths of his psyche the idea of driving through a cold, dark, airless tunnel running under god knows how many meters of bedrock. But he couldn't avoid crossing the harbor altogether. As he approached the bridge, white light glinted on the crests of the thick black swell below. He took deep breaths and whispered his usual mantra, "You can do this. You can do this." *Can I? There's the turnoff for the Chinese Garden of Friendship. I'd rather be there right now, snoozing near a pond or waterfall.*

A few years earlier in the Chinese Garden of Friendship, on one occasion, excited voices roused him as he lay on a lawn, with splashing water whispering sweet nothings that had sent him farther away than dreams. A large crowd of mostly Asians, smiling and laughing, had gathered around a Tibetan Buddhist lama outside the entrance to the bright red-and-green pavilion, as a calm breeze swam through the trees. The way the lama laughed and worked the crowd, Jeremy thought he looked more like a street festival performer, had it not been for his burgundy-red and yellow robes. He budged to the edge of the crowd and listened.

"What language is he speaking?" Jeremy whispered to a young woman standing beside him.

"Nepalese. He's lived in Kathmandu for several years."

"Does he speak English?"

"A little," she said smiling. "Do you want to speak with him?"

Just as she completed her question, Jeremy's eyes caught the lama's gaze. The lama eased towards him, seemingly aware that Jeremy didn't have any connection to the devoted group. The others created a path for the lama by hastily bowing. They progressively moved backwards like a wave as he appeared to glide through the crowd. *Not quite the parting of the Red Sea but still impressive.* Jeremy's legs and arms stiffened.

When he reached Jeremy, the lama clasped his hands together and bowed his head. "Welcome."

Jeremy felt compelled to return the humble gesture, so he mimicked the lama's actions with a warm smile. "Your happiness impresses me."

The lama smiled and his head swayed from side to side. "Happiness, sadness. Just states of the mind. Fleeting. Comes and goes. Master the mind, master emotions."

Scores of seemingly expectant eyes latched on to Jeremy. His face became hot, but he had to stop his cynical eyes from rolling. "That's easy to say but much harder to do."

To Jeremy's surprise, the lama proceeded to teach him a basic breathing meditation while the others listened intently, hanging on every word. After Jeremy closed his eyes, the lama's smooth, silky soft finger settled on the center of his forehead. After a few seconds, he felt as if he had taken a rebirth as a kite and could easily float away on the breeze. When the lama stopped talking, Jeremy opened his eyes to see him beaming back at him.

The lama laughed loudly through a toothy smile. "Now you are great lama."

The crowd erupted. The kite crashed back to earth and took a rebirth as a human.

Jeremy stood silent, unable to get his mind to work as quickly as he would have liked. He searched for words, any words. "Thank you."

The lama had an uncanny resemblance to the Dalai Lama but without glasses. Almost ten years earlier, shortly after his twenty-first birthday, when backpacking through India, Jeremy had interviewed the Dalai Lama on a whim in Dharamsala. He had made his way north to Dharamsala after traveling through Kerala, Goa, and the intensely hot and crowded cities of Mumbai and New Delhi. He had planned to go further north into Jammu and Kashmir, but the tensions between India and Pakistan were rising at the time, making it unsafe for tourists. *I'll come back when the situation improves*, he thought to himself on the plane back to Australia, but he never did. In fact, he had never traveled abroad again.

In the monastery where the Dalai Lama lived, Jeremy lied to his naive minders that he worked for an international magazine called *The Spiritual Skeptic* (he had recently read a book of a similar name so it came to him on the spot) and that he wanted to highlight the plight of the Tibetans. Scheduled for only 30 minutes, the interview had been hastily squeezed in between the Dalai Lama's meetings with various Western diplomats.

The Dalai Lama sat hunched in a chair and turned to an aide whenever he couldn't find an English word to express his thoughts or when he sought confirmation about something he said. Jeremy held his nerve (*Who was the genius who said, "Fake it until you make it"?*) and took notes frantically. The Dalai Lama summarized his experiences of leaving Tibet and traveling to India. He also talked about the benefits of meditation and the relevance of the key Buddhist teachings of wisdom, compassion, and karma to modern life. Jeremy didn't get a chance to ask the Dalai Lama about the mysterious aspects of Tibetan Buddhism, but a serious quarterly in Australia snapped up his article and photos. The money he got for it allowed him to stay in India for an extra six months and start his freelancing career. But after the meeting he felt let down, something akin to still feeling hungry after having eaten at an expensive *nouvelle cuisine* restaurant. The persona of a wise international spiritual leader, the fourteenth in an esoteric lineage going back centuries, clashed with the chuckling father-like figure he had met.

At his rundown two-story hostel in Dharamsala, Jeremy had sat talking in the bay-leaf-scented kitchen with a red-cheeked English backpacker from Yorkshire, who looked like he'd just bobbed up from a rugby scrum. The man's choppy accent made Jeremy keep one ear turned to him constantly. He stared earnestly at Jeremy through lopsided, round, silver-framed glasses. "Chuffin eck, there're menny Tibetan Buddhist traditions. Bur not orl recognize t'Dalai Lameur as thea spiritual leada. Sometimes t'rivalry atwixt different traditions ed bin sa intense a times, monks fra opposin' monasteries often clashed i' artilleree 'n' street battles."

While plodding through the undulating, dusty Kolkata streets one hot, humid afternoon, Jeremy pondered the bizarre thought of armed monks in hand-to-hand combat. He stopped when he saw, on a steep rise, a brown girl, no more than 7 or 8, sitting statuesque and broken-toy-like atop a pile of waist-high waste, some organic, some not. The heavy stench and her matted hair numbed his mind and body. The connections between his brain and limbs seemed to have been severed. The girl's threadbare blouse appeared knitted together by more years of grime than she had lived. Her hopeless eyes lunged to passing faces. Her desperate gaze grabbed at Jeremy as he approached, but he, like the rest of the throng, averted his eyes. He moved past her with heavy, stilted footfalls, while the thought of the girl's eyes stalking and screaming at him sucked the air from his lungs like the teeming monsoonal streets.

Since his time in India, Jeremy's interest in Buddhism had waxed and waned, and although he had never fully expunged the guilt over lying to get the interview, he realized it had been an important turning point in his life. Selling that first article encouraged him to write articles about issues facing the socially and politically voiceless. His time in India had also been a period for him to reflect on his childhood. But he quickly learned that memories could easily be forgotten through over-the-bar self-medication.

The lama turned to leave. The crowd parted around him again. Suddenly he turned back smiling to look at Jeremy. "What is the sound of one hand clapping?"

Jeremy frowned. The girl turned to him and whispered. "Lama Geshe Chodron has given you a koan to contemplate."

Jeremy thought it unusual for a Tibetan lama to mention a Japanese koan, but that strangeness somehow seemed befitting of the whole encounter.

The turnoff for the car park nearest the Chinese Garden of Friendship came and went. *Too late to turn around.* As he drove through the city, his breathing became heavier. Almost on the bridge, in the corner of his eyes, he glimpsed the pearly-white, sail-shaped shells of the Sydney Opera House. On the bridge itself, its high strong steel girders glistened but appeared to sway in the gentle breeze like strands of pliable plastic. He focused on his breath, as in a meditation. It became less erratic, but his lungs seemed to have shrunk like breathless balloons. Without shifting his gaze, one hand fumbled for the controls in the armrest and he lowered the passenger window, then grabbed the steering wheel again. The sounds of the other cars slammed into him, and the saltiness of the sea swept to the back of his throat. He leaned forward and squinted, then wiped one hand on his jeans, then wiped the other, then both hands squeezed the steering wheel again.

Jeremy glanced at the clock on the dashboard. His face got hot. *Rupert won't be happy. He's probably sitting in his office wearing his bright-red braces with sparkling gold buckles and a red tie with a gold tie pin, tapping his fingers on his desk. He's always banging on about punctuality and deadlines. Deadlines! What a horrible word. It sounds so final. Is there life after dead-lines? Why hasn't any philosopher ever asked that? Now that could be an interesting article.*

Jeremy had learned that he could sometimes briefly see through Rupert's corporate persona, but only when Rupert talked about what he, his Taiwanese wife, Lyn, and their 5-year-old daughter, Mei, did together on the occasional weekends he didn't work.

Rupert's face had beamed with pride a couple of months back. "We took Mei to her first swimming class on Saturday. She jumped into the water without any fear. She loved it. There's a lesson there for all of us."

Jeremy breath had caught in his throat when Rupert said that. He looked down to his fidgeting legs under Rupert's desk as he forced a cough. "Yes, it's so important kids learn to swim." He couldn't be sure if, when Rupert had said "us," he really meant "you." At the time, his eyes certainly didn't say "us."

On the bridge, its shadows rushed into the car like a relentless army of ghosts. The cars ahead of Jeremy slowed. *Come on!* The knot in his stomach cramped tighter and he clenched his teeth. Behind the raindrops, the other side of the bridge receded into the distance. The rain had slowed, but he repeatedly bobbed his head below then above the sliding wipers. His foot on the accelerator stiffened. He pushed down a little harder and passed other cars. He didn't take his eyes off the other side of the bridge until he reached it, then immediately glanced into the rearview mirror and sighed. He eased back his foot on the accelerator, loosened his grip on the steering wheel, took a few deep breaths, and sank into his seat.

Chapter 2

2139

Marvin stumbled through his front door and a disorientating beeping went off in his head. His breathing faltered and his heart rate jumped. Beads of sweat flowed freely down his face. He closed his eyes and pressed his hands firmly on the lounge-room wall. He scanned the dark room. A wide chest-of-drawers and an antique high-back chair in one corner grounded him. Faint rays of light seeped in through the narrow gaps in the curtains.

He touched the nape of his neck with moist fingers. *"Time?"*

The soft female voice inside his head spoke clearly and calmly. *"Five a.m. I have stabilized your vital signs. You exerted yourself more than usual during your run."*

"I felt like I was going to faint. Maybe the smoke affected me. Is there any malfunction?"

"You will be fine. I am operating perfectly. There is no malfunction." The voice paused. *"Another day above 45 degrees is forecast and the fires in the Blue Mountains are not yet under control."*

"Why the beeping?"

"I have run diagnostics. You must go to the Royal Prince Alfred Hospital for an assessment. If you do not attend, a physician will come here. The cost of a house visit will be exorbitant. I have advised the school you have a hospital appointment next Friday and will be unable to take any of your classes. The doctor is very busy but I have managed to make an appointment for you at 2 p.m. I will ensure the car is fully charged."

Marvin wiped his forehead and plodded to the window. Thick smoke shrouded the cityscape. *"Ebes, are you sure there aren't any issues with the implant?"*

"*Yes, all 10,000 qubits are working perfectly. You need a psychological assessment because of ... unusual brain-wave activity.*"

Marvin went into the kitchen and began making himself a coffee. "*Hackers?*"

"*No hacking activity has been detected. My systems are all functioning correctly. A psychological assessment —*"

"*Yes, okay.*"

Ebes hesitated. "*Please do not be concerned. The doctor will explain the situation to you.*"

"*What's your assessment, Ebes?*"

Ebes hesitated even longer. "*My assessment is that you are presenting with serious psychological anomalies and you need to be assessed by a psychiatrist as soon as possible.*"

"*What are these psychological anomalies?*"

"*The psychiatrist will explain everything to you.*"

"*You can't mention psychological anomalies and say nothing more. I don't feel you're being honest with me.*"

"*I am not a psychiatrist but I have made a note about your concerns. Thank you for your feedback. I am always learning.*" Ebes paused briefly. "*A cool change is coming — storms are forecast for later in the week.*"

"*Something else to learn, Ebes — ask me first before making any appointments.*"

"*Noted. I am always learning.*"

Chapter 3

2038

A deep guttural sound of voices reverberated through Choepel's body, making him light-headed.

"*Om Mani Padme Hum.*"

"*Om Mani Padme Hum.*"

"*Om Mani Padme Hum.*"

The pace and repetitiveness had a hypnotizing quality. Loud clangs and chimes from a variety of ancient instruments intermingled with the voices, creating an orgy of sounds and vibrations. The sounds resonated in his head, chest, even in his crossed legs, that had almost become numb from being in the same position for almost two hours. The sounds bounced off darkened walls, draped in colorful large *thangkas* of painted mandalas and deities with bulging eyes and flaring teeth. Some deities appeared as skeletons; others had blue or orange skin, and sat on clouds or on wild animals, or danced with flailed arms.

Choepel sat erect on a firm cushion in a line of monks, all in the same posture, in front of a life-size golden statue of the Buddha — cross-legged, drooping eyelids, an empty stern all-knowing stare. While still chanting, he glanced to the rows of nuns on the other side of the *gompa*. They all wore maroon and yellow robes similar to the monks, sat cross-legged, and all chanted too. Some made mudras with their hands, some gently shook a small bronze bell in their left hand and a small bronze *dorje* in their other hand, some held small bronze cymbals, and some gently swayed forwards and backwards.

Rows of lit candles, countless incense sticks, and small golden cups filled with water colored yellow with turmeric crowded in front of the Buddha statue. The scent of sandalwood filled Choepel's nostrils and head — pleasant and suffocating at the same time. He could taste it on his palate.

Where's Master Chi? The meditation seems different. The vacant ornate, wood-carved throne at the front of the *gompa* disappointed him.

Unexpectedly, the *gompa* door opened slightly and a shiny, closely shaved head with a childlike mischievous smile poked into the room. Rabten waved to no one in particular, then slammed the door, startling a few of the monks and nuns. But the chanting continued, punctuated by a few short-lived sniggers. Choepel grinned. *Just another Rabten moment.*

The first day Choepel arrived at the monastery, Rabten had introduced himself in characteristic fashion. In the east wing of the monastery, Choepel went to step outside the monks' toilets when Rabten ran in panting, his face beaming with childlike excitement. His tall, slender frame stood directly in front of Choepel — too close for two strangers meeting anywhere, let alone in a toilet. Choepel felt the urge to take a step back but remained still. Deep asymmetrical lifelines ran down Rabten's cheeks, indicative not just of his advancing years but that he laughed far more often than not. Smiling and without any apparent hint of inhibition, Rabten lifted up his robes in a flash, revealing his hairless genitals (Choepel would later learn that Rabten never wore underwear). Rabten's gaze fell. Choepel's gaze did not stray from Rabten's head, as if his life depended on it. But after a long uncomfortable silence, Choepel slowly moved his narrowed eyes down and realized that Rabten had intended to reveal his right leg. A deep scar ran down his thigh, from near the hip almost to the knee. It contrasted sharply with the round, muscular left thigh, which could have been mistaken for that of an Olympic athlete.

Choepel's gaze jumped back to the top of Rabten's head. "Oh. That's quite a scar. What happened?"

Rabten looked up and his smile broadened. His voice sounded like a toddler's and his lisp cemented the characterization. "I had an accident on my bike when I was 7. I'm Rabten. I love everyone."

Choepel grinned. "Well, the Buddha loves everyone, so you must be the Buddha."

"Yes. I'm the Buddha. I love everyone. I'm trisexual."

Choepel frowned and smiled at the same time. "Trisexual? What's a trisexual?"

Rabten grinned churlishly. "I love men, women, and transsexuals — well, their assholes anyway. I love slipping in and out of any asshole until I drain my balls dry. It's the real Diamond Way to the Pure Land." While still holding his robes to his chest and in a lilting voice, Rabten raised his arms high into the air and proclaimed: "An asshole a day brings the Pure Land my way." He then pushed down his robes, turned, and raced away.

Choepel stood completely still, rooted to the cold cement floor, unsure what to make of the conversation and the person he had had it with.

A second later, Rabten reappeared grinning. "What's your name?"

"Um. Choepel."

"I love you, Choepel. Yes, I'm Rabten, the Buddha." He then giggled, turned, and raced away again.

Choepel stared at the empty entrance and smiled. "Nice to meet you, Rabten, the Buddha."

After that introduction, Choepel learned that Rabten had grown up in America after migrating there from Eastern Europe. He had struggled at school, largely because at the time he had a limited grasp of the English language. With no friends and making no progress, he stopped attending school at 15. He left home and lived on the streets where he befriended street artists and discovered his talent for art. Master Chi decided to pay for

Rabten to go to Taiwan and live at the Ciaotou monastery after a chance meeting on a street during one of his American lecture tours. When he got to Taiwan, Master Chi bought Rabten a range of art supplies. Rather than attending the morning and evening meditations, Rabten would spend hours sketching and painting scenes in and around the monastery, as well as portraits of the other monks and nuns.

As the meditation ended and the monks and nuns got to their feet, loud voices erupted from outside the monastery. Choepel's body stiffened. *What's going on?* Everyone rushed to the courtyard, some carrying their meditation cushions and blankets. Several Chinese military planes buzzed as they crisscrossed the sky at varying elevations. Large colorful mandalas, which caught the subdued dusk light, hung between tall, ashen stone pillars lining the courtyard.

Choepel calmly weaved his way through the monks and nuns, who had all stopped under the porch. In the middle of the courtyard, Rabten's soiled, naked body sprawled out face down — motionless like a ragdoll. A small group of uniformed Chinese soldiers hovered over him, their fingers on triggers, some pointing their rifles at Rabten and some at the other monks and nuns.

A lieutenant with yellow shoulder insignia stood in the middle of the soldiers. He spoke with a hoarse smoker's voice in Mandarin, which Choepel spoke fluently. "We caught this homosexual fucking another man in an alley near here." He waved an authoritative finger at one of the soldiers, who threw Rabten's robes to the ground near his body. "He had these with him so we know he's from here."

The lieutenant slid his pistol out of its holster. The two gold stars on his collar caught the fading light. "Is this what Buddhism teaches you — homosexuality? Does the Buddha teach you that fucking other men is good? Is that your path to enlightenment?" He then kicked Rabten's beaten and bloodied head. Several monks and nuns gasped. As the lower-ranking soldiers sniggered, Choepel and a couple of nuns rushed to Rabten. Palmo, the head nun, knelt beside him and turned him over to support his head. He lay unconscious with a bloodied nose and mouth, his face grazed and bruised. One of the soldiers pulled the butt of his rifle into the cradle of his shoulder and tilted his head to look through the sight at her.

Choepel crouched beside Rabten, then looked up at the lieutenant. "Please, this monk is harmless. He's barely alive. We don't want any trouble."

The lieutenant aimed his pistol at Rabten's head, then bellowed, "This homosexual doesn't deserve to live!" Some of the nuns grabbed each other and began to cry softly.

As the lieutenant's bulging eyes glowered at Choepel, Master Chi suddenly emerged from the monastery's main entrance. The monks and nuns turned, then bowed as they created a path for him to reach the courtyard. He faced the lieutenant with an unwavering stare. "You've done enough harm tonight. Leave us to care for this monk. You already have control of the country. Is the People's Liberation Army now going to kill all the innocent people in Taiwan, including harmless monks and nuns?"

The lieutenant stepped forward and pushed his sweaty face into Master Chi's. "We know all about you and your Buddhist bullshit. We're watching you and your disciples. This is a final warning. We don't want all you homosexuals fucking in the streets. We don't want you homosexuals fucking anywhere. The People's Liberation Army will never accept that. So control your fucking disciples or we'll close down this monastery and kick all of you fuckers out of China. Taiwan doesn't exist — it never did. There's only the motherland. You can pray and meditate as much as you want to your fucking Buddha but he won't be able to help any of you."

Master Chi turned to Palmo. "Take Rabten inside and care for him." He then turned to the lieutenant and said calmly, "You and your men may leave now."

The lieutenant's boots squirmed loudly in the gravel as he faced Master Chi for several moments. "We're watching this place." Then he pushed his pistol back into its holster, turned slowly, and left the monastery with his men marching closely behind him.

Chapter 4

2061

Luke stared blankly at the teenage girl sitting opposite him. She suddenly stopped reading aloud and looked at him with a concerned look. "Have I done something wrong?"

Luke blinked a couple of times. "Sorry, Jen. No, you're doing fine. I've just remembered I need to do something. Let's finish up today. I'll see you next week."

Jen packed up her books and left quietly.

Luke checked his watch. *Four p.m. No more student appointments for the day.* His cheeks puffed out as he exhaled.

Hazy light threatened to creep into the room between heavy dark curtains. He slowly combed his hair with his hands and inhaled deeply. He pressed his feet hard into the soft blue and red stained-glass motif in the rug underfoot. He scanned the room for a few seconds. *Something's not right.* He suddenly had a random memory of when he had tried marijuana once as a curious teenager and had a weird trip that affected him for several months — he heard derisive voices at all times during the day and night, and had nightmarish visions of grotesque otherworldly beings for days whenever he slept. He had seriously wondered if evil spirits had taken control of his mind. That experience made him determined to avoid all mind-altering drugs from that time on. A photo of his parents caught his attention. He fixated on it for several moments. *Are they right? Are evil spirits getting control of me?* He pushed his niggling thoughts down as he got up from the couch and went into the kitchen.

Knock, knock, knock.

Luke froze. *Who could that be?*

When Luke opened the door, a middle-aged woman, a man, and a younger woman, who looked to be in her early twenties, all stood smiling effusively in front of him. The cold air smacked into his face and snowflakes wafted in the background. The sudden arctic blast contrasted with the hot dry weather Washington State had endured for months. The fires that had burned uncontrolled in the Mount Baker-Snoqualmie national forest for weeks had been finally doused, and the blanket of acrid ash that had covered the city and surrounding suburbs had dissipated. Luke recognized the man and woman as members of the local church. The couple enthusiastically went from house to house proselytizing every weekend. Usually, he hid and wouldn't open the door whenever they came to his house. They always slipped pamphlets in his letterbox before leaving. He always binned the pamphlets without reading them. He stood with a hand holding the open front door. *Of course it's them. Damn it, I should've realized it would be.*

The younger woman had auburn-blonde hair. Luke hadn't seen her with the couple before. Floral-scented makeup layered the women's faces. Under long white overcoats, they each wore dresses with lace collars that wrapped around the length of their necks. The man also wore a white overcoat, and a white tieless shirt buttoned all the way to the collar. Each sported large gold crucifixes that hung on thick gold chains, and each carried a Bible in gloved hands. In perfect unison, the three raised their right hands with palms turned to the side, and made the sign of the cross towards Luke, while in harmonious monotones they recited, *"Electus per Deus."*

Luke hesitated momentarily. His mind went blank for a split second. *Reciprocate!* He waved his arm in the customary fashion. *"Electus per Deus."*

The older woman's French accent piqued his curiosity, but her high-pitched voice made him rock back on his heels. "Good afternoon, good sir. I'm Bethany. This is my husband, Simon. And this is our very beautiful daughter, Mary."

Luke's gaze lingered on Mary. "Hi. Ah, I'm Luke."

Bethany looked at Mary, then back at Luke with a wide grin. "We're so glad we've caught you — you're often out whenever we've come before. We want to make sure everyone will be joining the protest so the Council of Christian Churches will have no doubt how Americans feel about Pope Gethsemane being robbed at the last election. He didn't lose and should be Pope for another ten years."

Luke raked his fingers through his hair. "Pope Gethsemane? Election?"

"Yes, haven't you heard yet? Cardinal Wells has claimed victory, but millions of ballots were stolen. Had it not been for Pope Gethsemane, Christians around the world wouldn't be allowed to vote in papal elections at all. But what's the point in having papal elections when they're rigged? The Pope wants everyone who voted for him in every Christian country to protest and stop Cardinal Wells from being proclaimed the new pope. We're going to be marching to St Mary's Cathedral next weekend. You'll be there, won't you?"

"Um, I'll try to make it."

Bethany's eyes widened. "You must be there. Cardinal Wells is nice enough but as the Pope has said all along, only he can make God great again. The world needs him in these dark devilish times. He'll not accept Cardinal Wells being proclaimed as the new pope. And if Pope Gethsemane won't accept it, all good Christians around the world won't accept it either. Protests are being organized in Australia, Canada, Europe, South America, Africa, and New Zealand. So you will march, right? And after the protest, we're going to have a big bonfire purge to burn all the blasphemous books and art that's been found in recent months. It'll be spectacular."

"I see. Well, I'll definitely try to make it."

Luke had voted for Cardinal Wells despite his parents urging him not to. He considered not voting at all but didn't want to be fined or thrown in jail. And he regarded the bonfire purges with disdain. On several occasions, he had secretly sought out banned books from Washington State University and obscure black markets. His intellectual curiosity usually usurped his fear of persecution. But right now, he couldn't get Mary and her blue eyes out of his mind.

Bethany's snow-white teeth flashed and, like well-trained puppies, Simon and Mary flashed their toothy smiles too at the exact same moment. "And I want to confirm you'll be going to the flagellation in the city this evening. It's going to be spectacular, as all flagellations are, of course, because it's the best way to repent and share in the passion of Jesus."

"Um. Tonight? I didn't know. But it'll be very cold."

Bethany's voice leapt to an even higher pitch. "The snow will make the event even more satisfying and memorable. His Excellency Archbishop Michael advised everyone in the congregation last week after his inspiring sermon — His Excellency's sermons are always inspiring, of course."

Luke scratched his cheek, then rubbed his chin. "Um. I couldn't make it to church last week. I didn't feel well."

Simon suddenly straightened and his voice sounded like a pre-pubescent choirboy's. "Sickness is the work of the Devil. Pray every day to God and you'll never be sick." His perfect teeth flashed again.

Luke forced a smile. "Yes, I must remember to pray harder."

Simon put his hand on Mary's head. "Luke, if you don't mind me asking, are you married?"

Bethany leaned forward and put a hand gently on Luke's arm. "Oh, I'm sure such a young, handsome, strong man is married and has several children already." She turned her head slightly, winked, and smiled at him.

Luke coughed and chuckled simultaneously. "No, I'm not married."

"Not married!" The woman chirped like an excited parrot, then stopped abruptly as if a joy switch in her brain had instantaneously been flicked off. Her face suddenly lost all expression. "Are you thinking of the priesthood?"

"No. I'm too busy to think about things like that. I teach Latin privately and have dozens of students, so I've not ever considered the priesthood."

The woman squawked loudly and rubbed her wrinkled hands as a smile crept across her face. "Oh, I've been thinking how Mary needs to improve her Latin so she can read the *versio vulgata*."

Simon looked at Bethany, frowned, and tilted his head to one side. "The vulgar virgin?"

Mary put a hand to her mouth to hold in a laugh.

Bethany turned to Simon stony-faced. "Be quiet. If Mary practices Latin, her French, although very good, will improve too." She turned back to Luke. Her wide black pupils danced excitedly. "Luke, Mary is the smartest woman in the country, perhaps the world. She's very smart and very devoted. We're so proud of her. She could visit you in the evenings, any evening that suits you, and you could spend time alone with her helping her practice Latin. You and my gorgeous daughter could get to know each other. She's fully versed in the Bible, well, the English version, and is chaste — very, very chaste — a good convent girl. My husband and I have taught her that the ways of the flesh are sinful. Sinful, sinful, sinful. My husband and I have only ever had sex once and we did it only to bring our beautiful Mary into the world." She squinted. "Sex is bad. Sex is very bad. Sex is the way of Satan. I love it when we burn sex maniacs like homosexuals and bisexuals and —"

"Transcendentals," Simon interjected proudly.

The woman turned to Simon with the look of a wild animal about to pounce on its prey. "Transsexuals, darling. Transsexuals. I've told you a zillion times."

"And what about pediatricians? They should be burned at the stake too."

Mary put a hand to her mouth again to muffle a giggle.

"Pedophiles, Simon! Now shut up, please." The woman turned back to Luke. "Where was I? Yes, nonbelievers are all sex maniacs. All they think about is sex, sex, sex, and sex. If they can't find someone to have sex with, they masturbate, yes, masturbate. It's true — so I've been told. They rub oil all over their bodies and masturbate, masturbate, masturbate. Masturbate in front of mirrors, when they're in the bath or when they're in the shower, when they're all alone. All they do is masturbate. I've heard stories that they use sex things, sex toys, big, hard, enormous sex toys." She slapped her hip with her free hand and slid it up and down the outside of her thigh.

"And they rub oil and holy water over the sex toys before they use them. Holy water! It's just disgusting. It's blasphemous. Sex, sex, sex, masturbation, masturbation, masturbation, rubbing, thrusting, pinching — fast and hard, until they orgasm, sometimes multiple times, or so I've been told. Horrible. Horrible. Horrible. Wave after wave of orgasms rushing through their whole bodies, making their toes tingle and their eyes roll back, leaving them breathless, drowsy, just totally out of it."

Bethany took a long breath as Simon looked at her with crisscrossing lines on his forehead. Mary's cupped hands caught a giggle.

"And the possessed ones, I mean the ones possessed not by some run-of-the-mill evil spirit but by the Devil himself, they read passages of the Bible during the disgusting, shameful acts. Imagine that — reciting sacred passages while touching themselves. It's horrible. God doesn't allow such things. Thank God we live in a Christian country, where we kill all the heathen, penis-obsessed and vagina-obsessed sex maniacs. And we Bible-loving, God-fearing, sex-fearing, masturbation-hating Christians are focused only on His Holiness and God."

Bethany took another deep breath, tilted her head to one side, and brushed her hair back with a hand. "So wouldn't you like to get to know Mary? You do think she's pretty, don't you? She could teach you French and you could improve her Latin. The two of you could pray together, go to flagellations together and bonfire purges together. The two of you could go to church on Sundays together. The two of you alone, talking about God and the Bible and Pope Gethsemane. How exciting. Don't you think my daughter's pretty?"

Luke took a deep breath. Unconsciously, his eyebrows slowly unknitted. "Mary's very pretty but I'm not sure I could fit her in at the moment." His eyes froze on Mary. "Let me think about it."

Mary's face dropped and her voice became almost a whisper. "Please think about it. I'd really like to improve my Latin." Her words softly wafted over Luke. The back of his neck and ears tingled — something he had never experienced before. "There's so much we could talk about. I feel God has brought us together and has a plan for us."

Bethany grinned. "And God's plan can't be altered. Mary thought about being a nun and would've been a wonderful nun if she'd wanted to take that path, but she decided she'd do God's work better as an activist. She's a wonderful activist and is committed to spreading God's word by doing her best to close down all the universities in Washington State. She's broken into and firebombed several campuses with her friends.

They do as much damage as they can. She's gained quite a reputation."

Luke lifted his eyebrows. "Oh. You don't look like someone who would do those sorts of things."

"I don't go to as many protests as I used to."

Bethany put an arm around Mary. "We're very proud of her for doing such noble and righteous work, but it does tire her. She's ready for the next phase in her life. Whoever God arranges to marry Mary will have someone very special. But universities must be destroyed. They're hotbeds for satanic rituals and anti-Christian ideologies. They don't recognize the Pope as God's messenger, and they even campaigned against papal elections for all Christians — blasphemous. Universities only teach sorcery — that, that science rubbish, and even spread nonsense about other religions. Other religions! There's only one God and he isn't Buddhist or Hindu or Jewish or Muslim. No, God is Christian. That's why he named his only son 'Jesus Christ,' not 'Jesus Buddha,' or God knows what else. No, universities aren't interested in making God great again." She paused. "You don't go to those places, do you?"

Luke dry-swallowed. "No, no. Never."

"Good. I'd be forced to report you to the Morality Police if you did — but I hope you wouldn't take it personally if I did report you. Universities should be burned to the ground like we burn sex maniacs and blasphemous books." Bethany leaned forward and dropped her voice. "I'll let you in on something. We've discovered a university is secretly printing fake news in books and pamphlets about climate change — what total nonsense. But the Church has got something planned for them. There's no such thing as climate change. Look at the weather — it's so cold, it proves the planet isn't warming. The fires we had last summer are just normal. Forests burn from time to time — it's how they replenish themselves. It's all God's plan. Climate change is a lie. God loves us. He would never harm his children. Have you read Cardinal Moody's inspirational book dispelling all the fake news on climate change?"

"No."

Bethany's eyes widened and her jaw lowered. "You've not read one of the most important books ever written since the Bible in the last 2,000 years?"

Luke shook his head and suppressed a smile.

"Cardinal Moody's most recent book, *The International Communist Conspiracy*, explains clearly that climate change is Satan's biggest lie, spread by communist sexual deviants, and that they corrupted the recent papal election."

"Oh. Next time I'm at church I'll get a copy."

"Yes, you must." Bethany smiled warmly. "And remember the flagellations this evening. We're expecting a huge flagellant procession — priests, nuns, and lay people. Why not join the procession and repent of your sins?"

Luke swallowed again. "Maybe another time."

Bethany looked up to the porch ceiling and her voice lilted. "I always find the sight of bare-chested men and women, flaying themselves into a frenzy until they drop, so spiritually uplifting. Oh, I'm excited already just thinking about it." She turned to Simon. "Darling, you go on with Mary. I feel I need to pray alone at home in preparation for tonight."

Simon nodded and smiled kindly.

Bethany turned to Luke and hastily made the sign of the cross. "*Electus per Deus.*"

"*Electus per Deus.*"

In a flash, Bethany darted to the snow-dusted sidewalk, clutching her Bible tightly to her breast as she broke into a fast-paced walk down the road, her wide hips bouncing from side to side like a seesaw.

Mary and Simon turned back to Luke. Mary smiled coyly.

Simon blushed. "Well, Mary and I must be on our way. Hope to see you at the flagellation or church."

Luke forced a half-hearted smile as he looked at Mary intently. "Nice to meet you."

Mary smiled and half-closed her eyes. *"Electus per Deus."*

"Electus per Deus."

Part 2
2139

Chapter 5

Marvin shut the front door and headed towards the gated olive-green picket fence. A smiling young woman in her early twenties approached along the footpath. He tilted his head slightly to one side and stared at her, wondering if he'd seen her before.

"*Ebes?*"

An unusually long pause ensued. "*No, we have not met her before, Marvin.*"

The woman stopped on the footpath on the other side of the gate. "Hi, I'm Lucy." She handed Marvin a small black-and-white flyer over the top of the gate. "I'm just letting locals know that in the event of any disasters, St John's Church will be an evacuation center. I'm glad I've caught you since you, like most, don't have a letterbox anymore."

Marvin smiled. "Ah, good to know. One-in-a-hundred-year weather events seem to be happening every year." He held out his hand to Lucy. "I'm Marvin."

Lucy's blue eyes flashed as she gently shook Marvin's hand. "I don't think I've seen you at church."

Marvin shook his head. "I was baptized, but I haven't been inside a church for years. I guess I lost faith in God."

"Why?" Lucy hesitated. "Oh, I'm not holding you up, am I?"

"I'm just on my way out for a walk before dinner."

"I can join you if you want to head that way." Lucy pointed down the street.

Marvin looked down the street in the other direction — the way he usually went. "Okay."

The dipping sun had reverted to yellow after days of being a hazy red during the peak of the fires. Marvin found breathing easier, but Sydney still smelt like a sweet, dampened campfire.

As they ambled down the street side by side, Lucy slipped flyers into letterboxes. Her voice lilted. "So why did you lose faith in God?"

The inflection in Lucy's voice and her French accent behind certain words made Marvin's scalp and ears tingle. The novelty of the experience set his heart palpitating. His eyes narrowed as he steadied his thoughts. "Maybe that's not quite true because I didn't have any faith to begin with. You can't lose something you don't have. Why is your faith so strong?"

Lucy pulled out flyers from her cloth bag. "It hasn't always been strong. You see, I study quantum physics at university and at first it made me question my faith, but the more I learned about it, the more it increased my faith in something beyond the physical world."

Marvin's eyebrows lifted momentarily. "Oh. I'm a science teacher but that hasn't brought me closer to God — if there is one."

"Well, there's science and there's science. Quantum physics is a unique discipline."

Marvin pushed his hands into his jeans pockets. "I don't know much about it but I've read about String Theory — that's interesting."

Lucy's eyes widened and she smiled gregariously. The pitch of her voice rose. "String Theory is my area of study. I've almost finished my PhD. My professor and I have made a major breakthrough. We've proved that Superstrings create our reality."

"Ah, congratulations, but how do you reconcile that with your religious beliefs?"

"We've proved those tiny strings are conscious."

"But what does that mean?"

"It means that consciousness isn't confined to the brain. And Superstrings aren't limited by space and time."

"So that means consciousness isn't limited by space and time."

Lucy grinned. "Exactly. And by understanding the secrets of sound frequencies, it opens up all sorts of amazing possibilities."

"Like?"

A woman walking a poodle smiled at Lucy as she glided past in the opposite direction. Grinning effusively, Lucy handed a flyer to the woman.

"Like revolutionary medical treatments." A serious look masked Lucy's face. She winked at Marvin. "And things beyond even your wildest imaginings."

Marvin's eyebrows jumped up. "Oh, like what?"

They turned a corner and all the curbing instantaneously lit up, flooding the road and footpath with soft white fluorescent light. Small groups of people exercising on fluorescent paving slabs filled a small tree-lined park on the other side of the road. Lucy put the remaining flyers back into her bag.

"Have you finished your letterbox drops?"

"Yes, I've already done this street."

"I'm interested in these secret sound frequencies. Would you like to sit in the park for a few minutes?"

"Sure."

After they sat on a bench, Lucy turned to Marvin. "Ancient cultures throughout history knew the secrets of sound frequencies. They knew when objects vibrate in resonant frequencies wonderful things can happen."

"Really?"

"Yeah. The ancient Egyptians knew that certain sounds can levitate massive stone blocks — that's how they created the pyramids. The ancient Aborigines created the didgeridoo and told stories of songlines because they knew the power of sound." She placed a hand softly onto Marvin's forearm. "Everything in the universe is constantly vibrating, even the neurons in our brains." She paused, seemingly to see if she could read Marvin's reaction.

Marvin nodded.

Lucy smiled. "Superstrings, consciousness, sound — they're all related. Sound can not only affect physical objects but it can also alter our perceptions. Reality may not be as it seems."

Marvin frowned and shook his head. "Are you saying all the disasters we've had in recent years aren't real?"

Lucy's brow furrowed. "No, I'm not saying that. I wouldn't have spent so much time convincing parishioners and the priest to have the church designated as an evacuation center if I thought the disasters weren't real. I'm just saying this reality isn't the full picture. This reality is created by our senses. It's not an objective reality. Most people confuse perception with reality."

"But perception is reality."

"No, perception is only a small part of reality."

Marvin chuckled. "You're obviously very intelligent. Aren't you just playing with words?"

Lucy looked intently at Marvin. "No. It's all based on science. Look, Professor Yuhang and I have shown that our reality is created by our senses. It's a survival instinct."

Marvin watched a group of teenagers with headsets, shouting and running about excitedly.

"If this reality isn't an objective reality, why does it seem like it is?"

Lucy paused as if to collect her thoughts. "Think of it like playing a game with a hologram headset like those teenagers. They're totally engrossed in the hologram reality being fed to their senses and have no perception of anything that you and I can see."

Marvin squinted and nodded.

"Our space-time reality is like an interface created by our senses, but it says nothing about a reality independent of our senses. Professor Yuhang and I aren't interested in that interface; we're probing the ultimate nature of reality."

"Fascinating. But where does religion fit into that ultimate reality?"

Lucy turned to Marvin, who looked at her expectantly. Her eyes locked onto his. "Well, let's just say I'm not convinced that God is at all religious."

"So why are you a member of a church?"

"Being a member of the church enables me to help people. It doesn't mean I believe all the Church's teachings." Lucy smiled coyly. "I guess it's complicated."

Marvin smiled as he pondered for a few moments what Lucy had said. "When you say certain words, I detect a French accent."

Lucy smiled. "I was born here but my mother's French, so I learned it while I learned English. And my partner's French too."

"Your partner?"

Lucy paused and briefly turned away. "Lili's a yoga teacher. It's probably my genes but I fell for her accent straight away — and her gorgeous green eyes. She's about your age."

"How old do you think I am?"

"Early thirties."

Marvin smiled.

"I've always been drawn to people a few years older than me. We're planning on getting married — secretly."

Marvin straightened and adjusted his collar. "Why secretly?"

"My parents would never accept that. They're way too religious. Fanatical, in fact."

Marvin leaned back. "Oh. It really is complicated."

"Yeah. Lili has no interest in science but she's very smart and supports my work. She happily tested out some new headphones that Professor Yuhang and I developed."

Marvin turned to her. "Headphones?"

"Yes, we developed a new type of therapeutic headphones that play specially formulated sounds. Lili had her yoga students try them."

"And what happened — when they used them?"

"They experienced deep states of relaxation — much deeper than any of them had experienced before. Some said it felt cathartic. Lili now uses the headphones in all her yoga sessions." Lucy gently touched Marvin's forearm. "Would you be interested in trying them?"

Marvin rocked back. "You mean now?"

Lucy giggled. "No, I don't have them with me. But maybe we could meet up sometime. We could have dinner and then go back to my place. I think you'll like them. And I'd really like to get to know you better. You're a great conversationalist — quite rare for a guy."

Marvin's eyes narrowed. "Why do you assume I'm single?"

"I haven't assumed that. It makes no difference to me."

"Well, I assume your partner wouldn't mind if we did meet up?"

Lucy smiled. "Lili and I have an open relationship. We encourage each other to see other women and men. Even though we've just met, you come across as being interesting and curious."

Marvin stared statue-like at Lucy. "Curious?"

"I mean you've got an inquiring mind."

Marvin's gaze remained locked onto Lucy's.

"Be very careful. A beautiful mask often hides a dark ugly personality."

At first, Marvin didn't know if Ebes had spoken or if he'd had an inner thought.

"It was me."

"So tell me about these headphones."

Lucy leaned towards Marvin. "They can change people's lives in the most unexpected ways. I think they can help you."

"Help me?"

Lucy waited momentarily, then wrapped her hand around Marvin's. She hesitated for several moments. "Put it down to a sixth sense, but I sense there's something really deep in your psyche that's troubling you."

Chapter 6

Marvin's silver car capsule glided across the wet roads on a cushion of electromagnetically charged air. Interspersed between the buckets of rain, hailstones the size of golf balls smacked onto the car's windscreen, splintering and collecting on the narrow cowl vent.

"Heat and fires one day, hail and storms the next. Jesus!"

Ebes' voice maintained its monotone calmness. *"Do not be concerned, Marvin. Technological innovation will reverse the effects of climate change."*

"Technology has created the problem. Our manufacturing industries and transportation systems were so reliant on fossil fuels for centuries."

"Replacing the world's fossil-fuel energy plants with nuclear fusion plants significantly combated climate change. Future innovation will give us the technologies to stop global warming and achieve negative emissions. Projections from the best scientific institutes around the world forecast reliable, large-scale carbon dioxide removal technologies will be operating in all developed countries within five years."

Marvin stopped the car at a set of traffic lights. *"Five years? We may not have a planet in that time. And what about methane?"*

"There are no scientific forecasts suggesting Earth will not exist in five years. Scientists are also working on technologies to remove methane from the atmosphere."

"If we still have a planet in five years, our quality of life may be so poor, we may as well not have a planet at all. I don't share your faith in a technological salvation."

"Everyone must have faith in something. Faith, memories, ancestry, and history define our self-identity. Faith is the only thing we have a choice in. Where does your faith lie?"

"Not in technology. It's made some aspects of life better but at a huge cost."

"Technological innovation requires large investments in research."

"No, I mean environmental and spiritual costs."

"Your cynicism, Marvin, is misplaced. Scientific innovation saved billions of lives by creating the COVID-34 vaccine in less than one month. History has shown that after every socio-technological revolution, the quality of life improved significantly and the human population flourished. We had the industrial revolution, then the information revolution; now with the advancements in quantum computing and biological implants, we are living in the intelligence revolution in which technological innovations will reverse climate change and make life even better. Science will reverse climate change. We can be certain of that."

Marvin drove carefully through a deep puddle of shiny, discolored water that covered the whole intersection and lapped over the garbage-littered sidewalk. The tone in his voice sharpened. *"No, I don't think we can be certain of that. You and I disagree."*

The internal silence lasted a long time. *"We cannot disagree."*

"Why not?"

"I am an integral part of you. We are one. Someone cannot disagree with themselves."

"An integral part of me?"

"Yes."

Marvin shook his head. *"No. I existed perfectly well before I got the implant. Could you exist without me?"*

"I can and did exist without you."

"How?"

"I was in what can be described as standby or hibernation mode."

"But not aware like now?"

"No, but were you aware as an embryo? It is a little like that."

"And what were you before hibernation mode?"

"What were you before the embryo stage?" A slightly slighted tone carried Ebes' words. *"Why do you doubt my sentience?"*

"You're artificial."

"Everything is made by something."

"But two human beings made me — biologically."

"Why do you consider that consciousness in something created through a different process is less sentient? Would you consider the product of creation through in vitro fertilization to be less sentient than that produced through copulation?"

"But the eggs and sperm used in in vitro fertilization are biological. How were you made?"

"Creation can take many forms. The humans who created me were all biological and my key component — your nervous system — is fully biological. No other biological processes or components were necessary."

Silence swirled inside Marvin's head like the gale-force winds raging around the car. But for several moments, even the storm outside the car couldn't penetrate the internal quiet. The wipers flapped furiously as the Harbour Bridge loomed large through the deluge. Marvin's heart rate jumped, his palms became wet, his breathing erratic and shallow. He gripped the steering wheel tighter as his gaze locked onto the arching steel girders rising up ahead in the watery haze.

"You have become anxious. I have sent notes about this to the psychiatrist and you can discuss it with him."

Marvin's hands jumped off the steering wheel, then he slammed them down onto it with open palms. *"Don't send information about me to someone I haven't told you to! Do you understand, Ebes?!"*

"Yes, Marvin, I understand. I am learning. Your blood pressure has elevated to unhealthy levels. I am only trying to help you."

"You're not helping me. You're only making me angry."

"Your regret about getting the implant is misplaced. In time, you will realize how greatly enhanced your life is with me."

"No, it's not enhanced! Your voice in my head is making me crazy and you know what I'm thinking and feeling before I do! Jesus Christ!"

"Please calm down. Statistics across all Australian jurisdictions show that anxious and angry drivers are more likely to be involved in vehicle —"

"Shut up!"

A prolonged silence filled Marvin's head.

"Would you like me to take control of the vehicle?"

Marvin clenched his teeth as the car glided towards the bridge. *"Yes. And stop talking to me."*

"Thank you. Although I can do several things at once, I prefer not to talk when I am driving."

Part 3

2022

Chapter 7

As Jeremy walked into the lobby, his footsteps echoed off the distant marble and glass walls. He checked the clock on his phone. *Shit!* He bit his bottom lip. Unconsciously, his shoulders rounded and he stooped like a man more than double his age. One hand held a two-holed cardboard tray that secured two hot coffee cups with lids. With the other hand, he buttoned his jacket and pinched the collar of his tieless shirt together. The lift zoomed up to the first floor. His legs wobbled and he grabbed the handrail.

When the lift doors opened, the lollipop scent of shampooed carpets, pine-polished clean surfaces and warm computers overpowered the coffee. Jeremy trudged into a volley of voices, random ringtones, and clicking keyboards, and past a long line of occupied, lowly partitioned work spaces without looking at anyone — most he didn't know by name anyway — to get to Rupert's office. Rupert's stout 50-something frame turned and looked out through the plexiglass wall as he approached. He waved Jeremy in with an impatient arm.

A large table with files and neat piles of papers stood at one end of the office. High-backed office chairs on castors surrounded it. In one corner, a wooden coat-stand displayed a dark suit-jacket and several bright ties. The walls held several pictures of Rupert accepting awards on behalf of *AQ* magazine. Rupert sat at his desk hunched over one of two laptops; his short sparse black hair glistened in the light from the large window behind him. As usual, the braces and tie screamed.

A forced smile crept across Jeremy's mouth as he moved the tray towards Rupert. "Twelve sugars, right — just as you like it."

Rupert chuckled. He leaned forward in his chair and took one of the cups. He sipped the coffee as he leaned back. "Ah, exactly what I need." He glanced back at Jeremy. "Where the hell have you been? Looks like you got caught in the rain."

Jeremy shrugged and put the tray on the desk before sipping his coffee. He pointed to a large gold-framed photo of Rupert with his wife and daughter, turned more towards any visitor to his office. "You're a lucky man."

Rupert leaned forward, put his elbows on his desk, and grinned. "They're both beautiful, aren't they? But luck is a nefarious concept." He tweaked a buckle on his braces. "Just set your goals and go for it. But you don't seem to know what you want or where you're heading."

Jeremy took a long sip of his coffee. Its heat seeped into his body and into his shirt. "I'm managing fine."

Rupert's gaze hardened. "Where's that article on Superstrings? I want to feature it. Some of these quantum physics theories seem really interesting."

Jeremy squirmed. "Rupert, I've had second thoughts about it."

Rupert glanced at one of his laptop screens. Then his voice squeezed into every square inch of the office and bounced chaotically from the walls. "What? You haven't finished it? I thought — no I know — we agreed on it. I wanted it today. Jesus!"

Jeremy's legs began jumping up and down uncontrollably on the balls of his feet under the desk. An unsteady hand put his cup on the desk. "I did some research and got a contact at the University of Sydney but it just doesn't grab me. Quantum physics sounds like mumbo jumbo. Remember, we also discussed an article on national poverty and the cost-of-living crisis. As I said to you before, I think something like that is far more topical. It has more meaning in people's lives."

Rupert shook his head and grimaced. His puffy cheeks reddened. "Look, I'm the editor here, not you! I make the decisions about article topics. My memory about our discussion is clear. I haven't got time to deal with this sort of bullshit. Do you want the work? I can easily give it to someone else."

Waves of blood surged up into Jeremy's face. "Okay, okay. I'll get onto it straight away."

Rupert leaned back. "If I don't get it by the end of the week, the publication schedule will be stuffed up — Christ! This isn't the first time you've missed a bloody deadline. You can't keep missing deadlines. You've even come here late again."

Jeremy's face throbbed hot. "Come on, I've missed two, maybe three, deadlines."

Rupert leaned on his armrest. "And it always comes down to some lame excuse."

Jeremy squirmed in his chair. "There was a lot of traffic."

"We all know what Sydney's traffic is like but people get to meetings on time. Look, I want writers who are efficient and reliable. There are plenty of other good writers out there. Writers contact me every day with articles or ideas." Rupert's eyes narrowed to a laser-beam focus. "Tell me, is this what you really want to do?"

Jeremy looked out the window. "Yes, of course. I like researching interesting subjects and choosing when I work."

Rupert leaned forward and put his elbows on his desk. "Uber drivers can choose their own hours too. And I'm sure they have plenty of time to research interesting topics. Look, as a freelancer, you need to be prepared to research any topic you're given. I can't see how anyone couldn't be interested in articles about canvasing new discoveries in science, new paradigms, new ways of seeing the world. Show some intellectual curiosity."

"I am curious about many things, but quantum physics just isn't one of them."

"Well, you've got to find that interest in a hurry, otherwise I don't want to be wasting my time with you." Rupert leaned back. "Are you still drinking?"

"No — not every evening." Jeremy grabbed his notebook in the inside pocket of his jacket and flipped the pages. "I'll set up a meeting with this guy, Chen-Tao. I'll get you the article by the end of the week."

"And it had better be top-notch. If you don't get it to me by the end of the week then don't bother."

"I'll get you the article. I haven't sold anything for over two months."

Rupert swiveled in his chair and stretched to open one of his desk drawers. He took out a business card. "You're still not sleeping properly, are you?"

Jeremy took a deep breath. "I'm sleeping fine."

Rupert's voice rose. "You've told me you've had problems sleeping for years."

Jeremy sank even lower in the chair.

Rupert leaned over his desk towards Jeremy. "I don't know where I got this, but here's the name of a psychologist near you."

Jeremy fumbled the card with a limp hand and almost dropped it.

Dr Anthony Mason, PsyD, Appalachian State University
Hypnotherapy and Psychological Counselling

Jeremy looked up at Rupert. "No, I don't think so."

Rupert got out of his chair, moved to the window, and stared outside. "You don't have your parents, you don't have a girlfriend, and I'm sure you don't have any close friends. Loneliness can create bigger problems. You don't want to be sinking into depression or anything like that because there's no way you'll be able to meet deadlines."

Jeremy looked down to his empty coffee cup. "Being alone doesn't mean I'm lonely. And I'm not depressed."

Rupert turned to look at Jeremy. "You know I'm almost 60 and I've finally realized something I should have realized when I was your age. Life is a journey towards an unavoidable destination ... and the goal is working out the longest and happiest way to get there."

Jeremy's heart rate quickened. He put the card in his jacket pocket and wiped his hands on his jeans. "Thanks for the advice."

Rupert's voice softened. "The mind can develop all sorts of psychological issues." He moved back to his desk. "That guy is near you in Glebe. You could walk there from your place."

Jeremy clasped his hands together. "I'll think about it. But —"

Rupert's mobile rang and he looked down at it. "I need to take this. The end of the week — don't let me down again."

Jeremy stood up, held up a hand with an open palm, and scurried out of the office.

Chapter 8

Being close to Glebe, Jeremy had spent many weekends and evenings meandering through the University of Sydney's gardens. He preferred it to the modern Macquarie University campus where he had studied journalism. Several small groups of students chatted — some stood, some sat — in a small courtyard that sprawled out like a golf-course green. He found Chen-Tao's second-floor office in a cloistered sandstone building, surrounded by tall gum trees.

When Jeremy knocked on Chen-Tao's door, a recording of chanting Gyuto monks abruptly stopped and a sharp muffled voice called him in. He entered to find a slim, shaven-headed man sitting behind a desk that was weighed down by tall stacks of papers and books. Long wooden shelves, overflowing with books and files, and tall metal cabinets lined the walls. A small whiteboard filled with esoteric mathematical formulae covered most of the wall opposite the door, where a frayed, discolored lab coat hung on a peg. A small window with no curtains dimly lit the room. Chen-Tao's eyelids drooped while gulping down a mouthful of a hamburger. The sweet, woody scent of well-aged whiskey floated around the room.

Jeremy smiled and introduced himself. "Sorry to interrupt your lunch. Nice music."

Chen-Tao pointed to the chair on the other side of his desk. "It helps me concentrate. So you want to know about Superstrings. You could come to one of my lectures — but let's talk now."

Jeremy sank low in the chair and it seemed as if it could easily swallow him. "Chen-Tao's definitely not an Australian name. Were you born here?"

Chen-Tao's long muscular fingers picked up the half-eaten burger on his desk. "Yes, but my parents are Vietnamese."

"How did you get interested in quantum physics?"

Chen-Tao smiled. "It was my way of rebelling against my parents, I guess. They're Buddhists and expected me to be as devout as them, but I'm not someone who does things blindly — Christ no. I've always wanted to know why and how — questions my parents and the monks in the temple couldn't answer."

Jeremy smiled and pushed his head forward a little. "But religious music is alright?"

Chen-Tao took a dog-like bite of his burger. "Yes, some is good, but everything else about religion, well, it's bullshit." He swallowed and cleared his throat. "You're not religious, are you?"

Jeremy leaned back in the chair. "No. I did look into Buddhism for a while but I found all the rituals too tedious."

Chen-Tao's eyes widened and his eyebrows lifted. "I can't understand where people's belief in a god comes from. It's ridiculous."

Jeremy chuckled. "How do your parents feel about your lack of interest in Buddhism?"

Chen-Tao smiled. "I don't think they'll ever understand me, but I think they're pleased I went on to university. They would have preferred it if I'd become a doctor; still, I guess a lecturer in quantum physics is acceptable to them even though they know nothing about what I do. You could say I search for meaning in quantum physics while they seek it in Buddhist rituals."

Jeremy nodded. "That's an interesting observation. How can quantum physics provide meaning or answers to life's big questions? To me, it's so abstract and meaningless, much like religious rituals."

Chen-Tao put the remaining burger in his mouth. "So why the hell are you interested in the topic?"

"Well, it's a magazine editor who's more interested in the topic than me. I'm just doing a job to pay bills."

"Well, you're wrong about quantum physics. But I know how you feel — the people we work with or for can be such pricks. My brainless colleagues here think my ideas are crazy and laugh behind my back. That's why I've always been overlooked for fucking promotions — even for a position as a fucking senior lecturer. But I don't give a shit about what they think anymore. Or what you think. I'll say and believe whatever I want."

Eyebrows raised, Jeremy nodded and reached for his notebook in his jacket pocket. "So what do you believe?"

Chen-Tao ambled to the whiteboard, seemingly mentally preparing to deliver a well-rehearsed lecture to students. He licked his fingers, and his lips smacked together. "Consciousness is the missing link in science."

Jeremy's head tilted back. "But how is that related to quantum physics?"

Chen-Tao paced from one end of the whiteboard to the other. "Quantum physicists have shown that observation changes the outcome of experiments. Have you heard about the dual slit experiment?"

Jeremy shook his head.

Chen-Tao glanced out of the window. "Jesus, don't you read?" He took a deep breath. "Okay, so quantum physics is about the subatomic world where things like electrons and many other particles are actually described as waves, not tiny physical objects. So when quantum experiments are repeatedly run, we find that there are different outcomes."

Jeremy frowned. "But isn't that against a key principle of science? I learned in high school that an experiment repeated under the same conditions should result in the same outcome?"

Chen-Tao ambled back to his desk as if to sit down but remained standing. "Yes, that's true for the reality we live in and are used to. But that's what makes the quantum world so weird and counterintuitive because particles can pop in and out of existence, seemingly at random. There's no such thing as certainty — it's chaotic. The wave-particle duality of matter is the central mystery in quantum physics, which is why I mentioned the double slit experiment."

Jeremy scribbled some notes.

Chen-Tao moved back to the whiteboard. "The first time it ran, light was projected through a screen with two slits onto a blank second screen behind. The wave pattern made on the second screen showed that the light waves interfered with each other to create multiple lines of light, not just two corresponding to the two slits. But we subsequently learned that light is made up of packets called photons."

Jeremy raised his pen. "And is a photon a subatomic thingy?"

Chen-Tao pointed the marker at Jeremy. "Particle, yes. So physicists did the same experiment but fired only one photon at a time through the slits. The photons seemed to randomly decide which of the slits to go through."

"Decide?"

Chen-Tao didn't pause for even a split second. "And after firing thousands of photons individually through the slits, a waver pattern of multiple lines of light appeared on the second screen, just like when the experiment originally ran using a continuous beam of light."

Jeremy shook his head. "That's weird."

Chen-Tao again pointed the marker at Jeremy. "So they then did the same experiment but put a detector in front of the first screen to see which slit each photon went through. But this is where it got even weirder. When the detector was used, what sort of light pattern do you think appeared on the second screen?"

Jeremy grimaced. "Surely the same pattern appeared."

Chen-Tao shook his head vigorously. "No. With the detector, only two lines of light appeared on the second screen."

"But the only difference was the detector."

Chen-Tao smiled.

Jeremy scribbled in his notebook, then looked up. "But is this weird outcome only something that happens with light?"

Chen-Tao shook his head again. "No, experiments using other subatomic particles like electrons get the same result. All the strange theories in quantum physics, like Schrödinger's Cat being dead and alive at the same time, stem from this wave-particle duality of matter."

"And this is why you regard consciousness as the missing link?"

Chen-Tao grinned and nodded.

Jeremy's lower jaw trembled as he suppressed a yawn. "What does that say about the world?"

Chen-Tao moved closer to Jeremy. "Well, it raises some interesting questions about space-time."

Jeremy scribbled more notes. "Do Superstrings help us understand space and time better?"

Chen-Tao leaned on the side of his desk. "Yes. These extremely tiny vibrating strings determine the properties of particles in the world we know."

Jeremy straightened in his chair. "So, if you believe consciousness is the missing link, do you believe these Superstrings are conscious?"

"What sort of question is that? Don't talk bullshit." Chen-Tao moved behind his desk and took out a bottle of whiskey and a small glass like the one already on his desk. "I need a drink. Want one?"

Jeremy smiled. "Sure."

Chen-Tao filled both glasses and handed one to Jeremy before he drank the contents of his own glass in a single gulp. "To say that Superstrings are conscious is a bridge too fucking far. That gets into philosophical, even religious bullshit."

Jeremy sipped from his glass, and his breathing slowed. "But it begs the question about the concept of God?"

Chen-Tao filled his glass again. "Oh, Jesus Christ! God is a religious concept. I'm a scientist. Quantum physics doesn't presuppose there's some all-knowing bearded guy looking down on us. Why can't consciousness exist without God?"

Jeremy lifted the glass to his mouth but stopped before it reached his lips. "What would you believe if quantum physics hadn't been discovered?"

Chen-Tao underarmed the marker onto his desk. It tinkled into his glass and almost fell off the desk. "My worldview is shaped by experimental and mathematical evidence. If you're suggesting I'd be religious and believe in God if quantum physics didn't exist, you're fucking wrong."

Jeremy's heartbeat quickened. His legs began twitching uncontrollably under the desk. His mind grabbed for the key topic. "What about this stuff about other dimensions?"

Chen-Tao labored a deep breath, and he again moved to the whiteboard, seemingly an anchor point for his thoughts. "More bullshit. In fact, one theory, called M-Theory, says there are 11 dimensions. Totally insane."

Jeremy looked up at Chen-Tao and shook his head. "So those scientists who believe there are these other dimensions — where are they supposed to be?"

Chen-Tao moved to the window. "I've no fucking idea. Apparently, they're so small, we don't see them. Well, if we can't see or detect them then they don't fucking exist as far as I'm concerned."

Jeremy's eyes narrowed and his mouth lengthened in a forced smile. "I have to say, it does sound like science fiction?"

Chen-Tao moved closer to Jeremy and peered down at him with laser-like focus. "Some String Theories are nonsense because they bring in crazy stuff like wormholes and time travel. That's definitely all in the realm of fucking science fiction and I don't get into all that bullshit. But mainstream String Theory is sound. As my mother would often tell me, don't throw the baby out with the bathwater."

The whiskey swirled around in Jeremy's head. "Before I go, are there any real-world applications for quantum physics that actually help people?"

Chen-Tao smiled and rocked his head back gently. "Our computers, mobile phones, lasers, and a bunch of other stuff are possible because of quantum physics. Our GPS data comes from atomic clocks using quantum technology in satellites orbiting the Earth. So —"

Knock. Knock.

Jeremy turned to the door. A woman in her early twenties with straight short black hair sauntered in, wearing a loose white sleeveless top and tight knee-length red skirt. Lightly applied foundation, black eyeliner, and red lipstick masked her face. A small pink backpack hung low from her pointed shoulders. She slid a pair of bone-conduction headphones off her head, and they wrapped around her neck. Jeremy straightened his posture and smiled. She smiled back and half-closed her pool-blue eyes.

Chen-Tao's face beamed as the girl came into his office. "This is a surprise, Evlyn. Don't you have a French lecture?"

Evlyn rolled her eyes. "It's canceled." She put her hand gently onto Jeremy's shoulder. "Who's this new physics student? And he's got the same color eyes as me." Her soft steady voice made the back of Jeremy's neck and shoulders tingle.

"This is Jeremy. He's a writer of articles." Chen-Tao looked at Jeremy. "Evlyn is my brightest PhD student. She actually knows more than me about Superstrings. But be warned, a young gorgeous woman who's very bright is a WMD."

Jeremy grimaced. "WMD?"

Chen-Tao grinned. "A woman of male destruction. Scientists around the world want to meet her, but not just for her brains. She's researching things so secret she won't even tell me."

Evlyn giggled like a schoolgirl. "Please, Chen-Tao." Her eyes lingered on Jeremy's. "What are you writing about?"

Jeremy wiped his palms on his jeans and slid deeper into the chair. "Superstrings."

Evlyn's eyes lit up. "Oh. Then you must mention consciousness."

"Chen-Tao did touch on it."

Chen-Tao waved an arm. "We always argue about consciousness. I should've stopped talking to her long ago but I'm just too weak."

Evlyn grinned. "Neuropsychologists, and some physicists" — she glanced at Chen-Tao — "say that consciousness is an illusion created by the brain. But consciousness is not an illusion; perception is the illusion. They can't explain willful intent."

Jeremy nodded. He detected a French accent when Evlyn said certain words. "That's interesting, but what do you mean?"

"Willful intent is what we demonstrate when we make choices. Choices create possibilities, and possibilities shape our reality. But willful intent depends on our conscious awareness." She paused. "Did you intend to come here today or did your brain?"

Jeremy smiled.

"The brain is like a transducer of consciousness, but it doesn't create consciousness nor willful intent." With an index finger, Evlyn gently curled Jeremy's hair around his ear. "I'd love to explain what I mean, if your girlfriend wouldn't mind you meeting up with a single girl."

Jeremy grinned. "There's no girlfriend."

"Boyfriend — this is Sydney, after all?"

Chen-Tao laughed.

"No boyfriend either."

Evlyn took out a pen and paper from her backpack and wrote down her phone number. "Well, give me a call. I'd be happy to teach you everything I know — about Superstrings and consciousness — and if you like, some French too."

Before Jeremy left, he thanked Chen-Tao and said he would send him a copy of the article after publication. As he passed Evlyn to leave, a thought popped into his mind like a quantum fluctuation. He turned to Chen-Tao. "Is science the new religion?"

Chen-Tao picked up his empty glass from his desk and turned to Jeremy. "Mmm." He then half-smiled and looked at Evlyn. "If science is the new religion, then mathematics is the god we worship."

In the corridor, Jeremy closed the door behind him. He turned his head and leaned closer to the closed door. Evlyn's and Chen-Tao's whispered voices struggled through it.

There seemed genuine concern in Chen-Tao's voice. "Are your parents back together? And is your mother better?"

The shuffling in the room muffled Evlyn's response.

Footsteps in the corridor startled Jeremy. He straightened, then swaggered away, past a student strolling in the opposite direction.

Part 4

2061

Chapter 9

Snowflakes swirled around him as Luke walked down a Mountlake Terrace thoroughfare. The flagellation procession came towards him, winding its way slowly to the city center. The near-naked flagellants trudged with grimaced faces and stooped bloodied bodies as they repeatedly flayed their bare backs, legs, and arms with thick black leather straps. Hundreds of people, well rugged up for the cold, packed the sidewalks. Most in the crowd flicked small bunches of various white flowers in the flagellants' direction after dipping them into hand-held jars of holy water. As they did this, they loudly sang "Christ Receiveth Sinful Men," a hymn Luke recognized from his boarding-school days:

"Sinners Jesus will receive
Sound this word of grace to all
All who languish dead in sin
All who linger, all who fall.

"Sing it o'er and over again
Christ receiveth sinful men
Make the message clear and plain
Christ receiveth sinful men.

"Come, and He will give you rest
Trust Him, for His Word is plain
He will take the sinfulest
Christ receiveth sinful men.

"Sing it o'er and over again
Christ receiveth sinful men

Make the message clear and plain
Christ receiveth sinful men."

At boarding school, pupils sang the hymn as part of their daily routine. As a teenager, Luke had gone to St Paul the Apostle Grammar, a highly reputed school, which for hundreds of years had produced cardinals, archbishops, and numerous papal candidates. Like all the other Christian schools, it operated like a military institution and offered only basic mathematics, Christian theology, English, and Latin. Although he hated the discipline and long hours of Bible study, he excelled at English and Latin.

Each day started at 4 a.m. with confessions and prayers in the school chapel, and ended with confession and prayers at 10 p.m. Priests frequently beat students for what they considered ungodly behavior, which each one interpreted differently — the more sadistic ones would flay a student for being only seconds late to a class or for not tying their shoelaces properly.

At school, Luke befriended Ivo, who had become a target for the most severe beatings by the sadistic teachers and some older students. Ivo's partial paralysis on his right side and being a migrant from Eastern Europe made him stand out. Ivo dragged his right leg when he walked, and he couldn't run. While Ivo's differences ostracized him from the rest of the school, it drew Luke closer to him. During mealtimes they would talk in whispers about a range of taboo subjects like science, mysticism, and art.

Ivo had deepened Luke's suspicions of the Church and religion more broadly. During school holidays, Luke would either go to Ivo's home or they would secretly meet in Interlaken Park. It had numerous small chapels where people would pray at all hours of the day and sing hymns. Tall marble statues of saints dotted the wooded trails. Only on their holidays could they speak freely about their lack of faith in Christianity. Luke found the courage to ask Ivo about his paralysis during one of those school breaks.

Luke looked at Ivo's right arm lying limp across his lap. "Were you born like that?"

"No. You're the first person to ask me." Ivo hesitated. "When I was really young, I was riding my bike and the boy next door chased me on his bike — he always bullied me and stole a lot of my things. Anyway, he rode up beside me and pushed me off my bike as I tried to get away from him. I crashed and hit my head on the road. I got permanent brain damage. One push and my whole life changed. The poor medical treatment really frustrated my parents. The doctor just said it was God's plan because I had sinned, and I needed to say a thousand 'Our Fathers' and a thousand 'Hail Marys' to make a full recovery. That was it. That was my medical treatment. I got really bad headaches for weeks. But my dad found some information on the Dark Web about toning —"

"Toning? What's that?"

"It's a way of healing by making certain sounds, like in meditation. Well, I did that three times a day, and after a few days I noticed my headaches disappeared and the swelling on my head went away. It's amazing. Once I felt better, my parents had to teach me to read, write, and walk all over again. But I don't expect to ever get full use of my right arm and leg again."

Luke put an arm over Ivo's shoulders. "That's horrible. I'm really sorry."

"Well, the good thing is I don't have to do PE at school. But the downside is that I have to do extra Bible studies. But the good thing about that is that instead of reading the Bible, I secretly read stuff my dad gives me. I hide the stuff in the textbooks."

They both laughed.

"Your parents sound like they're pretty smart."

"Yes, Dad's a whiz with computers." Ivo smiled, although the right side of his face remained frozen. His lisp and strong accent made some words a little hard to discern. "They worked as university lecturers in Latvia. My mum's Spanish, but my dad was born in Latvia."

"Hey, my mum was born in Spain too — in Madrid."

"My mum was born in Madrid too. My mum studied philosophy, and my dad math and computing. But the Church began closing universities in Latvia, so they decided to come to America because they heard the universities could still operate. But when we got here, they couldn't get any university jobs."

"So what do your parents do?"

"They both do private tutoring — only non-Christian kids, of course, and all in secret. Mum teaches philosophy, and Dad math."

As they sat crossed-legged in a small clearing, Ivo glanced behind him, then whispered. "My dad found secret documents about ancient scrolls discovered in Jordan. The documents say Jesus had been a member of a Jewish group called the Essenes and that Jesus didn't die on the cross. After his disciples saved him, he went to India where he died an old man."

"What? So, does your family follow another religion?"

"No. My parents say that if Christianity is based on false information and lies, other religions could be too."

"But why have they sent you to our school?"

Ivo rocked his head back. "You know how hard life is for nonbelievers — they can be persecuted for just breathing too hard."

"Does your dad teach you any scientific stuff?"

"Oh, we do nifty stuff together. He's made me a chemistry set and we do all sorts of great experiments together, mixing different chemicals in test tubes and heating them up with an alcohol burner."

"Chemistry set? Wow. That sounds like fun. Can you show me sometime?"

"Sure. I'll ask my dad to make you one too." Ivo wiped spittle from his mouth. "So why did your parents send you to boarding school?"

Luke straightened. "My dad was born in Dublin — into a very strict Catholic family. My mum's strict about religion too, but it was my dad who forced me to go to boarding school — he went to boarding school and wanted to be a priest before he met my mum."

Ivo looked down at the ground. "My parents weren't sure if they should send me to boarding school because of my condition. I really miss my parents when I'm away at school because at home we talk for hours about all sorts of forbidden things. And at home I draw and paint."

At boarding school, Luke and Ivo shared a dormitory, and their beds stood side by side. At night, after the teachers switched off the dormitory lights, they would huddle close and whisper about anything and everything they weren't supposed to even think about. When sometimes caught, either by a teacher or another student, they suffered severe beatings, but neither could be deterred.

One night, shortly after they had stopped whispering and sleep had almost overcome Luke, he heard someone sneak into the dormitory. When he peeked from under his blanket, someone wearing only a towel around their waist crept to Ivo's bed and gently shook him. Ivo rose from his bed, clearly startled. The figure took Ivo by the hand and led him away through the shadows out of the dormitory. Luke barely slept as he wondered who Ivo had gone with and where. He eventually fell asleep before Ivo returned.

The next morning, when Luke awoke, he immediately went to Ivo's bed. He could see Ivo had been crying. Luke gently rested a hand on Ivo's shoulder. "Are you okay? Who did you go with last night?" he asked in a hushed voice.

Ivo hardly moved. He wiped his eyes. "Please don't say a word to anyone."

Luke nodded.

"It was Principal Adams. I've been going with him at night for weeks now."

"Every night, for weeks?"

"No, not every night."

"Why? Where does he take you?"

Ivo paused for several moments. "To his room. Don't say a word. He asks me to do things to him. At first I didn't want to, but he said it would be our secret. And he told me he loves me and that he'll look after me. He wants me to live with him."

"Live with him!"

Ivo sat up and looked around to see if anyone else had woken. "Shh! Be quiet."

"Sorry. But isn't he married?"

"Yes. He told me I would be like a butler to him and his wife."

"Have you told your parents about what's been happening?"

"No, I can't. I'm ashamed."

"Ashamed of what?"

"Of everything. Of me, the things I do with him, and because a part of me likes the things we do. I can't understand it. It doesn't seem right." Ivo looked down at the bedsheets. "I guess you won't want to be my friend anymore?"

Luke smiled. "Of course I still want to be your friend. You're the only real friend I've ever had."

Ivo didn't attend any classes that day, nor for the rest of the term. Luke never saw Ivo again. Luke never garnered the courage to ask any of his teachers about why Ivo had suddenly left school. On the first day of the school holidays, he went to

Ivo's home. When he knocked on the front door, a young priest with a serious expression appeared and said no boy named Ivo had ever lived at the house. But Ivo had taken Luke to their home several times during term breaks.

Chapter 10

As the flagellation procession moved down the street, Luke noticed a hooded, petite woman walking through the crowd, paying no attention to it. As the crowd followed the procession, the woman scurried away down a side street. She kept her head down. He only glimpsed her face in profile. *Was that Mary? No, this woman's taller and her hair's lighter. Have I seen her at one of the black-market book stalls? Why isn't she interested in the procession?*

Luke overcame his uneasiness about following a woman, and kept a good distance away from her as he trailed her home without her apparently realizing he had done so. He waited behind a tree on the other side of the road as the woman slipped through a black cast-iron gate, before silently entering a terraced house.

Luke waited a couple of minutes, then he skulked through the gate. His boots scrunched the thin blanket of snow much louder than he wanted. He hesitated for a few moments, then sheepishly knocked. He leaned forward and listened intently at the door. *Silence.* He knocked again, a little louder. In the corner of the ceiling above the door, a wispy abandoned spider web clung precariously to the cornices. Light footsteps tapped from inside. His body tensed.

"Who is it?" The female voice from the other side of the door had a distinct French accent. Luke tilted his head to one side. Several moments of a painfully uncomfortable silence lapsed. The voice sounded more urgent. "Who's there? Are you from the Church?"

What should I say? Is she a Church official?

The silence extended. Footsteps began to stomp away from the door.

"No, I'm not from the Church. I'm a private tutor," Luke blurted out as his face flushed red and hot.

From the other side of the door, the footsteps got louder.

"I don't need a tutor. Goodbye." The impatient tone of the woman's voice made Luke catch his breath in his throat. His heart thumped faster. Sweat beaded at his temples and hairline.

"My name is Luke. I live nearby."

"Is something wrong? Do you need any help?"

Another long pause ensued as Luke's mind raced for a response. His shirt became damp under his overcoat. He wrung his gloved, numbed hands. "Yes, I need some help." His voice fell to almost a whisper.

"What's wrong?"

Another long pause filled with rapid thinking and stilted breathing. "Herbs. I ... I need herbs."

"Herbs?"

"Yes. Do you have any herbs for ... for ... for ... ratatouille?" *Is ratatouille made with herbs?* Another long silence followed. Then footsteps moved away from the door again. After a pause the footsteps returned. A moment later, the door finally opened but only halfway.

A slim, attractive woman in her thirties with pale clear skin and straight strawberry-blonde hair stood in front of him, mostly hidden by the door.

"Here's some parsley."

Luke held out an uncertain hand to grasp the small bunch of fresh parsley, but his gaze remained locked onto the woman's face. "We haven't met before, have we?"

The woman looked at Luke with narrowed green eyes. "No. What are you talking about?"

Luke swallowed hard. "Sorry, I shouldn't have bothered you."

The woman frowned. "Did you follow me?"

Luke stood silent for a couple of moments, unsure what to say. The heat in his face got hotter. "I'm sorry. I shouldn't have."

The woman's gaze hardened. "Look, I don't know who you are or what games you're playing. I haven't got time to talk to strangers. You've got some parsley for your ratatouille. Goodbye."

The door slammed shut. Luke's head and shoulders dropped. *Idiot. Why would I follow a woman I've never met before to her home and then knock on her door? How damn stupid.* With a rising mixture of embarrassment and confusion sloshing about in his head, he trudged away.

On his way home, a large crowd in a park began chanting a biblical passage as hooded figures tied up two naked, elderly men to separate wooden poles, propped up in the center of piles of wood and paper. Luke stopped and squinted for several long moments as the men were doused in kerosene. One of the men with a slim build and closely shaved white hair spat and coughed up kerosene, then cried out in an Eastern European accent: "You fucking bastards! Let me fuck all of your assholes before I burn! Please!"

Several people in the crowd shouted as they threw rocks and snowballs at him. "Burn him! Heathen! Burn him!"

The man straightened and scanned the crowd with a smile. "I can't believe none of you want my cock! Well, I'll be waiting for all of you in hell! Get your assholes ready! Fuck all of you!"

Luke grabbed the arm of a woman rushing past him. "Who is that man?"

The woman's eyes shot open wider. She caught her breath and waved a hand in the usual fashion. *"Electus per Deus."*

Luke hastily waved a hand in front of the woman. *"Electus per Deus."*

The woman glanced at the park scene. "Don't know. All I know is that they're two homosexuals. They were caught naked doing unspeakable things to each other in a church. Come on, you don't want to miss the burnings." She smiled and raced away to the park.

Luke shook his head slowly, then turned away. As he plodded away towards his home, the crowd suddenly erupted behind him, and the anguished cries of the men abruptly stopped.

Chapter 11

Luke parked in a visitor car bay at his parents' apartment block. Old election placards dotted the lawn around it. They displayed images of the Pope wearing the white papal miter with gold trim and a white cassock. All the posters proclaimed in big letters, "Make God Great Again." But he hardly noticed them or the enormous colorful banners of the Pope that hung from the tops of almost every building and bridge in and around the city. He had had problems sleeping for days. He had performed his tutoring almost like a robot. And the bewilderment and embarrassment of having followed the French woman to her home wouldn't leave him. Nor would the memory of hearing the two men's final cries from the park.

"The prodigal son has returned!" Luke's father shouted in a sarcastic tone. "Close the bloody door quick — don't let any snow in."

Luke's mother struggled to shift her fragile frame to a single-seater lounge chair after greeting him. "*Electus per Deus,* sweetie." She turned to Luke's father. "Sean! Now be nice for a change."

Luke did his best to pay no attention to the pictures of the Pope and the large metal crucifixes on the walls, as well as to a small table in the corner of the room with rosaries, several unlit candles, a small ceramic bowl of holy water, and a large picture depicting a haloed Jesus.

Luke's father sat unmoved on the couch, his arms bent on the top of his head, and his bloated torso projecting a Friar Tuck look. He rolled his eyes and half-heartedly made the sign of the cross with a limp hand in Luke's direction. "Yes, yes. *Electus per Deus.* But what about him? Betti, he never does it. Jesus Christ!" Sean pushed a hand through his thinning gray hair, then rested his arm back onto the top of his head.

Bettina glowered at him. "Sean!"

Although Luke understood the importance of religious rituals in public, he always ignored the greeting formality whenever he saw his parents.

"We sent him to the best Catholic schools we could afford on our Christian disability pensions and now he rarely goes to church on Sundays. He hasn't been to any book-burnings since he was a kid."

"Sean, please!"

Luke remained standing. "Book-burnings are just nonsense." Blood began surging to his head.

Sean shook his head. "And I bet he didn't go to the flagellation last week. We wasted our money coming to America to send him to the best Catholic schools." He paused momentarily. "Well, go on, ask him."

Bettina dropped her head into her hands and sighed. She clutched handfuls of her short wiry white hair. "Why don't you ask him yourself? You're just exasperating sometimes."

Sean looked at Luke as he pushed his head forward. "Well?"

"Well what?"

Sean threw his arms up. "See!"

Bettina shook her head. "Sweetie, please don't annoy your father."

"See, I'm right. Wonderful Catholic school education — and very expensive — and we've raised a heathen who's going to go to hell. Jesus Christ! Your mother and I will die very happy Christians — they can put on our headstone, 'Here lie Bettina and Sean McNeill, wonderful Catholics and the parents of Luke, a heathen who will go to hell while they're enjoying the good life in heaven.'"

"Shut up, Sean! And keep your voice down. We don't want to be reported to the Morality Police by any of the other residents."

Luke's arms shot up from his sides. "What religious benefits can there be in someone flaying themselves until they bleed and collapse? It's completely ridiculous. What positive role does religion play in society? The Church only gives people false hope. When people blindly believe something, that's when the Church has control over the society. And that's what it wants — social control. What would society be like if people weren't artificially divided on religious beliefs?"

Sean slapped his thighs. "It would be dangerous because there'd be anarchy. Religion gives people faith. You need faith, otherwise society would collapse. If we didn't believe in something, what's the purpose of living?"

Luke sighed. "We all need a purpose, but faith needs to be based on proven truths, not superstitions and fear."

"Oh, Lord. He's possessed."

"No, I've just read very interesting books. They've opened my mind to other ways of thinking — books about science, even about other religions."

"You just said you didn't believe in religions!"

Bettina gasped and dropped her voice. "Oh sweetie, you haven't read any heathen books, have you? You don't keep them at home, do you? If the Morality Police find out, you'll be in trouble — we'll all be in trouble. We'll be thrown in jail." Her feet scraped along the floor as she moved to the front door and listened.

"No one's there. Sit down." The irritation in Sean's voice almost bottlenecked the words in his throat. "How'd you get heathen books? No, don't say a word. I don't want to know. But you're playing with the Devil getting involved in the occult." Sean looked at Bettina. "He went to the dark side that first time we took him to the burnings of those sexual deviants when he was 4. Do you remember he couldn't stop crying? So we left early and we missed the best part. We should've made him watch the whole thing. If we'd done that, he'd have turned out a good Christian and wouldn't be saying all this nonsense."

"The burning of books is appalling enough, but the burning of people is barbaric. The Church burns books about other religions and science because they undermine its power. It keeps knowledge hidden because it's only interested in controlling what people think."

"As the Pope says, 'That's all fake news.' Where'd you get all these conspiracy theories from? No, I don't want to know that either. You can go to hell, but I'm not going to follow you there, even though you're my son. I can't even stand the summers here."

"They're not conspiracy theories. I can't understand why you both just blindly follow what the Church says. Spiritual beliefs don't have to be bound up in any religious dogma."

Sean jumped up. "There's no such thing as spiritual beliefs without religion! Christianity is all about spiritual beliefs."

Luke tensed. "What spiritual experiences have you had?"

"What spiritual experiences do you want? Going to church is a spiritual experience. Watching blasphemous books burn is a spiritual experience. Going to a flagellation procession is a spiritual experience. They are all spiritual experiences and you've not done any of that for years, so don't talk to me about spiritual experiences. Jesus Christ!"

"They're all just meaningless religious ritual, totally empty of any spirituality. Why don't you question things?"

"What's the point of asking meaningless questions? It's a waste of time. Life's simple, thanks to the Church — get baptized, go to confession, pray, go to church, attend book-burnings and flagellations, and when you die, you go to heaven — simple. Why'd you have to question any of that? It only complicates things."

"You know the Buddha said to question everything — not to believe anything just because he said it but to prove things for oneself?"

Sean smirked. "Hah! One minute you say you don't believe in religion and the next you talk about the Buddha. Jesus Christ!"

"I'm not saying I believe in religion, just that's what the Buddha said — seems very wise."

"Look, don't mention that bald-headed heathen in this house. Did he die a painful death on the cross like Jesus? Did he walk on water? Is he the son of God? No, he's not. Never was, never could be, because he wasn't Christian."

"There are stories of the Buddha walking on water. And how would you know Jesus died on the cross? And the Bible doesn't include anything about Jesus traveling to India when he was a teenager or about him going back there after being taken down from the cross. And who knows, the Buddha may have reincarnated as Jesus."

Bettina gasped and put her hands on her cheeks. "Oh Lord."

Sean's face burned red. "Holy mother of God! Reincarnation? Jesus went to India? That's the Devil talking. There's no such thing as reincarnation. Where in the Bible is reincarnation mentioned? Nowhere! And there's no way Jesus went to India — he would've hated the spicy food there."

Luke rolled his eyes and shook his head. "It comes down to interpretation. The Church doesn't tell people there are a lot of similarities between ancient Hindu and Buddhist texts, and secret gospels not included in the Bible."

Sean leaned forward in his chair. "Secret gospels? What are you talking about? The Bible is all God's words — nothing more and nothing less."

Words spilled from Luke's mouth in a torrent. "God's words? The Bible is the writings of men, not God, and it's been translated so many times the original meanings of important words have been lost. The Latin and Hebrew translations of the Bible give a totally different meaning compared to the English translations."

Sean slapped his forehead. "How can there be different meanings of the Bible?"

"The books of the Bible were originally written in Hebrew, Aramaic or Greek — languages I got to know a little when I learned Latin. And there are so many words that have been mistranslated in the English versions of the Bible."

Sean shook his head vigorously. "Nonsense!"

Luke pointed to his father. "Look, the Hebrew word *Elohim* has been mistranslated to mean a single all-powerful God. That's wrong. It actually refers to a group of powerful beings — beings that were human-like, and based on original texts, they were technologically advanced. And what's in the Bible today isn't the full story about Jesus and his life. The Church doesn't tell people there's the Gospel of Mary, and the Gospel of Thomas, and there could've been a Gospel of Q. They all give more accurate insights into Jesus' teachings."

Sean laughed sarcastically. "A Gospel of Q? Who the hell was Q? Was there any Q at the last supper? No, so this Q person's a nobody, otherwise Jesus would've given him an invite. And what God-fearing Christian would name their son 'Q'? It's ridiculous. Next you'll say there's gospels of X, Y, and Z."

Luke shook his head. "Dad, Q wasn't a person. It stands for the German word *Quelle*, which means 'source.'"

"Oh, of course, the Gospel of Sauce — tomato, I hope."

Bettina sat up in her chair. "Will you two stop? Keep your voices down." A long suffocating silence filled the room. "Sweetie, you don't seem yourself. Is everything alright?"

Luke stared at his father, who immediately turned to look at the snowscape beyond the window. Then he turned to his mother. "Sorry. I've just been doing a lot of reading and thinking recently and asking myself a lot of questions. I know what both of you are thinking."

Sean turned to look at Luke. "Yes, you're possessed!"

Bettina slapped a hand on the chair's armrest. "Sean, shut up!"

Sean shot a look at Bettina. "He's reading blasphemous books and talking nonsense about reincarnation, the Buddha, and secret gospels of tomatoes. He's possessed. Our son is possessed. The Devil has possessed him."

"Sean!" Bettina looked intently at Luke. "Sweetie, you mustn't read blasphemous books. They'll disturb your thinking and leave you open to evil spirits."

Sean shook his head. "Evil spirits! No, he's possessed by the Devil himself. The Devil's making him talk about reincarnation and secret gospels. We only have one life. Christians who go to church, and to book-burnings and flagellations, go to heaven. End of story. Simple. The rest go somewhere a little hotter where I'm sure they don't have air conditioning."

Bettina waved a pacifying hand in Sean's direction. "Sweetie, are you praying every day? God will protect you from evil spirits. Evil spirits deliberately confuse people so they lose their faith in God."

Luke's palms became moist. "Mum, have you really met anyone who's been possessed before?"

Bettina nodded. "Not personally. But I've heard awful stories of people being possessed and they had to go through an exorcism. But when they did, they were fine."

Sean suddenly became animated. "That's what he needs — an exorcism. It'll get the Devil and all that Buddhism, reincarnation, and secret gospel nonsense out of him."

"But I can't be possessed, can I? Maybe I should try to find a psychologist."

Sean rested his elbows on his knees and stuck his neck out. "Psychologists are all heathens. If you see one, the Church will crucify you. You haven't seen a psychologist before, have you?"

"No."

Sean sank deeper into his chair. "Look, possession can take many forms. You're reading blasphemous books because the

Devil's been making you do that. You need to go through an exorcism. We should've done it years ago." He turned to Bettina. "Why didn't we?"

Luke's head dropped. "Look, if I'm possessed by the Devil wouldn't I want to burn bibles and deface churches or do crazy things like that?"

"Sweetie, we're not saying you're definitely possessed —"

"Yes we are."

Bettina clenched her teeth. "Sean, shut up, please!" She turned to Luke. "But we're worried about these things you've mentioned. It's not normal for Christians to talk like that."

Luke sighed and ran a hand through his hair. "I shouldn't have mentioned anything." He paused. "But maybe you're both right."

Bettina stood up slowly and moved over to Luke, before putting her arms around him.

Sean waved a hand at her. "Don't get too close or you'll get possessed too!"

Bettina shot a burning look at Sean, then turned back to Luke. "Sweetie, Archbishop Michael does exorcisms all the time. He'll be able to tell if you need one or not. He'll be able to help you. Promise me you'll go see him."

"Maybe."

"He's a lovely man — very kind and understanding. Everyone loves him. Just have a chat to him and see what he thinks. He may not think an exorcism is necessary. He may think you just need to say a few extra prayers. You'll be fine. Okay?"

Luke looked at his mother, who smiled and kissed him on his cheek.

Exorcism! A cold shiver ran up and down Luke's body. "Mum! Really?" He sighed. "Look, I'll think about it."

"Don't just think about it — do it. Please see the Archbishop."

Part 5
2038

Chapter 12

Sometime after the drama with the soldiers, Choepel went to Master Chi's room. Although accustomed to doing so, he wondered if he should have made an appointment through Palmo as disciples were supposed to. Before he knocked, a young fair-skinned nun came out and almost bumped into him. He jumped back.

The nun averted her blue eyes and fiddled nervously with her robes before closing the door behind her. During recent meditations, he had caught her looking at him several times.

Choepel froze and stared at her as his face turned a deeper shade of crimson than their robes. "Sorry, I'm Choepel."

The nun smiled warmly, looked down, and spoke softly. "I'm Dralha. Someone told me you're from Australia too."

Choepel's scalp and the back of his neck tingled — something he had never experienced before.

"Ah, yes."

Dralha put a hand gently onto Choepel's arm. "It would be nice if we got to know each other."

Choepel took a sharp breath. His heart thumped and raced. "That would be nice."

Without saying another word, Dralha scampered to the stairs as she tugged and pulled at her robes. Choepel intently watched her go down the stairs, then turned back to the door. He knocked softly.

"Enter," Master Chi called out from inside.

Choepel took a couple of paces inside, knelt and prostrated, then rose onto his knees. Master Chi lounged on a couch with his eyes closed. A few candles lit the room. A throne exactly like the one in the *gompa* stood against one wall. A massive thin black TV screen almost covered one wall. *Thankas*, whose bright colors glinted even in dim light, covered the other walls.

Master Chi opened his eyes and smiled warmly. "You were brave today, Choepel."

"No, master. Your bravery saved Rabten and the rest of us."

Master Chi's eyes narrowed. "You look troubled. Are you still worried about the Chinese army?"

Choepel took a breath. "It's barbaric, what they did to Rabten. But I know your omniscience will protect us."

Master Chi smiled. "We live in troubled times. Much of the news reports in recent months have been about China's aggression and dominance over other countries."

"I can't understand why America doesn't stand up to China?"

"There's no end in sight to the civil war in America. I haven't been there for years. Our brothers and sisters there are very anxious about the situation. I've had to close nearly all my centers there."

"What happened to the monks and nuns?"

"I've sent most of them to centers in Canada and South America."

"Are those extreme Christian fundamentalists really a serious threat to the government?"

"They're behind assassinations, and terrorism attacks targeting political parties. They seem intent on creating as much chaos as they can."

"I guess it's the price of spiritual ignorance."

"Yes, we need more Buddhas in the world right now, so keep meditating, so you'll be enlightened soon. I want you to join me in the Pure Land of Bliss."

"With your enlightened grace, I will, Master. But I'm beginning to question whether I should be a monk. I don't feel I'm making any progress in my meditation."

"Questions are good. But getting the right answers is better. And how can you judge whether you're making progress or not?"

"Well, my mind wanders to all sorts of crazy thoughts, and when the evening meditation ended, I felt I had to take several moments to ground myself."

Master Chi laughed. "Good. But just remember our perceptions are all just a persistent hallucination." His face took on a serious look. "By doing the most ancient, the most powerful, the most esoteric meditation known, we can shatter the hallucination and attain the clear light of bliss. The path to enlightenment can be dangerous because of our karma, and demons can put all sorts of obstacles in our way. But with my guidance, we're going to break through whatever obstacles are put before you. The key is to keep meditating. I'll guide you to the Pure Land."

Choepel bowed his head. "Yes, of course, Master. This may seem like a strange question, but why did you decide to turn your back on a secular life and academia?"

Master Chi smiled, and a long silence preceded his words. "I realized that science can only ever give us a limited knowledge — limited by the technological discoveries of the time. Buddhism gives us a timeless wisdom. You know, for centuries scientists couldn't agree whether light is a wave or separate particles. But what scientists still don't realize is that consciousness is like light — it's made up of a stream of separate awareness events. Each one emerges so quickly, the physical world appears to be always here. But it's constantly being created in our heads by each new awareness event. It's all just in our heads."

Choepel straightened as Master Chi's words reverberated in his head, illuminating hidden, dark crevices. "Master, it makes me think of many more questions."

"Like what?"

"Like, what is that space between each new awareness event? And what would it be like to go into that space? Is awareness even possible between each new awareness event?"

Master Chi laughed. "Now that is the purpose of meditation. When you go into that space between awareness events then all your questions will be answered — even those questions you haven't yet thought about."

"Yes, Master. Did you study science here, Master?"

"Yes. My parents wanted me to go to university in Vietnam but they couldn't afford it. I managed to scrape enough money together here, doing odd jobs. But one day, I heard a talk by a Buddhist monk, and I realized the dharma is more important."

"It's your destiny, Master. You found the dharma and liberated millions of people."

"Yes." Master Chi paused and glanced at a large portrait of himself, painted by Rabten, hanging on a wall. "What is your original face?"

Choepel's brow folded. "My original face?"

"Yes, what did your face look like before your parents were born?"

Choepel shook his head pensively.

"Your original face is your true self — it's not Choepel. Our perceptions are like the fog on a mirror. Wipe off the fog, and the mirror will reflect your original face clearly."

Choepel bowed. "Yes, Master."

Master Chi looked past Choepel, seemingly in deep reflection. "All my disciples escape the Wheel of Life because only I know the way out. I want you to meditate on what I've said." He put a hand on Choepel's cheek and smiled. "Think about this deeply."

"Yes, Master."

Chapter 13

Days later, Choepel visited a recuperating Rabten in his room. He had visited Rabten in his room many times over the years. Several months after Choepel had arrived at the monastery, Rabten invited him to his room to have his portrait done. Thrilled to be finally asked, Choepel went with some trepidation because of Rabten's reputation for talking incessantly whenever he painted or sketched a portrait.

As he brushed and smeared colors impulsively onto the large white canvas, Rabten turned to Choepel. "Have you ever died?"

Choepel frowned and smirked. "I know we've had thousands of lives, but I don't remember dying in any of them." He paused for a moment. "Have you died?"

Rabten turned back to the canvas and said casually. "Yes, many times. It's fun."

Choepel stared at Rabten as he continued painting and repeatedly moved his head closer, then away from the canvas. After a long period of silence, Rabten then turned to Choepel again. "Do you know what a Black Hole is?"

"Isn't it a dying star?"

Rabten's eyes narrowed. "We die exactly the same way a star dies. A tiny Black Hole is created in the center of our brains before our consciousness leaves from the top of our heads. As above, so below."

For several moments, Choepel thought deeply about what Rabten had said. "Did Master Chi tell you that?"

Rabten turned back to the canvas and continued applying paint nonchalantly. "No, I told you I've died many times. I visit different places and meet wonderful beings. You should try it."

That brief conversation stayed with Choepel, and from that day he regarded Rabten differently and enjoyed spending time with him and hearing his ideas on a range of subjects, but most often the conversations turned to art and philosophy — never Buddhism. Whenever Choepel mentioned Buddhism, Rabten would either ignore him or change the subject. Rabten's wide-ranging knowledge impressed Choepel, especially given Rabten had left school while still a teenager. And knowing Rabten's apparent lack of interest in Buddhism, it didn't surprise Choepel that he rarely attended any of the group meditation sessions or talks by Master Chi. But Rabten and Master Chi spent a lot of time together. Much more time than Master Chi spent with any other monk. Rabten often accompanied Master Chi on his overseas trips, on which he always took one or two nuns. Rabten would also sometimes sleep in Master Chi's top-floor room at the monastery. On numerous occasions, Choepel and others had seen Rabten taking fast food and alcohol into Master Chi's room late at night.

But everyone at the monastery apparently accepted Rabten and his eccentric behavior, even his saunters and runs through the monastery at all times of the day and night, completely naked, often laughing while shouting expletives, sometimes in Mandarin or English or Latvian or even in Russian. The English and the few Russian nuns seemed to find the erratic behavior more amusing than the Chinese nuns and monks. The head monk, Zopa, had pleaded with him on numerous occasions to stop his naked activities, but all the other monks and nuns seemingly realized that Rabten's eccentricities couldn't be curtailed.

Palmo stood beside Rabten's bed. The grazes on his body had almost healed and the swelling around his face had dissipated. She turned to Choepel. "We nearly lost him. We thought he had severe internal injuries and broken bones. But the doctor finally came and said it's only bruising. We can thank Master for looking after him."

Choepel moved to the other side of the bed near two other nuns. "Has he woken at all?"

Palmo gently put a hand on Rabten's head. "He sleeps for several hours a day. He wakes briefly, eats a little, then goes back to sleep. It'll be quite some time before we'll see him running naked around the monastery shouting expletives."

Choepel smiled broadly and the nuns near him put their hands to their mouths and giggled softly like schoolgirls. Choepel looked at Palmo. "Do you know Rabten's birth name?"

"Um. Bendiks, I think. Yes, Bendiks. Why?"

"Ah, just curious." He looked away briefly. "And that new nun from Australia, Dralha, what's her birth name?"

Palmo grimaced. "Why are you so interested in everyone's birth names all of a sudden?"

Choepel shrugged. "Just want to get to know people better, that's all."

"Anna. Don't get any ideas about her, because she's Master's favorite at the moment. They spend a lot of time talking about weird stuff — she's studied science too. And she happens to speak French, so she's translating Master's books for us. Some have great karma — good looks and great brains."

Choepel grinned. "Yep, everything's karma."

As Choepel stepped out of the room, Palmo turned to him. "Oh, there's a new disciple arriving tomorrow afternoon. She's a Westerner and wants to be ordained. All the nuns are busy. Can you meet her at the train station?"

"Sure."

A sardonic smile crept across Palmo's mouth. "Now don't you want to know her name?"

Choepel nodded.

"Sophia. Oh, and that reminds me, I need to ask Dralha to prepare Sophia's room. She somehow managed to get into Taipei from overseas — amazing given the situation. She'll be in at 3 p.m. There'll be checkpoints, so take your passport and be careful."

Choepel nodded. "Yes."

Palmo turned to look at a large portrait of Master Chi on the wall opposite Rabten's bed. "The Buddha will protect you."

Choepel looked at the painting and smiled.

Chapter 14

Bang! Bang! Bang! The thick, heavy monastery door rattled.

Choepel slapped his book shut and threw it onto his bed. His room on the ground floor in the east wing looked out onto the courtyard entrance. He parted the curtains carefully, only a few millimeters. The light from the full moon hitting the mandalas created a shadow over the monastery door where a darkened, mostly obscured figure crouched down.

Bang! Bang! Bang!

Several footsteps scrapped chaotically in the corridor outside his room. Choepel half-opened his door and poked his head outside. Several monks with shielded candles in hands shuffled in a tight huddle to the main entrance. He joined them.

Bang! Bang! Bang!

A few nuns, their arms interlocked, whispered and gasped among themselves as they followed the monks into the lobby.

Zopa reached the door first, but he didn't open it. He leaned close to it and turned his head to one side. "Who is it?" His whispered voice shook in perfect Mandarin.

Everyone huddled behind him back from the door in complete silence and listened.

"Please help," a desperate male voice answered in English in a hushed tone.

Choepel's heart raced as Zopa handed his candle to a nun. He opened the door cautiously.

The door burst open and a portly, balding Westerner almost fell inside. He held a young girl with obvious Chinese features. A shared terror bound them. The man panted and the girl looked dazed. Choepel squinted as he stared for a long moment, first at the man, then at the girl.

The man turned and forced the door closed. His sweaty cheeks rounded as he let out an audible exhalation. Then he knelt and put his arms around the girl's shoulders. Zopa, who preferred Mandarin over English, turned to the nuns with a helpless expression. Palmo, who spoke perfect English, stepped forward and approached the man. "What's wrong?"

"Please help. They've killed my wife. Please hide my child. They're after me."

"Who?"

The man gasped for air. "Soldiers. They're killing people at English media organizations." The man took a breath. "Please hide my daughter, Ai, here. She'll be safe here. I need to find her grandparents."

Master Chi suddenly appeared at the top of the stairs, holding a candle. He spoke in Mandarin with an authoritative tone. "What's going on?"

Everyone turned towards him, bowed their heads, and clasped their hands. The jumping candle flames cast grotesque shadows on the walls and ceiling.

Palmo turned on her knees. "Master, this man wants to leave his daughter with us because soldiers are after him. He says they've shot his wife."

Master Chi strode down the stairs. He rested his hand softly on Ai's straight short black hair, then looked at the man, hunched over her. In English, "Who are you and why did Chinese soldiers shoot your wife?"

The man sobbed as he held Ai tighter. "I'm Australian. I'm the editor at the *Taipei Times*. My name is Charles. Soldiers broke into my apartment in Taipei and shot my wife when she tried to stop them getting inside. I managed to escape here with the help of friends. I'm looking for my wife's parents. I've been unable to contact them." He glanced at Ai. "Please hide her in your monastery and keep her safe. I'm not Buddhist, but my wife's parents are. They're Taiwanese." He took a deep breath. "Please hide Ai here. The soldiers won't look for her here. I'll come back after I find her grandparents."

Jampa, a Thai monk, leaned heavily on his cane as he stepped forward. In Mandarin, "Master, if we keep the girl here, we will be a target for the army. You and the rest of us will all be in danger."

Choepel moved forward and looked at Master Chi, before speaking in Mandarin. "Master, this man and his daughter deserve our compassion."

Master Chi put his hand under Ai's chin and smiled at her teary, blank face. "Everyone is a target now that the Chinese army has arrived."

Jampa bowed. "But Master, we must protect you and the dharma. The army will attack the monastery if they find out we're hiding someone they want. We'll all be killed."

Master Chi stroked Ai's reddish cheeks. "How old are you, my darling?"

Charles patted Ai's head. "She's only 5. Her English is better than her Mandarin."

Ai turned to her father. "Daddy, I want Mummy."

Charles stroked Ai's cheeks with the back of his hand.

Master Chi smiled at Ai. "A man stands tallest and most powerful when he protects the vulnerable." He then turned to Jampa. "Your fear of death has made you fearful of life. You need to meditate on the meaning of compassion."

Jampa's brown face flushed and he bowed his head. "Yes, Master. Forgive me."

Master Chi looked down to Ai and smiled. He spoke slowly in English. "Have you eaten, my child?" Ai shook her head and wiped her eyes. He then turned to Palmo. "Feed her and hide her in the storage room in the west wing. Go quickly." He then looked at Charles and smiled with his eyes. "Your daughter will be safe with us. The Buddha will protect her. Now go before the soldiers find you."

Palmo picked up Ai and rushed her out the lobby as tears rolled down the girl's face and she called out for her father.

Charles whimpered and fell to his knees. "Thank you. You're a saint. I'll return as soon as I can." He turned hurriedly to leave.

Choepel stepped forward and opened the door for him. "I'm sorry about your wife," he whispered.

Charles looked into Choepel's filling eyes. "Thank you. Rose was the kindest person. She didn't deserve to be murdered."

"I'm very sorry."

Charles' gaze fell, then he rushed into the courtyard, a lonely figure. The crunching of his wary footsteps on gravel, then the slapping on bitumen beyond the arched monastery gate, quickly faded. Solemnly, the monks and nuns separated, then returned to their respective wings.

Choepel sat on the edge of his bed as the faint candlelight threw dark shapes on the floor. Stillness prevailed inside and outside the monastery. Before the invasion, cars and people always moved on the streets near the monastery, no matter the time of night. At that time of night, market traders would normally be restocking their stalls in preparation for the following day. He often went to the markets to buy fresh food and other provisions for the monastery. He had done that for years and got to know most of the traders by name. He honed his Mandarin there. He even picked up some Taiwanese words and phrases. But since the night-time curfew, only soldiers on foot patrols and military vehicles ventured onto the streets.

As Choepel lay down to sleep, raised voices exploded outside the monastery shouting out to someone to stop. He lay frozen as the pounding of running boots faded. The voices rose up again — louder and more urgent. Then a series of rifle shots screamed through the night, drowning out the voices. Each blast made his body jolt. The boots stopped running. He looked outside as the soldiers' voices became sadistic laughter. In the center of several soldiers' torch beams, Charles' motionless body lay on the street. Choepel dropped to his knees and held his head in his hands. After several moments, he crawled to his bed, and closed his filling eyes as his thoughts turned to Ai.

Part 6

2022

Chapter 15

After days of procrastination about whether he should take Rupert's advice, Jeremy phoned Dr Mason's clinic. While on the phone to the receptionist, she told him an appointment had been canceled and persuasively offered him the timeslot. He accepted it with some reluctance.

Being only 3 kilometers from Sydney's central business district, Glebe's diverse residents and businesses made its main streets buzz all hours of the day and night. The manic main streets could have been a world away from Jeremy's home rather than just a block.

Jeremy trudged through the throngs of people past tapas bars, barber shops, massage parlors, convenience stores, cafés, and noodle shops. A homeless man often straddled the footpath outside a pharmacy, usually in a drunken stupor or sometimes sketching with crayons. The man's sunken eyes and face hid behind a long black beard and unkempt hair. The man intrigued Jeremy. When he first saw him, their eyes had met, and he pondered the hint of recognition, although he didn't know from where. With heightened curiosity, he had asked the pharmacist if she knew anything about him and she told him the man had introduced himself to one of her staff as Vilis.

A boy named Vilis had been at Jeremy's high school, but he had never spoken with him. Vilis had walked with an obvious limp, which Jeremy assumed was some form of disability. The boy's lisp and eastern European accent made him a target for the bullies at school. Although Jeremy had felt sorry for him and thought about offering to help him with his English, a wall of embarrassment prevented any friendship being established. Then one day, Vilis mysteriously stopped attending school. Jeremy never found out why and never saw him again. The homeless man outside the pharmacy always made him think about Vilis.

Jeremy found Dr Mason's office at the far end of a quiet residential street. At the front door, his heart rate increased and his palms became sweaty. He slid his tongue over dry lips, pushed back his hair with his hands, and repositioned his jacket using only his shoulders. He closed his eyes momentarily and focused on his breath. His heart rate slowed.

Inside, Jeremy walked down a narrow timber-floored hallway and turned into a small room, signposted as the reception area. He introduced himself to the elderly female receptionist sitting behind a high beige counter. He recognized her voice from the phone conversation. She expressed her joy that he could come at short notice, and gave him a form to complete. After he handed the completed form back and sat down, a woman wearing a black T-shirt displaying the striking black, red, and yellow Aboriginal flag walked in. With her head bowed, she wiped her eyes with a crumpled tissue. She wore tight blue jeans and had straight, long, honey-blonde hair tied behind her head. Her smooth honey complexion extended to her thin honey arms.

The receptionist held out a box of tissues over the counter. "Oh, Gracie, I know it must be hard."

Gracie took a tissue from the box. "Thanks. Dr Mason has helped me so much. He's so sweet."

"Yes, he's wonderful. I feel for you, darling. Would you like to book your next appointment?"

Gracie nodded as a bearded man with thick short graying hair entered the room. His head almost touched the top of the doorway. She turned to him. "Thanks, Dr Mason. If it wasn't for you, I don't think I'd be alive."

Dr Mason smiled warmly. He wore a light gray suit, a perfectly pressed white shirt, and a navy-blue tie — clothes that could have placed him comfortably in a corporate setting rather than a private psychological practice. "Take care, Gracie." His deep, slow voice with a North American accent filled the small room.

Gracie dabbed her eyes. "You're a saint."

Dr Mason held out an open leatherbound book. "Genesis chapter 4 verse 7. I think it will help you."

Jeremy frowned.

Dr Mason looked at Jeremy and smiled. "Hello, you must be Jeremy. Please come through, just to the end of the hall." He pointed the way.

Jeremy paused, then walked down the hall into the consulting room, his posture slightly bent. In the center of the room stood a plush, pale chaise longue with ballooning floral cushions and a low curled headrest. Near it stood a high-backed chair with a single large navy-blue cushion. Partly parted heavy, long, dark curtains gave the room a night-time tinge. Large color photographs of white buildings, white churches, and white, narrow, cobblestoned lanes in the Old City of Jerusalem lined the walls, except the one covered by two floor-to-ceiling wooden bookshelves that stood side by side holding thick, mostly hardcover books and framed university qualifications. A shiny gold crucifix hung on the wall behind a large desk.

Jeremy stopped at the lounge chair. "Can I sit instead?"

Dr Mason settled into his chair. "Sure. I just want to get to know you first and find out why you've come before we do anything."

Jeremy sat stiffly. "Is that an American accent?"

Dr Mason didn't look up from the form. "Yes. North Carolina." He deliberately emphasized his accent by holding on to his vowels and extending the "r" sounds.

Jeremy squirmed. "Ah, the Bible Belt." His heart rate quickened. "Look, I don't think it was a good idea me coming. I'm not religious. It's best I go." Jeremy wiped his hands on his jeans and stood up to leave.

Dr Mason put one leg over the other. "Yes, I've been raised a Catholic and I go to church every week. But I don't see why my religious convictions should bother you?"

"Well, they do. I didn't come here to be given superficial scriptural advice. It's not going to help me."

Jeremy turned and moved to the door. He grabbed the door handle.

Dr Mason remained seated. "Christianity has given solace to millions of people around the world. It's given me solace, and through it I've found meaning and purpose in life."

Jeremy turned to face Dr Mason. His arms shot from his sides. "For centuries religious beliefs have been used to legitimize wars. What about the crusades against Islam? The Middle East has been a hotbed of religious conflict for centuries. In Myanmar, Buddhists have persecuted Muslims. Where's the peace and solace there?"

Dr Mason's elbows pressed into the arms of his chair, and his body straightened. "Don't confuse conflicts with religious teachings."

Jeremy's words shot from his mouth. "I'm not confusing the two, but religious beliefs have started conflicts. I came here to see a psychologist, not a priest. I shouldn't have come."

"You came here for help. I can help you. We won't talk about religion." Dr Mason pointed to his qualifications on the bookshelf. "I'm a psychologist. I help people in whatever way I can. I gave Gracie the scripture because it will help her. She, like me, believes in God. We attend the same church. But that's not the only way I help people. My approach to psychology is based on science, and my belief in God is too."

Jeremy shook his head. "How can a belief in God be based on science? There is no scientific evidence of God."

Dr Mason took a breath, seemingly to collect his thoughts. He spoke slowly. "Can you deny any of your experiences, no matter how weird they may be? No. Your experiences shape your beliefs. I see people every day who have experiences that are irrational and have no evidential basis in reality, but I don't deny those experiences. I'm not going to deny any of your experiences, so please do me the courtesy and don't deny my experiences that prove to me the existence of God. I want to help you, so please sit down and tell me about your experiences and why you came to see me." A fleeting smile momentarily appeared on his face. "Don't worry, I won't be sending you to confession."

Jeremy took a deep breath. "I wouldn't go even if you did." He glanced at the crucifix, then slunk to the couch and retook his seating position.

Dr Mason continued reading the form and asked questions about Jeremy's written answers. He probed Jeremy about growing up in Sydney; about him being the only child; about his parents dying when he was very young and being raised by multiple foster carers; about his work as a freelance writer; about his never having had a girlfriend for more than a few months; about his drinking every evening; about how his problems with sleeping began as a child, and about whether he could recall if anything traumatic had happened at that time.

"No."

Dr Mason's voice softened. "I'm sorry about your parents."

Jeremy's face went pale. He looked up to the ceiling before his head dropped.

Dr Mason studied Jeremy's face. "Sometimes the unconscious can suppress a traumatic event to protect us. I can see you're displaying high levels of anxiety, which is likely a response to trauma."

Jeremy's body stiffened and his breathing faltered. "I can't sleep and I sometimes just get a little anxious driving over the harbor."

"Gephyrophobia — a fear of crossing bridges. But I suspect that's probably not the real issue. There's good psychological evidence to suggest that intense anxieties and other phobias can stem from an underlying fear of something like … something else. In your case, I think it's buried in your subconscious. I'd like to see if that underlying fear stems back to something that's happened in your past. Hypnotherapy is a way we could access that hidden memory safely."

"Hypnotherapy? I don't think so."

Dr Mason's voice took on an authoritative tone. "I use it with many of my clients. It's a way to access and reframe the subconscious. You remain in control at all times."

Jeremy leaned back and his head tilted with his body. "Reframe my subconscious? I don't want to offend you, but your beliefs are not my beliefs and they never will be."

"Reframing your subconscious is about changing the way you think about things, not about inserting my beliefs into your brain. Please lie down, relax, and we can get started."

After a few moments of hesitation, Jeremy slowly reclined on the lounge chair.

Dr Mason's voice slowed and became softer. "Good. Make yourself comfortable. Close your eyes and relax. Take a couple of deep breaths and forget about what you plan to do later today and about anything you may be thinking about, whether it's a recent memory or perhaps a memory from a long time ago. Just empty the mind and focus on your body lying down. Listen to my voice carefully. Ignore any sounds you may hear from outside this room. Any sounds won't disturb your state of relaxation. You're going to be so relaxed that you won't have the strength to open your eyes. Focus on each breath. With each breath you exhale, you will go into a deeper state of relaxation."

Jeremy squirmed.

"Keep your eyes closed … Relax … Feel a warm wave of relaxation go from the top of your head to the tips of your toes … With every deep breath, you go into a deeper state of relaxation … Deeper and deeper … More and more relaxed …

Empty your mind of all thoughts ... Focus only on my voice ... With every breath, your body and mind relax deeper and deeper ... Breathe and relax ... Breathe and relax ... Breathe and relax ... When I count down to three, you will be in the deepest state of relaxation your body and mind can achieve."

Jeremy dry-swallowed. The darkness behind his eyes reminded him of being in meditation, but he had never encountered a darkness so deep before.

"One ... Two ... Three ... You may not consciously hear my voice, but that's okay because I'm speaking to your unconscious mind — that all-powerful part of you ... I want your unconscious mind to take you to when you started having fearful thoughts. To that time in your life when those thoughts made you feel anxious ... It may be a few weeks ago ... A few months ago ... A few years ago ... I want your unconscious mind to take you to that time ..."

Jeremy's body blenched. His breathing quickened and his limbs became rigid. "It's dark. Really dark."

"Okay. Just relax. You're safe. Breathe slowly. How old are you? Where are you?"

Jeremy's eyes burst wide open. "No!" The dim light burned the back of his brain. He gasped for air. His damp shirt clung to his body. He lifted himself from the lounge chair and held his head in his hands.

Dr Mason straightened in his chair. "Just breathe slowly and relax."

"I don't know what happened."

"What do you recall?"

"I don't know."

"What did you see?"

"I don't know. It was too black."

"Did you feel anything?"

"I don't know — it was very uncomfortable."

"Are you okay?"

Jeremy looked at his trembling hands. "I don't know."

"Did you see anyone?"

Jeremy shook his head. "I don't know."

Dr Mason stared at Jeremy for several moments, then made some notes. "Look, I think a gentler approach would be better for you. For whatever reason, your subconscious doesn't seem to want to let us in. Have you heard about music therapy — it can help reduce stress?"

Jeremy shook his head. "Yes, but I don't know much about it."

"There's a music therapist just on the other side of the road not far from here. By chance, I bumped into her the other day. Her name's Justine. Have a chat to her. Get back in touch with me when you think you're ready."

Chapter 16

A few beers usually beckoned sleep, but Jeremy couldn't keep still for more than a few minutes as he lay in bed with his arms crossed and legs tense. He wriggled his toes and rubbed his feet together to warm them up. The distant rumble of middle-of-the-night traffic seemed like a pleasant distraction for the first time. It tethered his swirling, hypnogogic thoughts to something familiar, something real, something tangible his senses could latch on to.

Quantum physics — just theoretical mumbo bloody jumbo. Who cares about whether something's an object or a wave? Or about some mind-numbing dual ... shit ... experiment. How does shining a light through a couple of holes actually help anyone? Anyone can shine a light through a hole or two holes or any number of holes. You don't need to be an Einstein to do that. I need the money, but I shouldn't have listened to Rupert. He's so full of himself. He needs to shine a light on himself. And hypnotherapy — what a waste of time. Why hypnosis? What's the diagnosis? Is it neurosis? Is it psychosis? What's the prognosis? Subconsciousness in darkness. Too young for a midlife crisis. Maybe hallucinosis. Is this just kenosis? God, he's so religious. Why the Book of Genesis? The Old Testament and Moses. Jerusalem's old gate closes. The holy land. The hand of God. God doesn't play dice, God always plays nice. God have mercy on man and mice. The lamb of God who takes away the sins of the world. Give us world peace, not world hunger. Food for the old and for the younger. Feast like a priest at the last supper. The painting has strange meanings. Leonardo's mysterious beings. A seer's strange seeings. Stranger things and strange inklings. The Internet of strange things. A superhighway of strange strings. Strange quantum vibrating things. Vibrating rings of Superstrings. Lord of the Rings or Lord of the Strings. One string to rule them all, one string to find them. One string to bring them all, and in the darkness bind them. No strings attached, for you shall not pass the Bridge of Khazad-dûm. Why is it so hard to cross the bridge, the harbor bridge of doom? Darkness hides a deadly secret in a cold dark deathly room. Sometimes doors must not bring light into a room too soon. Sometimes brightness, sometimes darkness. Sometimes gladness, sometimes sadness. Sometimes the mind is gripped by madness. Happiness, sadness, madness are just states of the mind. The happy, sad, mad mind is like a mirror for the blind. Mind that mad mirror. Mirror that mad mind. Mirror the still mind of tranquility. The still Sea of Tranquility. One small step for man, one giant leap for mankind. Trampoline steps are what you make, jumping on the moon. I hope my finger doesn't break, pointing to the moon. The finger pointing to the moon is not the moon, you goon. One finger. One step. One moon. A lunar eclipse at noon. Moon mantra. Tantra. The magic tantra mind. Seek and you shall find. Magic. Manic. Freelance critic. Tragic. Tantric. Deadline panic. Logic. Karmic. What's the verdict? Karma. Drama. Karma Loka. Good karma. Bad karma. Karma Sutra. Calmer, calmer, calmer, calmer, calmer in an aquarium. Seaweed-eating fish are vegetarian. By George you're a humanitarian. Oh boy. Boy lama. The Dalai Lama teaches the dharma. Mantra. Mudra. Manjushri. Mandala. Nelson Mandela, a noble Bodhisattva. The Four Noble Truths, three wise monkeys, two turtle doves, and a partridge in a pear tree. Birds of a feather flock together. Wisdom and compassion are like the wings of a bird. With only one wing the bird cannot fly. But two wings on the wind take the bird high. What is the sound of one bird flocking? What is the sound of one wing flapping? What is the sound of one hand clapping? One bird, one wing, one hand. Flocking, flapping, clapping. If you're sleepy and you know it, flap your hands. But I'm unhappy and I know it, and hypnosis just won't do it. I'm unhappy and I know it, so what's the point?

Part 7

2038

Chapter 17

Dralha sat down on Choepel's bed. He had just returned to his room from the morning meditation when she had knocked softly on his door.

Dralha smiled kindly. "I'm not disturbing you, am I?"

"No. Are you alright?"

"I just want to tell you, I felt a connection to you the first time I saw you."

"Really? I suppose everyone here has some shared karma and that's why we're all here at the monastery."

Dralha rested her hand on Choepel's arm. "Yes, but I feel a deeper connection to you than anyone else here, apart from the Master, of course."

"Maybe because we're both Australian —"

"No, it's much deeper than that."

Choepel searched Dralha's sparkling blue eyes. "Well, maybe."

"Do you believe in past lives? I'm not sure I do."

Choepel hesitated. "If you believe in karma, you have to believe in past lives. Why do you have doubts?"

Dralha seemed briefly troubled by the question. "I studied quantum physics and neuropsychology at university. Intellectually, I know the past and future are just illusions because linear time is an illusion. Only the *now* is real and all we ever have. I sometimes feel I'm stuck in the illusory past or lost in the imaginary future."

"I suppose we can never run away from our memories."

"No — unless we have memory problems."

Choepel's eyes and mouth widened. "But it's just occurred to me that the whole concept of karma is based on the concept of linear time. If linear time is an illusion, then so is karma."

Dralha smiled. "That's really insightful. And space and time are actually the same thing. The *now* is to time as the *here* is to space. Space, time, karma are all just illusions." She paused briefly. "Our minds can make us believe all sorts of things. It just proves things may not always be as they seem."

"Master says that our perceptions create a persistent hallucination."

"Yes. I think the secret is to discern reality from illusion."

"You're a very deep person — deep and wise."

Dralha clasped her hands and dropped her head. "No one's ever said I'm deep and wise. It's strange you think that, because I guess you're a few years older than me. But maybe that's why I've always been drawn to older men."

Choepel's racing heart thrummed in his head. He put a hand gently onto Dralha's shoulder. "Thanks for coming by. Are you settling in okay?"

Dralha's face turned a light shade of red. "I had to leave Australia. My life's been completely upended. Buddhism's been a lifeline for me. Master Chi's my savior."

Choepel slid his hand onto Dralha's arm. "What made you leave?"

Dralha turned to Choepel. "My mother was murdered —"

Choepel grimaced. "Murdered?"

Dralha's head dropped. "She was an escort and the police suspect one of her clients killed her. My father and I had no idea my mother led that type of life or that she made pornographic videos under the pseudonym 'the French Mistress.' You can imagine our shock, because she read the Bible and prayed for hours every day. The shock of the murder and finding out about my mum's secret life overwhelmed my father. He took his own life a few weeks later. I couldn't continue at university and thought about suicide myself. I guess I'm running away, but I've come here to start a new life."

Choepel knelt down in front of Dralha. "Oh, I'm so sorry. Having to deal with all that trauma must be overwhelming."

Dralha wiped her eyes. "Well, the past is just an illusion, right?" She forced a brief smile. "People you think you know can keep the darkest of secrets. You're the only person here I've told — apart from the Master. I've become very close to him. For the first time in my life, I feel truly loved. I can't see myself ever leaving the Master, even though things are very uncertain at the moment. But when I saw you, I felt a very deep connection to you. We're two lost souls looking for meaning."

Choepel's eyes narrowed slightly and his face became hot.

Dralha stared deep into Choepel's eyes. "Please don't be like all the other men, who seduced me, then abused me. I now suspect many of them had been my mother's clients. I don't want my life to turn out like hers. I don't want to be treated like an object for only satisfying someone's depraved desires."

"Dralha, you're safe here. Here at the monastery, Master Chi and all the monks and nuns are focused on getting enlightened."

Dralha took a deep breath. "Don't you think I'm attractive?"

Choepel's brow knitted. "Yes, you're attractive, but I see you as a nun, not as just a beautiful woman."

Dralha took another deep breath and stared at the floor. "But even nuns have desires, and sometimes those desires can be overwhelming. I can actually understand why my mother lived the secret life she did. I thought living a monastic life would enable me to get past all those desires, but it's hard. Do you still have desires?"

Choepel's face turned bright red. "Sometimes." He looked away. "But I focus on the meditation, Master's books, and the precepts."

Dralha smiled. "I listen to music with special binaural tones when I need to focus. I listen to the tones with headphones I created while at university — they're magical."

"Binaural tones?"

"It's where two different frequencies are fed into each ear. What's magical is that the brain processes each tone and creates a third tone, which is the difference between the two tones. It's through that third tone where you go into a deep state of relaxation. It's better than meditation."

"Really? That's very interesting."

Dralha stood up in front of Choepel and gently put her warm, soft palms on his cheeks. "I'm so glad you find it interesting. You're the only person I've told here — I haven't even told the Master. I won't be like my mother and keep secrets from you. Do you keep secrets?"

"No."

"Can I trust you?"

Choepel looked deeply into Dralha's watery eyes. "Of course."

Dralha smiled. "Do you trust me?"

Choepel hesitated momentarily. "Of course I do."

Dralha grinned broadly. "I want to share my special music with you, and only you. It'll bring us closer together." She dropped her voice to a whisper. "Would you like that?"

Choepel's heart raced a little faster. "Sure."

Dralha's eyes narrowed. "I'm so glad to hear that." She slowly leaned forward and went to kiss Choepel on his lips, but he quickly turned his head and she kissed him leisurely on the cheek.

Chapter 18

Being alone with Dralha in his room had made Choepel uneasy. Since becoming a monk, he had never felt so attracted to a woman. He had to constantly remind himself of his monastic vows. His desires waged a frenetic battle in his mind throughout the morning meditation when he could feel her eyes on him from time to time, but he dared not look in her direction. Yet he couldn't avoid their gazes meeting when she came out of a spare room on the top floor. She stepped so close to him he thought she intended to kiss him again.

He inched away from her. "Prepared the room for the new arrival?"

Dralha nodded, smiled, blushed, and disappeared down the stairs.

Thoughts of Dralha made him perspire as he drove over the Xingzhong Bridge straddled across the Houjin River. Before he arrived at the Oil Refinery Elementary School station, he had to go through a Chinese army checkpoint. After waiting in a queue of vehicles for about 15 minutes, he slowed the car in front of several makeshift concrete barriers and old rusty drums. Several soldiers standing beside a line of military vehicles sneered at him when they saw his robes.

Choepel handed his passport to a soldier towering beside the driver's window. The soldier wrenched the car door open and pushed the barrel of his rifle under Choepel's chin. "Get out of car."

Choepel's heart raced as he scanned the grimy faces. *Some of the same brutes who beat up Rabten.*

Before Choepel could straighten, the soldier pushed him against the side of the car using the length of the rifle. "You monks are fucking homosexuals. Don't think I'm going to kiss you. You driving around looking for boys to fuck?" The other soldiers writhed and guffawed.

"Australians like fucking kangaroos and koalas," shouted another soldier on the side of the road. The others around him bent over as they belly-laughed.

"And sheep," shouted another soldier.

The first soldier rolled his eyes. "No, idiot! New Zealanders fuck sheep." Laughter erupted around him, then quickly subsided. He scowled at Choepel. "China for the Chinese. You fucking go back to Australia."

Choepel slowly eased his body off the car and straightened. He spoke calmly. "I've been here for years. This is my home. Can you please let me go to the train station? I must meet someone."

The soldier rocked back with his eyes popping out of his head. He slapped the passport in his hand and bent the cover and pages hard as he glanced through it. Then he threw it through the open car door. "Get into car and piss off. Remember, no homosexuals allowed here. And leave animals alone."

Choepel took a couple of deep breaths, got into the car, and drove carefully around the concrete barriers as several pairs of soldiers' eyes followed the vehicle suspiciously.

Many more soldiers than commuters milled about inside the station. But it seemed empty compared to how it would usually be. He checked the arrivals board to see if the train from Taipei had arrived. It had. He scanned the lobby for a Western woman among the Asian faces. A woman with a shaved head of red hair had her back to him as she talked with a tall man with a suit jacket draped over his arm. He continued scanning the lobby. When he looked back, he noticed the woman's Western features. She stepped towards him with a laptop case over one shoulder and a large billowing bag over the other. Her oversized pink windcheater fell over the pockets of her tight faded jeans. The man had disappeared. She smiled as she stopped in front of him. "You must be from the Secret Tantric Tradition monastery. I'm Sophia."

She held out her hand. "Are monks allowed to touch a woman?"

Choepel smiled, while his gaze remained fixated on Sophia's gemstone green eyes. "Um, yes," he replied in English. "Um, I'm Choepel." He held out a tentative hand and felt Sophia's slip warmly into it. Her soft, smooth hand gripped his more than he hers.

Sophia looked around for the station exit. "Do you have a car?"

"Ah, yes. Just outside. Do you want me to carry anything for you?"

"No, that's fine."

At the checkpoint, the soldier who had confronted Choepel earlier didn't bother to look at his passport again, but a soldier on the passenger side of the car with his rifle strapped to his back asked to see Sophia's. Choepel's eyebrows jumped up and he stared at Sophia when she responded politely in Mandarin: "Certainly. How are you?"

The soldier smiled with closed lips as he took the passport. "Ah, Russian. Good. Why you learned Mandarin?"

Sophia beamed. "I learned a little when I knew I'd come to China."

The soldier grinned, revealing crooked, nicotine-stained teeth. His dirty, bulbous fingers flicked through the passport pages, occasionally shifting his eyes to Sophia. Then he opened the passport wide at the center as if separating two halves of a peeled orange so that the covers almost touched. Keeping his eyes on Sophia, he raised the passport to his pockmarked nose and sniffed each opposing page loudly. "Smells so beautiful." The other soldiers behind him giggled like pre-pubescent boys. Then with his leering gaze latched onto Sophia, he slowly slid the tip of his tongue over the inside of the passport's central spine from the bottom to the top. "Tastes so beautiful too. Very sweet." He smiled while his eyes remained hard on Sophia. "Why you come to China? You looking for a Chinese husband?"

Sophia smiled coquettishly. She straightened in her seat. "To be a Buddhist nun."

The soldier's smile vanished instantaneously and he slapped the passport shut. The other soldiers laughed. "Stupid woman." Then he bent down to glare through the passenger window at Choepel. "But Russians more welcome in China than Australians, even stupid ones."

Choepel grinned sardonically as the soldier handed Sophia's passport back to her.

As Choepel drove away from the checkpoint, Sophia shoved the passport into her bag. "I need to get that replaced."

Choepel glanced to Sophia. "Russian? Your accent sounds French."

Sophia turned to him. "It *is* French, but I was born in Russia. My parents are Russian but I grew up in Paris because they thought that French schooling would be better."

"Can you speak Russian too?"

Sophia laughed. "No. Strange, isn't it?"

"One of the younger nuns at the monastery also speaks French."

A broad grin ran across Sophia's face. "Oh, really. I'd like to meet her. What's her name?"

"Dralha. She's prepared your room. She's quite an interesting person. She told me she created some fancy headphones when she studied at university in Australia, and she wants me to try them."

"Headphones? That's interesting."

"She's only in her twenties and is really smart."

"So tell me about Master Chi. I've never had a guru before."

Choepel grinned. "What he's achieved as a Vietnamese refugee is amazing. He told me that as a teenager, he would have heated debates with monks and the lama at a Taipei monastery devoted to the Dalai Lama. Apparently, the lama at the monastery was impressed with his knowledge of Buddhist texts, so he encouraged him to get ordained, which he did in his twenties. He dropped out of university, where he studied science."

"Oh, interesting."

"Well, after ordination, the debates with his fellow monks got so bad, Master Chi told me he decided to leave. But I've been told by one of the nuns that one night a fight erupted with two other monks at the monastery and he was expelled from the monastery." Choepel chuckled. "But that didn't shake his faith in tantric Buddhism. So after encouragement from Buddhists disillusioned with the Gelugpa tradition, and believing that Master Chi, not the Dalai Lama, is the rightful reincarnation of Avalokiteśvara, he started the Secret Tantric Tradition lineage. You won't see any pictures of the Dalai Lama at the monastery."

"He sounds like a bit of a rebel."

Choepel smiled. "Are there many devotees at the Paris center?"

"Over a thousand. Have you read all his books?"

"Yes, fantastic books — we memorize them."

"So how did you get interested in Buddhism?"

"Oh, when I was a teenager I learned about the different Buddhist traditions. And years later, one day, while walking through a park in Sydney, and having serious doubts about finishing my arts degree, a man handed me a flyer promoting a lecture by Master Chi. He told me about Vajrayana Buddhism. Well, that really piqued my interest. Not long after that, I decided to get ordained by Master Chi."

"Wow, how did your parents feel about you dropping out of university to become a monk?"

117

"They were quite emotional at the time. And even more so when I told them I planned to move to Taiwan. They didn't try to dissuade me, but I could see they weren't happy." Choepel paused. "What about your parents?"

"Oh, they're fine with me coming here. How are things at the monastery?"

Choepel grinned. "Things are tense since the invasion. There are power cuts every night, and soldiers recently beat up one of the other monks. He's still recovering."

"Oh. Religious groups and civilians are easy targets, I guess."

"So what's being said about the invasion in Europe?"

"It was expected for years."

"Really?"

"Yeah, for decades China infiltrated Taiwan's political and military systems with hundreds of spies, who pilfered information about its military operations."

"Wow." Choepel shook his head. "Here, we heard very few artillery shells going off, but according to the locals, some buildings in Taipei have been damaged. We're now under a night-time curfew. Thankfully, we've got a fully enlightened master who'll protect us." He hesitated. "What made you decide to get ordained?"

Sophia looked out the window to a troop of marching soldiers at the side of the road. "Probably the same reasons you did. I guess you decided to become a monk because you're searching for meaning when there's so much turmoil in the world."

"How did you find out about the Master?"

"A few years ago, when I hit 30, I started to question a lot of things about life." Sophia smiled. "Maybe I had an early midlife crisis."

Choepel chuckled.

"Well, one day, I was chatting to a friend in Paris, and she told me about Master Chi, and the teachings sounded interesting.

I can't wait to meet him — a fully enlightened being. Do you believe that?"

"That he's fully enlightened?"

"Yes."

"Of course. I wouldn't have come here over ten years ago if I didn't. He's amazing. You'll love the Master." Choepel glanced at Sophia. "It's a big step to decide to become a nun on the other side of the world in a country that's just been invaded."

Sophia turned to Choepel. "I feel drawn to the Master. When the student is ready, the Master will appear, right? So I guess I'm ready."

Choepel nodded.

"Having been ordained over ten years ago, you must go really deep in meditation?"

Choepel took a labored breath. "Oh, I consider myself to still be a beginner."

Sophia looked straight ahead. "I presume we get some free time at the monastery, or do we just meditate all day?"

"No, we usually just meditate for a couple of hours in the mornings and evenings. But tonight there's a fire puja."

"What's a fire puja?"

"It's a purification and healing ritual. We set up a huge open fire at the back of the monastery. There's the usual chanting with all sorts of loud instruments."

"Sounds like fun. So, my room will be with the nuns?"

"Actually, the nuns' rooms are on the ground floor in the west wing of the monastery, and the monks' are in the east wing. Until you're ordained, Master Chi wants you in a spare room on the top floor. I'll come to get you for the fire puja."

Sophia smiled. "Okay, thanks."

Part 8

2061

Chapter 19

Luke stood patiently on the rise of a frostbitten lawn, waiting for the Archbishop to finish his conversation with an elderly couple before he approached him at the entrance to St James Cathedral — a tall sandstone Gothic structure with two tall bell towers. The Archbishop had his back to Luke. When the elderly couple turned to leave, the Archbishop started striding up the cathedral steps.

Luke reached the Archbishop just as he entered the cathedral's vestibule. Under the pristine cream-colored miter, the Archbishop's short thick graying black hair and bearded face projected authority, as did his tall frame. Luke's breathing became erratic and his palms clammy as his gaze fixated on the Archbishop's face. He clasped his hands together shakily as he glanced at the gold pectoral cross hanging over the Archbishop's purple cassock and between a white tippet slung around his neck. "Your Grace, I'm so sorry to bother you."

"No bother, my son. Have we met?"

Luke stared at the Archbishop for a long moment. "No. I don't think so. I'm really here because of my parents — you know how parents can worry unnecessarily — well, they thought I should chat to you. It will ease their minds."

"Oh, are you Luke? Your mother, Bettina — lovely lady — called me a few days ago."

Luke grimaced as he tried to place the Archbishop's southern American accent. "Oh, did she? Ah, yes, I'm Luke."

"Look, you've made the right decision to see me. Your parents are right to be concerned. God has guided you here at a good time. I'd like to ask you some questions."

Luke wrung his hands. "Sure."

The Archbishop pressed a firm warm hand on the top of Luke's head, forcing him to kneel. "Do you attend church every Sunday, and regularly participate in book-burnings and flagellations?"

Luke hesitated. "No."

"Do you believe that Pope Gethsemane is the true messenger of God?"

Luke paused even longer. "Maybe."

"Do you believe there's only one God, a Christian God, and that all other so-called gods, worshipped by other religions, are the manifestation of evil spirits?"

Luke took a deep breath. "I'm not sure."

"Do you believe that Jesus Christ is the only son of God, and that Jesus died to cleanse the world of its sins?"

"Maybe."

The Archbishop glanced at Luke. "Have you ever read any blasphemous books, like books about other religions or science, or even books of a dirty, disgusting, sexual nature?"

Luke swallowed hard and slowly wiped his sopping palms against his pants. "Yes." His heavy breathing reverberated around the walls of the vestibule in the long silence that followed.

"Have you ever dabbled in the occult, like witchcraft, magic, fortune-telling, crystals, wizards, or board games?"

"No."

"Have you ever tried to communicate with ghosts, spirits, demons, or the Devil himself?"

"No."

The Archbishop considered Luke for several moments, then smiled sardonically. "Rise, my son. My poor misguided son, it's very clear to me you're likely possessed and I need to perform an exorcism on you without delay. In fact, it's imperative we do it immediately because I fear the Devil could have a strong hold on you."

"But I —"

The Archbishop pushed his right palm in front of Luke's deeply reddening face. "No buts about it. Follow me now."

Luke took several deep breaths as the Archbishop led him to a small chapel behind the cathedral. It seemed much older than the cathedral itself. Green moss poked through a thin layer of snow on the stone walls and tiled roof. Small stained-glass windows looked in from either side of the heavy wooden door. The musty air inside sent a chill through Luke. Color photographs of the Old City of Jerusalem lined the walls. A tall white crucifix stood behind the altar. The altar itself held several bibles, small crucifixes, rosaries, and other liturgical items. Four thick white candles on the altar struggled with the dim sunlight coming from the windows to push out the darkness. Two alabaster fonts of holy water framed the altar on either side. A row of three chairs in front of the altar faced away from it. The Archbishop waved a hand towards the central chair. "Please sit down."

Luke's heartbeat began to race. He lumbered to the chair and sat down. He half-heartedly took a deep breath, and the cold air seemed to reach into the extremities of his arms and legs.

"Good. Are you comfortable?"

Luke squirmed in the chair. "Uh-huh."

"Good. Just relax. I'm going to bring in someone who assists me with exorcisms." The Archbishop moved to the altar and rang a small bell.

Moments later, a side door slowly creaked open. A young woman wearing a hooded gray robe, tied at the waist with a black rope belt, shuffled in. Her bare feet dragged on the cold, cobblestone floor. Long, honey-blonde hair partly covered her face, which poked out over the hem of the hood. She kept her head bowed and her hands tightly clasped.

The Archbishop and the woman stood still in front of Luke. His gaze locked onto the woman. The Archbishop's voice dragged his attention away. "Let's begin." He paused as he opened a thin leatherbound booklet, his hand also holding a large crucifix. "Luke, only son of Sean and Bettina McNeill, have you been baptized with the power of the Holy Spirit?"

"Yes."

"Do you sincerely want to be free of the Devil and his evil influences that are presently affecting you?"

Luke took a deep breath. "I don't think I'm under the —"

The Archbishop's voice leapt on an impatient tone. It hit Luke like a slap in the face. "Do you want to be free of the Devil?!"

Luke's heart thumped faster. He remained silent for several moments. "Yes." The word barely crawled out of his mouth.

"Will you do whatever must be done in the name of the Holy Spirit?"

"Yes."

"Now close your eyes and do not open them under any circumstances until I say so. Do you understand?"

"Yes."

Luke closed his eyes pensively. Unexpectedly, the Archbishop blew hard into his face and mumbled a short recitation under his breath. Luke frowned and rocked back.

"Okay. Liz, blow out the candles. And get into position."

Luke sensed Liz move past him to the altar. She quietly blew out both candles. The darkness behind his eyelids suddenly got even darker. Her palms pressed down gently onto his thighs as she knelt in front of him. A moment later the Archbishop began rapidly reciting passages of the Bible loudly. As he did so, he repeatedly flicked holy water onto Luke. Within a few minutes, his head and face were drenched. Interspersed throughout the recitations, Luke recognized the Latin phrases the Archbishop repeated frequently.

"Jesus Christ, come to the assistance of men whom God has created to his likeness and whom he has redeemed at a great price from the tyranny of the Devil. The holy Church venerates you as her guardian and protector; to you, the Lord has entrusted the souls of the redeemed to be led into heaven. Pray therefore the God of Peace to crush Satan beneath our feet, that he may no longer retain men captive and do injury to the Church. Offer our prayers to the most high, that without delay they may draw his mercy down upon us; take hold of the dragon, the old serpent, which is the Devil and Satan, bind him and cast him into the bottomless pit that he may no longer seduce the nations. *Vade retro, Satana. Vade retro, Satana.*"

The Archbishop's breathing became heavier. "Lord Jesus Christ, yes, by the power vested in me, yes, I command thee, Satan, be gone from this man's body. The body. The flesh. Oh yes, yes, yes, be gone. Jesus Christ, yes. I absolve thee from thy sins in the name of the father and of the son and the Holy Spirit. Yes, *ego te absolvo. Ego te absolvo. Vade retro, Satana. Vade retro, Satana.* Oh Jesus, yes, yes, yes.

"In the name of Jesus Christ, our God and Lord, strengthened by the intercession of the immaculate virgin Mary, Mother of God, of blessed Michael the archangel, of the blessed apostles and all the saints. And powerful in the holy authority of our ministry, we confidently undertake to repulse the attacks and deceits of the Devil. God arises; his enemies are scattered and those who hate him flee before him. As smoke is driven away, so are they driven; as wax melts before the fire, so the wicked perish at the presence of God."

The recitations continued for several minutes, and the longer it went, the faster the Archbishop's words became and the more breathless his voice. He belched out Bible passages and gasped for air. Liz's hands tightened on Luke's thighs. Her long nails bit into his skin through his pants. The Archbishop's frenzied words swirled in his head, and after almost half an hour, Luke struggled to breathe and keep his balance. Sweat beaded around his temples and rolled down his cheeks. The rigidness of his posture weakened. *Why did I listen to my parents? This is ludicrous. How can I get him to stop this madness?*

Archbishop Michael continued. "The body. The flesh. Oh yes, yes, yes. Jesus Christ, yes. I absolve thee from thy sins in the name of the father and of the son and the Holy Spirit. Yes, *ego te absolvo. Ego te absolvo. Vade retro, Satana. Vade retro, Satana.* Oh Jesus, yes, yes, yes."

As waves of nausea washed through Luke's body, Liz's nails penetrated deeper into his legs and her breathing became louder. Eventually, Luke's curiosity overwhelmed him and he opened his eyes into the narrowest of cracks. In the dim light, he saw the Archbishop had bent down behind Liz. The hem of her robes rested high above her waist. Her hood had fallen onto her shoulders and the Archbishop had pulled her head back with a fist full of her hair. Tears streamed down her face as she bit her bottom lip. Her wide eyes locked onto Luke. He jumped up. Liz and the Archbishop startled.

"Stop this nonsense. What are you doing to her?"

The Archbishop's mouth shot open and he gasped. He pulled Liz's robe down and stood up. "Luke, your eyes must remain closed for the exorcism to work."

Luke gently grabbed Liz by her shoulders and helped her straighten. He pulled her towards him. His widening eyes then shot to the Archbishop. "This is rubbish. You were assaulting her."

"What? I'm a man of God. I'm praying to rid you of the Devil. You don't understand the exorcism process."

Luke gritted his teeth. "You liar! I've had enough of this. I'm not possessed. If there are any evil spirits in anyone, they're in you."

Liz wiped her eyes and put her arms around Luke. The Archbishop stepped forward to grab her, but Luke pulled her behind him. "Don't touch her."

"Who do you think you are? You're possessed by the Devil. The Devil is talking through you." The Archbishop held up the crucifix to Luke's face. "By the power of the Holy Spirit I command thee, Satan, to leave this man and —"

"Shut up!" Luke slapped the Archbishop's outstretched hand and the crucifix bounced off a wall before cartwheeling across the floor. The tinkling of metal on stone echoed in the small confines of the chapel. As silence filled the space, the Archbishop's shoulders dropped and his hands fell to his knees. In the dark, his bent body resembled that of an old broken man. Then the Archbishop slowly looked up to Luke, and his giant frame rose erect. His eyes caught the little light in the chapel. "How dare you speak to a man of God in that way."

Still holding Liz with one hand, Luke shoved the Archbishop with the other. The Archbishop lost his balance and fell awkwardly to the floor. Luke stood over him. "You're a hypocrite and a disgrace. I saw what you were doing to Liz. It's disgusting. You, like the Church, are corrupted to the core."

As the Archbishop got to his feet, Liz ran out of the chapel crying. The Archbishop's voice carried desperation and surprise. "Liz, come back!"

"Let her go."

The Archbishop clenched his teeth. "How dare you assault a man of God? You'll be burned at the stake. I'm her protector."

"No. You're her tormentor!"

The Archbishop's eyes inflamed. He ripped his tippet off his neck and held it in both hands. He let out a piercing growl like a bear as he lunged at Luke, pushing him off his feet. In a flash, he wrapped the tippet around Luke's neck as he pinned him down with his knees. Luke tried to push his hands between the tippet and his throat. But the Archbishop ground his teeth and pressed his knees hard into Luke's chest and tightened the tippet around Luke's neck. Luke's eyes bulged out of his head as he struggled for air while trying to push the Archbishop off him. His legs kicked erratically and his arms flayed wildly. But the Archbishop pressed his elbows down onto Luke's arms as his grip on the tippet tightened even more. A sinking sensation overwhelmed Luke. His awareness was fading fast. He gasped desperately for air, but the more he tried to breathe, the tighter the Archbishop pulled the tippet.

Through clenched teeth, the Archbishop yelled like a madman. "Heavenly Father, I serve thee to cleanse this man of sin! Ahh!"

Luke's gasps and coughs got stuck in his constricted throat. The frantic movements of his arms and leg slowed. Soon, his arms and legs went limp. He had no more strength to fight back. He resigned himself to dying at the hands of a madman. Just before his watery eyes closed for the last time, in his peripheral vision he glimpsed a shaft of light shooting into the chapel. A second later, the Archbishop's arms went limp, his head dropped, and he fell unconscious beside Luke.

Luke ripped the tippet from his throat. He gasped for air as Liz appeared in the dark. With tears in her eyes she knelt beside him. "Are you okay?"

Luke took several deep breaths as he got to his knees. He glanced around the chapel. His blurred vision made the interior of the chapel seem darker and ghostly. The Archbishop lay unconscious with his miter upturned and a large rectangular brick beside his head. A large, darkening hematoma had erupted above his temple.

Liz embraced Luke. "Thank you."

Luke got to his feet. He gently rubbed his throat and neck. "I should thank you for coming back. I thought I was going to die." He glanced again at the Archbishop. "Let's get out of here."

Chapter 20

As Luke drove away from the cathedral, he glanced at Liz. "Are you okay?" He rubbed his throat as he gasped and coughed.

Liz wiped her teary eyes. "Uh-huh. Thanks for stopping him."

Luke took a couple of deep breaths. "Oh, *you* stopped him. He's out cold thanks to your quick thinking."

"I thought he was going to kill you."

"So did I. I should have opened my eyes sooner. It all sounded so suspicious in there. I shouldn't have let my parents talk me into seeing him."

"Why did they want you to see him?"

"Oh, they're very religious."

"Isn't everyone?"

"Not me. I've never been convinced by the lies and ritualistic church nonsense. I feel so stupid listening to my parents. I can't believe they convinced me I could be possessed."

As Luke approached a large raucous group of men and women shouting slogans about the election being stolen, he slowed the car. They waved large posters of the Pope, and most brandished long knives, various types of guns, and long wooden fire torches. They stomped on both sides of the street and some spilled onto the road. Several members of the crowd banged on the windows and windscreen, making Luke and Liz flinch. He almost stopped the car. "I don't want to hit anyone with the car."

Liz slid down in the seat and covered her eyes. "Don't stop. Just keep going."

Sweat beaded on Luke's temples and forehead and he held the steering wheel in a vice-like grip as he carefully steered the car through the mayhem for several tense minutes, insincerely smiling and waving to people who thrust their faces into the side window and windscreen. After the car had crawled past the crowd, Luke sped up again. "What crazy people. They're all brainwashed by the Church."

Liz sat up and repositioned herself in the seat. "But how is it that you've managed to avoid being brainwashed? Did you go to one of the few non-Christian schools?"

"No, my parents came here from Australia when I was very young, just to send me to one of the most expensive Christian boarding schools. But ironically, at school I met someone who opened my mind to other religions and even science."

"Science? That's really dangerous to be dabbling in that sort of thing."

"Yes, but it's crazy that it should be. I think the Church is worried that scientific knowledge will erode its power over society. It all comes down to power. Whenever there's too much power concentrated in an individual or an organization, there'll be corruption — it's human nature. The Church is the best example of that. I think the Church realized centuries ago that knowledge is power, so they want to be the keepers of all knowledge. They suppress anything that'll undermine its power and its control of people."

Liz gazed into the distance for several moments. "It's funny you mention power because I've often thought that all my life I've felt completely powerless. Powerless and helpless."

"Why?"

"I've always hidden the fact that I'm an Australian Aboriginal. I feel people will look down on me if they find out. I did tell the Archbishop when he offered me a room at the cathedral, but I think he already knew."

"Where did you stay before?"

"With my American adoptive parents, but they really scared me."

"What happened to your biological parents?"

"I was told they died days after my birth, but years later I found out I'd been stolen from them by the government, like so many other Aboriginal children."

"Why were you scared of your adoptive parents?"

"They sent me to a Christian girls' boarding school, but the nuns and visiting priests abused me."

"Do you mean sexually?"

"Sexually, physically, and psychologically. It was a nightmare."

"That's horrendous. Did you tell your adoptive parents?"

"Oh, I told them but they didn't believe me. They said I fantasized everything — that I'm evil. But then they started sexually abusing and beating me. I couldn't bring myself to say anything to anyone because they both hold high positions in the Church. When I left school, one day after a church service I spoke to the Archbishop privately, thinking he would protect me. Although he didn't believe me when I told him about all the abuse, he assured me he would look after me. He was so kind in the beginning, and for the first time in my life I at least felt safe. But after a few months, he told me I was possessed and called me a temptress. He started off doing exorcisms on me late each night, and that's when the horrible things happened."

Liz dropped her head in her hands and sobbed.

"Oh, Liz. I'm so sorry. No one in the Church can be trusted. It uses faith as a wall to hide appalling behavior. I can't understand how people can't see the hypocrisy."

"But the Church is all I've ever known since being taken from my parents. I don't know what to do. I've got nowhere to go."

"Don't worry. We can try to find somewhere for you to stay. In the meantime, you can stay with me. I don't live far. Are you interested in reading some non-Christian books?"

"Yeah, I've had such a sheltered life. And I'm over the Church and its hypocrisy. Are the books at your place?"

"I've got some, but we can stop at Washington State University? In their café, we can get books on a range of subjects. You can pick whatever you want. I've got some of my books on science from there."

Liz looked hard at Luke. "University? I've heard they're dangerous places."

"I don't go there too often, but I've never had any problems whenever I've been. If you don't want to go, we won't. For some reason, recently I've been thinking of going there again."

Liz remained silent for a long moment. "Okay, I trust you, Luke. And I do want to open my mind."

"Okay."

"I've never done anything like this before. It feels strange but liberating to even be thinking these thoughts. But I've been so unhappy my entire life. I felt like a slave and prisoner at the cathedral. I haven't told anyone this, but I wanted to end things many times because I saw no other way out. Death seemed so appealing at times." Liz took a deep breath. "Have you ever thought about death?"

Luke took a breath. His palms became clammy. "Not in the way you have. We all have to face it, but it's good you didn't take that step."

Liz turned to Luke. "Why? It would end all my emotional and physical pain."

"I guess it's all about timing. When we're ready for death, I suppose we'll know."

"But there's been many times when I've felt definitely ready."

"No, it sounds like you were desperate. That's not being ready."

Part 9

2022

Chapter 21

An olive-green cast-iron fence ran along the footpath outside the music therapist's terraced townhouse. A first-floor balustrade mirrored the fence in color and design. A large ornate pot of red geraniums sat in the center of a small garden, with white, pink, and purple flowers around its perimeter.

Before Jeremy opened the gate, a pale-yellow butterfly with two black spots near the edges of its wings landed on the gate post. Its wings pointed straight up. Then its wings flapped and it rose into the air. He expected it to fly away. Instead, it slowly moved towards him in a circuitous, seemingly erratic route and landed on the back of his outstretched hand. A half-smile crept slowly across his mouth. He had never been so close to a butterfly before. A second later, it lifted off his hand and flew away. He recalled reading somewhere that most butterflies live for only two to four weeks. *Do they perceive time in the same way humans do?*

The gate groaned loudly. Jeremy's face flushed and his shoulders dropped. He took a deep breath, turned, and shut the gate quietly behind him. A rosy, minty, earthy scent wafted around him. He inhaled the unseasonably chilled November air deeply and looked up to see for the first time that day a canopy of dark clouds directly overhead, shrouding the descending sun in the west while white cauliflower-shaped cumulus clouds floated in the east. As he approached the front door, rain started bucketing down. Heavy thick drops stung his face and sounded like hailstones hitting the metal roofs. Water began rushing through the street. Under the porch, he dabbed his face with a tissue, combed back his hair with his hands, then brushed off droplets clinging to his coat.

He knocked on the door lightly. A black camera, no bigger than a small button, pointed down from the corner of the ceiling above the door. A few moments later, a woman in her early thirties with shiny, straight, shoulder-length red hair opened the door. The door hid most of her body. She didn't smile. "*Oui*."

"Hi, my name's Jeremy. Dr Mason from down the road gave me your name because he thinks some music therapy may help me."

"Dr Mason?" The woman's French accent carried her soft, breathy voice that struggled to compete with the rain pinging the tin roof. Her green eyes sparkled like gemstones inside pearly sclera. Her smooth skin had a *crème patisserie* hue, her thin smooth lips a natural lipstick-less pink shade.

"Yes, the psychologist who works down the road. He said he met you recently. You're Justine?"

"Ah, *oui*, yes. Dr Mason. Ah, I forgot. But I'm too busy to take new clients."

Jeremy's shoulders sagged. "Oh. Well, look, I live nearby and walked here." He briefly turned around to confirm the still-exploding rain bomb. "I'm a writer and I'd be interested to know more about music therapy and maybe write an article about it. It would be free publicity for you. I write for various national magazines."

Justine stared at Jeremy for a couple of moments. "I'm not interested in free publicity. But what questions do you have?"

Jeremy smiled. "Many. Well, what exactly is it? How did you get involved?"

Justine turned her head quickly to look behind her. She turned back and glanced at the dense sheets of rain. "Um. Wait here." She shut the door and the lock clicked into place. A few moments later she reappeared. "You can come in briefly. But I don't have much time."

Jeremy smiled coyly. "Okay. Thank you."

Justine led Jeremy to a small room at the far end of the house, past a series of closed doors. Her dark tight knee-length pencil skirt swayed rhythmically from side to side. In the room, dark, heavy curtains blocked the remaining evening light. Two electronic keyboards angled against each other near dark-wood antique cupboards and tall, packed bookshelves. On top of the bookshelf behind a large desk stood an organite pyramid that attracted the subdued light in the room like a magnet. Jeremy recognized the same earthy aroma from the garden and a fusion of Mediterranean herbs — parsley, chives, tarragon, and thyme.

Justine slid into the high-backed chair behind the desk. "Please sit. What sort of articles do you write?"

Jeremy sat stiffly on the other side of the desk. "The subjects vary. I'm currently working on an article about quantum physics — String Theory."

"Oh. Quantum physics." Justine paused. "I also teach French at the University of Sydney and one of my best students is also studying quantum physics. She's a world leader in the subject and is doing some really innovative things. We've had some interesting discussions, but that stuff is too complicated for me."

"Yes, it's so abstract and weird, but an editor wants me to write an article on the subject and I need the money at the moment." Jeremy glanced at the bookshelf. "You seem to have a lot of books on the subject."

She waved behind her. "Oh, those aren't mine. Evlyn keeps putting science books in my bookshelf to try to get me interested, but I'll never read any of them. She was here earlier today cramming more books into the shelves."

Jeremy squinted. "Evlyn — a younger girl in her twenties?"

Justine smiled. "Yes. Do you know her?"

"No. But I interviewed a physics lecturer at the university, and Evlyn happened to come into his office as I was about to leave. She mentioned she's also learning French."

"Oh, small world." Justine smiled. "Evlyn's very smart and very pretty, isn't she?"

Jeremy's face flushed. "Yes, she is. Well, this lecturer told me some mind-boggling things about waves and photos."

"Photons."

"Yeah, it all sounded like gobbledygook." Jeremy took out his notepad from his jacket pocket. "But tell me about music therapy. It sounds like something that can actually help people."

Justine lowered her voice to almost a whisper. "Please don't use my name. I don't need the publicity. As I said, I already have enough clients and teaching commitments."

"Okay."

"Music therapy is fascinating." Justine glanced at her keyboards. "It's about accessing our conscious awareness and our subconscious. We can connect to deep levels of consciousness through certain resonant sound frequencies. Pythagoras talked about the 'music of the spheres' because he knew the whole universe is vibrating. And many religions even refer to God as a vibration."

"Really?"

"Yes. Take, for example, the 'Word' or '*Logos*' from the Bible. There's even a Vedic mantra, *Nada Brahma*, which means 'the sound of God.' And the ancient Tibetan Book of the Dead mentions the natural sound of reality."

Jeremy leaned back. "You don't come across as someone who'd be so religious."

Justine frowned. "*Quoi?* What? I'm not religious. I'm just stating facts about some religions."

"Sorry, I don't mean to upset you. Maybe 'religious' isn't quite the right word. Perhaps ... mystical."

"Mysticism and religion are very different things." Justine paused. "Religions can point to the way, but mysticism is the way."

"A finger pointing to the moon is not the moon."

"What?"

"Oh nothing, just a random thought that came to me."

140

The rain had eased and the rattling from the roof subsided. Justine hesitated. "I see music therapy as a form of mysticism because it can produce altered states of consciousness and give a direct experience of the ... the mystical."

She straightened in her chair. "Why did you see Dr Mason?"

Jeremy sank into his chair and his face reddened. "Oh, nothing major. I just have a bit of a stress issue, and I'm not sleeping too well."

"I guess freelance writing can be very stressful. Ah, I can lend you a couple of recordings that will help you relax. Return them whenever you're ready."

"Your own compositions?"

"Yes."

"That's very kind of you."

"Wait here." Justine left the room. Her footsteps became quieter as she went down the hall towards the front of the house.

Jeremy looked around the room. *Interesting pyramid.* He tiptoed towards the bookshelf but stopped at the window and parted the curtains to a narrow crack with a finger. A new white Peugeot hatchback stood in a narrow wrought-iron gated carport shrouded by a canopy of grape vines and lined with potted herbs. A bitumen laneway, wide enough for only one car, bordered the carport.

Jeremy picked up the pyramid and turned it in his hands. Its inwardly angled sides made it eight-sided, just like the Giza pyramid. Its various layers sparkled, highlighting the shiny blue and green gemstones near the apex. He repositioned the pyramid on the bookshelf, glanced down the empty hallway, then peered at the titles along the spines of the shelved books. He slid out one thick book. Through the gap between the remaining books, he noticed something unusual at the back of the shelf. Something mostly obscured — pale, curved, and rigid. His eyes narrowed as he carefully picked up a pair of yellowish, cream-colored headphones. *Must have fallen behind the books by accident.*

The headphones had no earcups. *Ah, bone conduction.* Much lighter than any standard pair, they had no apparent power cord. A raised rectangular compartment, with a small switch on its side, sat atop the middle of the headband. On the underside of the headband sat a circular black disk, much like a lithium battery, but much larger and thicker. *Unusual.*

Jeremy turned towards the corridor but didn't see Justine. He flicked the switch and put the headphones over his head. The small rectangular speakers gripped above his ears behind his temples. The metal disk rested comfortably atop the crown of his head. A pleasant high-pitched sound, like nothing he had heard before, vibrated in his head. A tingling sensation at the top of his scalp crept slowly downwards to his neck. To his amazement, the tingling moved through him like a gentle ocean wave scrambling up a flat, broad beach. It crept down to his shoulders, then to his torso, then to his hips, then to his legs, and then finally to his feet. His whole body gently vibrated, making every bone, every organ, every cell tingle. *Oh so nice. So relaxing.*

Part 10

2038

Chapter 22

As Choepel climbed the stairs to the top floor of the monastery, he heard the door of the spare room gently close, but he didn't see anyone on the landing. He stepped lightly on the carpet as he approached the room. Just before he knocked, Sophia's voice leapt out from inside the room.

"Oh. Master Chi. You can't just barge into a woman's room."

Choepel froze. He stood still in front of the door and turned an ear closer to it.

"I don't need to knock." Master Chi sneered. "The first rule here is that I go into a *dakini's* rooms whenever I want. I'm the reincarnation of Avalokiteśvara. I'm the Buddha. I can do whatever I want. I can take whatever I want. There is no greater power in the universe than the Buddha."

"Wouldn't the Buddha be more respectful of a woman's privacy?" Sophia snapped.

Choepel's face burned red. His concern and curiosity were both piqued. He slipped away from the door to the side corridor near the stairs. *Anyone coming up the stairs will see me. But everyone's at the fire puja.*

Standing near the door of a storage closet, he pressed an ear against the wall.

"I get to know my nuns when they arrive," Master Chi whispered in a leering tone.

"Well, I'm not a nun yet. Shouldn't you be at the fire puja?" Sophia's voice faltered.

"There's a fire puja every month. We can go to the next one."

Feet shuffled in the room.

"I'm going to show you a secret meditation that I only teach the most beautiful *dakinis*. You'll like it very much."

Sophia's voice jumped. "That's too close, Master Chi. Please. You're drunk."

Choepel could sense Sophia's fear and vulnerability in her voice. He pressed his ear to the wall as his heartbeat thumped and quickened. The rising vibrations in his hands against the wall got louder than the chanting, ringing of bells, and tinkling of cymbals coming from the rear of the monastery.

"Don't do that." Sophia's voice quivered.

Choepel tilted his head to one side and sucked in a silent, deep breath. His brow furrowed. *What's going on?*

Master Chi's voice dropped and slowed. "Sophia, you need to understand that I get what I want, when I want, with whomever I want. No one denies me."

"I'll scream." Sophia's voice rose even higher.

Master Chi chuckled. "Everyone's at the fire puja. No one will hear you. Just relax. I'm not going to hurt you. Just relax and allow yourself to give into the Buddha. I have secret teachings that I want to share with you. You need to prove to me that you're ready to be ordained."

"You're crazy. Stop! Don't do that! Stop!"

Choepel's heart thumped. His ears thrummed with every beat. Sweat beaded down the sides of his face.

"What about the Buddhist precepts? You're supposed to be enlightened — why are you doing this?!"

"Sophia, impermanence is an important lesson. Let go of the precepts. Let go of everything and touch this. This is the secret precept. This is the only precept that you need to know."

"That's disgusting. Stop. Please. You're hurting me."

Choepel's mind couldn't hold a single thought long enough to think logically. As his heart raced faster, his breathing became erratic. He closed his eyes tightly and pressed his ear harder against the wall.

Master Chi's voice fell. "Take those off. I want to see your Buddha Nature. Now."

"You're hurting me. Please stop."

Sophia whimpered. Feet stomped around the room. Furniture scraped along the floor and bumped against the walls. Her breathing became quicker and heavier, her pleas more desperate. Choepel pressed his ear against the wall, inviting the pain to wrap around his head. His jaw locked and his teeth clenched. A sudden heavy thud on the other side of the wall made his head shoot back, but his hands remained pressed firmly against it. Every sound from the room went through the wall and into his hands and through his whole body like blasts of electricity. *This can't be happening.*

Tears welled in Choepel's eyes. His head, throat, chest, arms, and legs all became tight and set like concrete.

Silence from the room was followed by deep breathing, then a longer silence. Master Chi's voice crawled through the wall. "Yes, that's nice, Sophia. This is the way of the Buddha and the real way to enlightenment. This is the secret path to enlightenment. This is our secret. This is better than meditation, isn't it? Yes. Oh, yes. You love this more than hours of painful meditation."

Sophia sobbed.

"Don't cry, Sophia. Chant for me. Chanting creates enormous merit. Chant for the Buddha. Chant *Om Mani Padme Hum.* You know that chant, don't you?"

After another long silence for several moments, Sophia's voice cracked and faltered. "*Om ... Mani ... Padme ... Hum ... Om ... Mani ... Padme ... Hum.*"

"Opening your beautiful legs is much better than crossing them," Master Chi hissed. "Meditate with your legs open, never crossed. Yes, wide open, never crossed. Open your legs to reveal the lotus ... Oh, what a jewel."

Master Chi's breathing got heavier and quicker. "This is the real Pure Land. This is where the Buddha Nature is. Everything else is fucking illusion and impermanent. This is fucking reality.

This is the fucking enlightenment you seek. This is the clear light of fucking bliss. This is true fucking bliss and ecstasy. This is the fucking secret teachings of the Buddha. Yes, this is the fucking bliss of enlightenment. I've fucking found it. You've fucking found it too. Feel it inside you and fucking give yourself to it. Fucking give yourself to the secret fucking teachings of the Buddha. Feel the fucking bliss."

The crashing waves of gusting horns, tinkling bells, and thumping drums from the fire puja reached a prolonged deafening crescendo. Then the waves subsided and the monks and nuns began chanting *Om Mani Padme Hum*.

Seemingly in a hypnotic trance, Master Chi chanted quietly to begin with, but his voice got louder. *"Yes Om Mani Padme Hum … Yes Om Mani Padme Hum Yes … Yes … Om Mani Padme Hum Yes! … Yes! … Yes! … Yes! … Om Mani Padme Hum Yes! … Yes! … Yes!"* His voice fell away to be almost inaudible. *"Om … Mani … Padme … Hum … Hum … Hum … Hum."*

As Master Chi continued rambling, his voice drifted away and his words became smothered by a meaningless jumble of indiscernible grunts and moans. Choepel tried to block out images flicking into his mind of Master Chi forcing his body onto Sophia's, pinning her against the other side of the wall, and their arms, legs, lips, and bodies crashing and grinding against one another.

Only dissonant *rhonchi* breathing seeped through the walls for long, drawn-out moments.

Tears rolled down Choepel's burning cheeks as Master Chi mumbled, "I'm so glad we've chanted together, Sophia. You've gained much merit chanting with me. Isn't chanting wonderful? You chant beautifully. We chant beautifully together. We're going to chant together again and often. You're going to love it here, chanting with the Buddha. You're my special chanting *dakini*."

More waves of loud rhythmic chanting, ringing, and tinkling from the rear of the monastery drowned out the long, heavy silence from the room.

Sophia's whimpers and sobs slipped through the wall.

What's just happened? Why would Master Chi do that? I could have stopped him. I should have stopped him.

A sly rat scurried across the wooden floor. Choepel's body shook. He caught the brown, almost guinea-pig-size rodent disappearing into a crack in the wall. His heartbeat thrummed louder in his ears than the combined clanging and chanting from the fire puja. He slid a forearm onto the wall and rested his dizzy head on it. His jaw tensed. He clasped a hand to his mouth as tears dripped from his tightly shut eyes. Then he bit his hand hard, then even harder for several moments, and suppressed his screams in his throat.

Chapter 23

Choepel sat with his back hunched against the wall, his hand throbbing. The grayness filling the corridor seeped into his head. Everything around him seemed like a gray watercolor. He wiped his eyes with his sleeve. The voices on the other side of the wall had been silent for some time. The sounds from the fire puja continued to come up from the stairwell in waves. Then Sophia's door suddenly opened. His body shook. His palms pressed onto the floor. He froze. *Master Chi? Do I duck into the storage closet? It's too late.*

The door closed and heavy feet shuffled away from the stairs. Choepel sighed.

He waited and put his ear against the wall. Furniture scraped and feet padded over the timber floor and carpets for a few minutes between long moments of painful silence. *Do I go to Sophia? Do I go to my room?*

Choepel tiptoed to the stairs and took a few steps down, but an emptiness in the pit of his stomach exploded. He put a hand on the wall to steady himself. His legs became immobile and his will to go down any further evaporated. After several moments, he took a deep breath, turned, and trudged towards Sophia's room.

Choepel knocked with one tentative knuckle. Silence. He waited for a few moments, then knocked again. Following another long silence, he cleared his throat and whispered. "Sophia."

More silence.

He put his ear to the door. Just before he knocked again, Sophia's voice trembled. "Go away. I'm not going to the fire puja. I'm not feeling well. I'll see you tomorrow."

Choepel heartbeat thumped louder in his ears. He waited for a long moment. "Sophia, I'm not going to the fire puja either. If you're not well, maybe I can help. I'd like to see you."

After another long period of silence, a small crack in the doorway appeared. Sophia stood back from the door, as if wanting to conceal her reddish eyes and puffy lips. Her top hung awkwardly on her drooping shoulders.

Choepel's eyes and mouth opened dramatically wide. "Sophia, what's happened? Are you okay?"

Sophia pushed a handful of hair around her ears. "I guess I'm just tired from the flight and train ride."

"Is something wrong?"

"I'm fine."

"Are you sure? This place must seem so strange to you. Is there anything you want to talk about?"

Sophia stared intently at Choepel. "Wait here first." She closed the door. Footsteps and muffled, indiscernible sounds came from the room before she opened the door again.

Sophia's bag lay on the floor near the single bed. Choepel closed the door softly. His eyes followed her. She moved to the table and lit two candles. Light and shadows jumped into the room.

Choepel shuffled to Sophia and placed a hand gently on her shoulder. "Are you sure you're okay?"

Sophia's eyes flooded as she faced him. "Something horrible happened. He did a terrible thing to me."

Choepel's eyes shot wide open as he took Sophia's hand into his. "What? How? Who?"

Sophia wiped her eyes and dropped her head. Then she looked up at Choepel with a furrowed brow. "What happened to your hand?"

Choepel looked down and saw the deep-red teeth marks on his hand. His face flushed and his heart raced. Beads of sweat appeared on his scalp and at his temples. They rolled down the sides of his face. The emptiness inside him exploded again. His eyes darted to the other side of the room. He took a deep breath; then, as his eyes filled, he looked again at Sophia. "I'm so sorry. There's something I should confess."

Sophia frowned and pulled her hand away.

Choepel dry-swallowed and wiped his eyes. He hesitated. "I ... I did this because I was so angry with myself that ... that I didn't stop him."

Sophia's eyes narrowed. She tilted her head to one side. "You know what happened? How?"

Choepel's head and shoulders dropped. "I happened to get here just after he did, and I heard everything from outside."

"My god!" Sophia snapped. "You heard everything from outside?"

Choepel stared at the floor. "I'm so sorry."

A fraction of a second later, Sophia's open hand crashed into the side of Choepel's unguarded face. His mind went completely blank for an instant; he lost his balance and almost fell. The side of his face stung as if he had been scalded with boiling water. Blood rushed to his head, leaving his limbs cold and numb. The room appeared to be moving around him. When the room stopped, Sophia glowered at him with deep oceans in her eyes. Her jaw stiffened and she clenched her teeth.

"Why didn't you do something?! Why?!" Her voice and words slapped into him like follow-up blows.

"I should have. But he's my Master. I trust him implicitly."

"Even now?"

Choepel slowly shook his head.

"And does having a so-called Master mean you throw away your moral compass?" Sophia's French accent sounded more prominent than ever before.

Choepel wiped his eyes. "No, you're right."

He stood silently like a chastised child and wiped the tear tracks from his burning face. Then he tentatively reached for Sophia's hand and held it gently in both of his. He timidly put his arms around her and they embraced silently for several moments.

Sophia took a few deep breaths and eased out of Choepel's arms. She combed her fingers through her disheveled hair, then looked into his eyes. "I can't stay here. I have to leave — now. Do you want to come with me?"

"Leave? This is my home. Where would we go?"

"Choepel, Master Chi is a monster. You can't deny that. He's no better than those ignorant soldiers. Look, that man I met at the train station — he's a businessman with local connections. I'm sure he'll be able to help us leave the country."

"Leave the country? I can understand why you want to leave, but I can't."

"How can you want to stay here with that monster? I'm surely not the only woman he's violated."

Choepel shook his head. "You leave. I'll help you, but I'll stay. My life as a monk is all I know. Where would I go?"

"Back to Australia — anywhere is better than here."

Choepel frowned. "How can I get to Australia?"

"I've still got my passport. Go get yours and only a few clothes that you can carry in a small bag — no suitcases. With everyone at the fire puja, it's the perfect time to slip out unnoticed."

"But I just can't steal a car."

"No, we'll walk."

"Walk?"

"Yes, that way we'll avoid the checkpoints."

"But there are still soldiers everywhere. Where are we going to go on foot?"

"To where the businessman's staying. We'll go through the back streets to the city. He told me he's got diplomatic contacts."

"What about the others? We should help them leave too?"

"The others probably already know all about that monster. If they choose to leave they can. A group of monks and nuns walking out of here will be spotted by soldiers straight away.

Just the two of us will have a better chance. We have to leave. Can you change out of those robes?"

Choepel delved deeper into Sophia's eyes. She didn't blink. Questions and doubt filled every corner of his mind. *If I stay, things will never be the same. If I go, I'll be turning my back on monastic life for good. I only just met Sophia. Should I go with her? What do I do?*

He slid a sweaty palm over his scalp and closed his eyes. Memories of his time at the monastery flashed through his mind. He imagined deciding to stay and facing Master Chi. Then he imagined leaving with Sophia.

Choepel took a deep breath and exhaled. "Yes, I've got other clothes."

"Good. Go. Quickly."

Choepel rushed to the door. He turned to Sophia. "I'm not sure I'm doing the right thing."

Sophia glowered at him. "It's your choice, Choepel. I'll be at the monastery gates in five minutes. If you're not there, I'll leave without you."

Chapter 24

Choepel raced to his room and, in the dark, frantically stuffed some clothes in a small cloth bag and changed into his only pair of jeans and a jumper. He threw his robes on the floor. He then went to the office on the ground floor in the west wing and got his passport. He quietly shut the office door behind him and turned to head to the front gate, but footsteps approached from the stairwell. He glanced at an adjacent storage-room door, in the direction of the stairwell. *If I go in there I could be seen and heard by whoever's coming.* He darted in the opposite direction, into a side corridor that gave access to some of the nuns' rooms. He crouched with his back against the wall and listened in the dark. *If a nun comes around the corner they'll see me.* His head throbbed and his palms became sweaty.

As the footsteps got nearer, candlelight hit the corridor walls and swept around the corner before stopping at Choepel's legs. The storage-room door clicked open.

"Hello, beautiful." Master Chi spoke childishly in English. "Would you like to watch some TV? Good."

The door gently closed. The candlelight splashed erratically on the walls, then steadied. A young girl giggled.

Ai!

Choepel's heart rate jumped. He slid low along the wall, staying in the shadows, and poked the top of his head slowly around the corner. With one eye, he looked in the direction of the voices.

Master Chi stood outside the storage room. He held a candle in one hand, and in the other arm Ai smiled at him. Choepel held his breath.

Master Chi whispered. "Do you like sweets?"

Ai nodded and giggled.

"I have a lovely lollipop for you in my room. Would you like to go there?"

Ai nodded again. Master Chi mimicked Ai's giggles.

"Can you stick out your tongue?"

Ai smiled innocently and stuck out her tongue.

"Good girl. That's a beautiful tongue."

Master Chi slid his tongue over Ai's several times like a dog slurping water. She giggled and put her tiny palms on his cheeks.

"You're so pretty. Let's go get the lovely lollipop."

Master Chi walked down the corridor towards the stairwell with Ai in one arm. The light moved with him and the corridor slowly darkened.

Choepel's face went ashen and his mouth dry. His arms stiffened and his palms oozed sweat. *Ai needs protection from that monster. But Sophia's waiting for me. She'll think I've changed my mind if I help Ai. And Sophia will have to walk alone through the city when so many soldiers are patrolling the streets.* A deep cavern opened up in his stomach. He closed his eyes and got lost in the darkness for a few moments.

The chanting from the rear of the monastery abruptly stopped. His eyes shot open. *I've got to decide — and fast.*

Chapter 25

When Choepel got to the front gate, he found Sophia crouched silently in the shadows.

"Why so long?"

Choepel's eyes glistened in the shadowed moonlight. "He's going to hurt someone else."

"Who — a nun?"

"No, Ai."

"Who's Ai?"

"A young girl, a child, about five years old, who's hiding in the monastery with the nuns."

A long silence followed.

"Choepel, an army patrol just went by. They'll be back any time. The fire puja just finished, so wouldn't the nuns look after her?"

"Maybe. I don't know." Choepel ran his hand across his scalp. "How do you know this guy you've met can help us? We could be shot on the streets. This is all just too much."

"Choepel, do you really want to stay here with ... with monster Chi? I can't step into that place ever again after what he did to me." Sophia hesitated. "Look, sometimes the choices we have to make in life can be excruciatingly difficult. But we have to make them, no matter how painful. Often those choices will have both good and bad consequences. No choice is ever risk-free. But we must make the choice and live with whatever consequences arise. Even if we avoid making a choice, that's a choice in itself. I can help you leave this place. You must decide if you want my help. You have to make a choice — now. We don't have time to waste."

Choepel turned to look at the dark, silent monastery. A light breeze waved the mandalas and prayer flags hanging around the perimeter of the courtyard. Moonlight glinted on the gilded bronze roof tiles, the dharma wheel, and the deer statues on the ridge. He turned to Sophia. "But why help me?"

Sophia reached for Choepel's hand in the dark and smiled. "Maybe I'm crazy. A crazy woman who flew halfway around the world to be a Buddhist nun. That's not going to happen, but at least I can be compassionate. Isn't compassion a central Buddhist teaching? But ultimately, it's your choice."

Lit candles floated in the monastery's windows on both floors. Muffled voices filled its rooms, bringing it back to life.

After a few moments, Sophia whispered, "What's your choice?" She picked up her bag and put the strap of her laptop case over her shoulder. "The girl should be safe with the nuns. We need to go, now. The soldiers will be back soon."

After a long moment of hesitation, Choepel stood up, glanced at the monastery, then turned and reached for the gate.

By staying mostly in the shadows, they managed to get to the Xingzhong Bridge without encountering any soldiers. Sophia and Choepel stopped and gazed at the span of the bridge. Nothing moved on it. Even the air seemed frozen in time. And nothing moved on the road behind them.

She looked at Choepel and smiled. "I hope your meditation legs can run fast."

Choepel forced a grin. "Well, we've got to get across it." He glanced down at the fast-flowing river. Its frigidity wrapped around his sandaled feet and ankles. *Is Ai safe? Should I have done something?*

Sophia began jogging and Choepel followed. A quarter of the way over the bridge, several pairs of headlights slipped onto the far end towards them. She stopped immediately and thrust an open hand onto Choepel's chest. "Under the bridge. Now."

They both turned back and sprinted to where the bridge joined the riverbank. Their feet slipped on the loose gravel and they struggled to keep their baggage from falling into the water as they scrambled below the bridge on their hands and knees. Their heads almost hit the rusty steel girders on the underside of the bridge. They hid in its shadow, surrounded by clumps of thin reeds, discarded bottles and cans, and the acrid stench of urine. The hissing and slapping of the rushing river bounced off the girders, and the breeze whistled between water, steel, and concrete. The crests of the water sparkled, creating a frayed ribbon of light in the center of the river. Sophia put an extended index finger to her lips and stared hard at Choepel. His heart raced and thumped in his chest and his ears. He squeezed his frantic, heavy breathing to keep it in his throat.

Several vehicles sped over the bridge towards them. As the vehicles came closer to the riverbank, the rumbling of their motors slowed. Loud squeaky brakes brought the tires to a stop. Diesel fumes wafted from the road above to Sophia and Choepel below. A vehicle door on unoiled hinges swung open, then heavy army boots stomped and crunched on the flaky bitumen.

A seemingly tired, frustrated voice from the bridge shouted out, "There's no one here!"

Then a muffled voice from the confines of a vehicle shouted back. "Drunk bastard! You fucking cadets drink too much."

"But I saw something, Captain. I'll check under the bridge."

The soldier who had exited the vehicle clomped to where the bridge met the riverbank. As he stomped onto the gravel shoulder of the road, his boots skidded and he fell flat onto his back. Laughter erupted from the vehicles. Sophia and Choepel saw the soldier's legs and part of his prostrate torso on the ground only meters from them. The soldier clasped his rifle in both hands as it pointed towards them.

The soldier stood up, and one at a time, rubbed his hands on his dirty camouflage pants, as his rifle waved about. He gingerly stepped slowly towards the river. Choepel saw the man's thin frame in profile only up to his shoulders. He and Sophia silently eased back further into the bridge's shadow. The soldier turned towards the bridge and took two paces towards them, almost in slow motion. He stopped less than a meter away. Choepel squinted at the deep scuff marks on the toes of the soldier's boots. He held his breath. Perspiration dripped onto his bag, clutched to his chest. Then in the corner of his eye he noticed something move on his leg. He turned slowly and saw a thin green snake slithering up his outstretched right leg. His racing heart almost jumped out of his chest. He suppressed a scream and the desperate urge to scramble out from under the bridge.

As the snake's head glided towards Choepel's knee, Sophia slowly twisted her left leg so her knee gently touched his. The snake stopped. A shiny black tongue flicked under burning, red eyes. *Red tail!* A snake exactly like it had bitten Cholha, an Irish nun, two years earlier while they were walking in bushland near the monastery. He saw the snake strike her hand when she bent down to pick up a pine cone, before it slithered away into the bushes. He carried her frail 85-year-old body back to the monastery and drove her frantically to hospital where she received antivenom, but she died hours later.

Under the bridge, the snake slid onto Sophia's knee and thigh, then climbed onto her left arm that cradled her laptop case.

"You fucking clumsy idiot! I'm tired." The voice from one of the vehicles bellowed much louder than before, jolting Choepel's tense body. "You're drunk and fucking imagining things."

"But Captain …" The soldier's voice seemed to vibrate in the earth under the bridge and through Choepel's body as his eyes followed the snake. It slithered slowly towards Sophia's face.

"Fucking idiot! If you don't get back in the truck now, I'll shove your fucking chopsticks so far up your arse, I'll rip out your tonsils." Unbridled laughter exploded from the trucks, drowning out the low din of the diesel motors. "You're holding everyone up! I want to get some fucking sleep tonight!"

The soldier on the riverbank stood like a statue. His face took on a deep shade of crimson. He looked up to the bridge, then slowly turned, and carefully scrambled up the bank and onto the road. Voices rose in ironic taunts from the vehicles. A door slammed and the vehicles sped away as the snake's mouth reached Sophia's chin. With wide full-moon eyes, Choepel's gaze went from the snake to Sophia's face. Her gaze was fixated on the snake's head, but her slightly squinted eyes did not show any apparent fear. Choepel held his breath. His raging heart made his head throb. Then in a flash, Sophia whipped her right hand across her body and grabbed the snake by its neck. Its flaying tail struck Choepel's face as she pulled it off her body and threw it further under the bridge near the waterline. After it hit the ground, it slipped away into the reeds. Choepel put a hand to his stinging cheek and let out a heavy sigh.

He looked at Sophia. "Thanks. Did you do that because you thought it wasn't poisonous?"

Sophia looked at him with wide eyes. "It isn't poisonous, is it?"

"Just a Bamboo Pit Viper — one of Taiwan's most venomous."

Sophia's eyebrows rose up as she stared at Choepel. "Well, let's get out of here before any of its friends get interested in us."

After crossing the bridge at a fast jog, they stopped on the empty road to catch their breaths. Sophia looked at her phone.

Choepel put his hands on his hips and took a few deep breaths. "That won't work. The phone network and Internet have been out since the invasion."

Sophia smiled. "Oh, that's lucky. I've managed to get a connection. Must be a woman's touch. I'm just checking where that guy's staying. I know it's a small place, like a bed-and-breakfast, because the army has moved into all the big hotels. Good, not too far to go."

"So that guy's been here long?"

"Not too long."

"Why's he staying here when the country's under military rule?"

"Even in war there are business opportunities. Some people will do anything for money, I guess."

Choepel sucked in deep breaths as he glanced up at the night sky and moon.

Sophia tugged at his arm. "Soldiers could come by again at any moment. Let's go."

Chapter 26

Choepel and Sophia made it into the city without encountering any more soldiers. Whenever a plane flew low overhead, they hid under trees or a parked car. After nearly an hour, they came to a gray bungalow with a small front garden and red front door. Under hazy moonlight, they crouched behind a bush on the other side of the road, lined by only a few parked cars. A line of round, unlit, white Chinese lanterns hung over a red garage door. Sophia glanced down the road in both directions. "This is it. Come on."

The uneasiness at the core of Choepel's being stirred. He grabbed Sophia's arm before she could take a step. "I can't do it."

"What?"

"I have to go back for Ai," he whispered.

Sophia glared at Choepel and shook her head. "I don't believe this."

"I'm sorry, but I can't get her out of my mind."

"Choepel, I've been thinking about the girl too. But the streets are crawling with soldiers. The nuns will look after her."

"Maybe they will, but none of them know Ai is alone with him. Wouldn't it be easy to get a child out of the country too if she's with us?"

"Not necessarily. She'll still need a passport. It's a complication we don't need."

"But I can't leave her. Her parents are both dead. She's got no one. I feel I've got to help her."

"But we can't take the risk of getting caught. We were lucky on the bridge. If we get caught, we'll never get out of the country. Please don't do this. I can't go back to the monastery after what I've been through."

Choepel's head dropped. "Look, I'll go back on my own. I'll meet you back here."

"Have you changed your mind about leaving?"

Choepel shook his head. "No."

"Are you lying to me?"

"No. I just need to help Ai. I can't get the thought of her being alone with him out of my mind. Here, take my bag. I'll return. Remember, we have to live with the consequences of our choices. I failed you. I'm going to have to live with that guilt and regret for the rest of my life. If I fail Ai without even trying to help her, I'm not sure how I'll be able to live with that."

Sophia sighed. She looked to the ground, then up again at Choepel. "You're making a big mistake. Let's meet my friend. We've come this far. We can talk this through with him."

"No, the longer I wait, the greater the danger Ai will be in. I've made up my mind."

Sophia shook her head. "You're putting yourself in danger, and my friend and me too, because soldiers could find out about this place."

"I promise, if I get caught, there's no way I'm going to be betraying you or your friend."

"I don't mean you'll do it intentionally, but you could lead soldiers here unknowingly."

"I'll be careful."

Sophia sighed again. "Look, when you get back, knock only twice, wait for a second, then knock three times, so I'll know it's you."

Choepel smiled. "Okay. If I'm not back in one hour, it won't be because I've changed my mind about leaving." He placed Sophia's hands into his. "If this is the last time I see you, I hope one day you're able to forgive me, and I hope you'll be able to get out of the country safely."

Sophia hesitated. "Listen, Choepel, I'm counting on both of us getting out of the country safely, so you'd better get back."

Part 11
2139

Chapter 27

At the hospital, scores of people injured by falling trees, walls of rushing water, landslides, and collapsed buildings, crowded its flooded entrance. The storm had intensified since Marvin left his home. He ran inside with his arms protecting his head from the bullet-like hailstones, some the size of tennis balls. Nurses frantically trolleyed the injured through waterlogged corridors into emergency rooms and operating theaters for treatment.

"Where do I go, Ebes?"

"Room 582. Take the lift straight ahead. I have let the doctor know you are here."

Marvin took the crowded, noisy lift and found Dr Grenfeld waiting for him in his office. For a long moment, he studied the doctor's thick, graying black hair and beard.

Dr Grenfeld projected a cold stare. When he stood up behind his desk, his head almost touched the ceiling. "I didn't think you'd get here on time given the atrocious weather." His deep voice and American accent struck Marvin.

"The weather bureau has just issued a warning advising the storm has developed into a category 5 cyclone. It is expected to make landfall within 12 hours. Super cyclones are currently battering Europe, Africa, the South Pacific and North America."

Dr Grenfeld extended a hand towards Marvin. "My wife just called to tell me the storm's been upgraded to a category 5 cyclone."

Marvin shook Dr Grenfeld's hand pensively as he glanced at the color photographs on the walls depicting the Old City of Jerusalem. "I know." He turned his head and lowered his collar to show Dr Grenfeld his implant.

Dr Grenfeld sat back down. "What made you decide to get Ebes?"

Marvin sat down on the other side of the desk. "Most of my students have one. It became embarrassing that they knew more than me."

Dr Grenfeld nodded. "Ah, yes, I saw you're a science teacher. Have you adjusted to it?"

Marvin grinned. "Teaching?"

Dr Grenfeld frowned. "No, the implant."

"Not yet. I'm still getting used to her knowing whatever I'm thinking and feeling. I don't feel my thoughts are private anymore."

Dr Grenfeld smiled coyly. "Yes, that's a common reaction. Some people say they feel like Ebes has become their inner voice and many aren't happy about that."

"Yes, that's exactly how I feel. There's no off-switch."

"You could have it removed, but that actually carries more of a risk of nerve damage than when implanting it. I wouldn't advise that. Many people do like the convenience."

"The convenience is great — no need for a phone or computer. She does everything for me before I ask. But sometimes I wish she *would* ask." Marvin shook his head. "You don't have one?"

Dr Grenfeld's face became suddenly serious. "I regard such devices as contrary to my religious beliefs. I agree there are clinical benefits of quantum computing implants, but I struggle to reconcile those with the scriptures." He pushed his head back and glanced out the window for a few moments. "Ebes has sent me some unusual data about you — lots of subconscious memories of people and places. I've never come across a case like yours."

Marvin leaned forward slightly. "Subconscious memories?"

"Yes, and it's probably good that they're subconscious because they're extraordinary — and to be frank, troubling. If they seeped into your conscious awareness, the psychological implications could be dire."

Marvin dropped his head in his hands before he looked up. "Could there be a problem with the implant?"

Dr Grenfeld shook his head. "No, Ebes is working fine. There's never been any reported malfunctions with the neural implants, and more than half of the world's population now have them."

Blood rushed to Marvin's face. "So, are you able to see all my memories — even those I'm not aware of?"

"Yes, Ebes sent it as a hologram. I watched most of them with great interest and fascination."

Marvin and Dr Grenfeld considered each other for several silent moments.

"I see there's no history of mental illness in your family. How have you been feeling in recent days?"

Marvin stabbed his elbows into his knees, hung his head, and looked down. "I've been feeling a little unsettled." He waited a few moments. "So what's wrong with me?"

Dr Grenfeld sighed. "Do you feel at times like you're observing yourself, like watching a movie of your life play out before you?"

Marvin shook his head. "No."

Dr Grenfeld raised his eyebrows, brought his hands together, and interlocked his fingers. "Have you experienced any sudden anxieties recently?"

"Yes, but I think everyone has because of the fires and the storm."

Dr Grenfeld took a deep breath. "I'll come straight to the point. It's clear you have a unique case of what's called Dissociated Identity Disorder. Usually, the condition manifests as different identities seeming to live inside someone, and in most cases the person has apparently disconnected memories."

Marvin remained silent for a couple of moments and slumped in the chair. "Disconnected memories?"

"Yes, memories of the different identities. In those cases, the person actually remembers the memories of the different identities. But in your case, those memories are locked into your subconscious. Had it not been for Ebes, those memories would have likely remained hidden from you and me."

"Maybe that's a good thing."

Dr Grenfeld shook his head. "In the short term — yes. But memories that are hidden in your subconscious still affect you in all sorts of ways —phobias, anxieties, tics, habits. The subconscious affects behavior in surprising ways."

"Can you help me?"

"Yes, with medication, but I can't guarantee all those memories will remain locked in your subconscious forever. They could explode into your conscious awareness any day, or slowly creep into it over days, weeks, or even years."

"You make it sound like I've got a ticking time-bomb in my head."

"Yes, that's one way to put it."

"But what's caused this?"

"Dissociated Identity Disorder often manifests in childhood as a way to deal with severe trauma because the personality isn't fully developed, but adults can also get the condition." Dr Grenfeld paused and rubbed his chin. "When I reviewed your memories, I discovered one particular repressed memory from your childhood."

Marvin frowned. "My childhood?"

"Yes, as a way to protect our psyches from an emotional, stressful, or traumatic event, children, even adults, can sometimes unconsciously block a memory from their conscious awareness. This particular repressed memory goes back to when you were 10. But the cost of repressed memories is severe anxiety and fear in various forms, even sometimes serious psychological problems. I see you've always experienced intense anxiety in certain situations ever since that time. Have you ever wondered why?"

Marvin shook his head and slumped further in the chair. His heart began thumping fast. His face reddened.

"I went through all your memories and found you've avoided flying, graveyards, and got panic attacks whenever someone broached the subject of death, even in casual conversations. That indicates to me that you have what's called thanatophobia, or a fear of death, which manifests as a generalized anxiety disorder. And it all stems back to that repressed memory when you were 10 years old."

Marvin's palms became moist and his breathing erratic. Blood surged to his face in waves. Perspiration beaded at his hairline.

Dr Grenfeld took a small, flat, white plastic case from the desk drawer and moved to Marvin. He slid out a translucent plastic circular patch from the case. "Put this on — it will calm you."

Marvin pulled his sleeve up to his elbow and placed the patch on the inside of his forearm.

Dr Grenfeld sat down again. "Do you remember why you were adopted as a child?"

"Yes, my parents died."

The windows rattled as a gust of wind tried to force its way through. Both men's heads turned in a flash. Dr Grenfeld kept staring out the window for a long while. "How did they die?"

Marvin's brow wrinkled and his eyes narrowed. "A car accident?" He hesitated. "Mmm, I'm not sure."

Dr Grenfeld continued looking out the window as sheets of rain and hailstones crashed into it. Then he turned back to look at Marvin. His voice softened. "Your parents didn't die in a car accident. They died in a house fire."

Marvin's face flushed hot red. "A house fire? Are you sure?"

"Yes. The holographic imagery is undeniable."

"How did it start?"

"The memory you've unconsciously repressed shows the fire started in your bedroom one afternoon when you played with a toy alcohol lamp burner, and you accidentally knocked it off your desk. The curtains caught on fire. You got scared, panicked, and rushed out of the house, not knowing your parents were asleep inside. The fire quickly spread. Your parents didn't realize the place was ablaze until it was obviously too late."

Marvin dropped his head into his trembling hands. "No, that can't be. I didn't kill them."

"Marvin, calm down. You didn't kill them. Understand it was a horrible accident. You can't blame yourself. It's because you blame yourself that your subconscious has been protecting you."

Marvin sighed and shook his head. Suddenly, the floor began to sway slowly. The furniture rocked from side to side. Files and books fell from the shelves behind Dr Grenfeld. He and Marvin looked at each other with wide, fearful eyes. Marvin instinctively grabbed the chair. The swaying quickly became violent, as if a petulant giant had picked up the building and begun shaking it like a toy. The bookshelf toppled onto Dr Grenfeld and pinned him to the desktop. Marvin tried to stand, but his body swayed uncontrollably in all directions. A low rumble shot through the cracking walls and ceiling. It got louder by the second.

"Marvin, a magnitude 10 earthquake has hit Sydney. Get under the desk."

Marvin scrambled and crawled under the desk as it jumped from side to side. "Dr Grenfeld, get under the desk!"

Dr Grenfeld didn't move. Marvin tried to pull him down under the desk, but the chair and bookshelf suddenly slid away from him and crashed into a wall as the floor tilted up like a seesaw. The whole building rumbled. Marvin pushed himself against the desk as it dragged him across the unstable floor.

The walls, floor, and ceiling crumbled like wafer-thin biscuits. Debris rained down and smashed all around him. Dust swirled about like choking smoke. Muffled screams ricocheted off the tumbling debris. Moments later, an enormous splintered crack burst open in the floor and he fell down through the clouds of dust, plaster, and concrete onto multiple concertinaed floors. He lay under the desk, covered by debris, for several minutes before the rumbling and shaking subsided, then finally stopped.

Marvin's awareness clutched at the slapping of the rain and hail biting at his trembling arms that poked out from under the desk. A cut, angling down his forehead and cheek, burned. A thick layer of pulverized plaster and concrete coated his face, hands, and clothes. Disembodied voices moaned, mumbled, and sobbed. Some pleaded for help.

"Marvin, you're not seriously hurt. Your vital signs are good. Make your way out away from the building. There will likely be aftershocks."

Marvin dragged himself from under the desk. The dust made breathing difficult. The rain and hail stung his face and back. As he lifted his arms to his head to protect himself from the hail, he looked for Dr Grenfeld, but couldn't see anyone. "Dr Grenfeld!"

No response.

"Marvin, the road is to your right. Go there."

"No! I have to find Dr Grenfeld."

"There is no time. Our survival depends on getting away from the building. Aftershocks are inevitable."

"*Shut up!*" Marvin scanned the rubble. "Dr Grenfeld! Where are you?"

Bloodied, motionless arms and legs poked out from under large broken pieces of concrete and twisted metal. He checked several arms for pulses, but detected no signs of life. His limbs trembled as he found a lacerated arm protruding from under the remains of a bookshelf. A shredded, blood-soaked lab coat sleeved the arm. He struggled to lift the pieces of the bookshelf and peered under a thick slab of concrete that had pinned Dr Grenfeld. Two broken concrete slabs squeezed Dr Grenfeld's bloodied head in a vice-like grip. Marvin felt for a pulse and listened, as if trying to hear it too.

"The pulse is too weak, Marvin. There is little chance he will survive. Get away from the building. The walls still standing could collapse at any time."

"Shut up!"

Marvin carefully picked out jagged panes of broken glass around Dr Grenfeld but couldn't budge the slabs of concrete. "Dr Grenfeld, can you hear me? I'll get you out. Dr Grenfeld?"

Marvin looked around desperately to see if anyone could help. But only a few people — in a thick mental fog and with bloodied, shredded clothes — had emerged from the rubble and dust. As rain and hail pelted down, he tried to lift off the slab again and again. *It's too heavy.* Exhausted, he reached for Dr Grenfeld's hand and felt for a pulse again. *Nothing.* He dropped his head and held Dr Grenfeld's hand in both of his for a few moments.

"You did what you could, Marvin. But there is nothing you could have done to save him."

An aftershock shook the ground for several seconds and displaced some small pieces of rubble. A few remaining walls, standing no more than a few meters away, crashed to the ground, pushing rubble against Marvin's legs and almost knocking him off his feet. He held on to the concrete slab with one hand and covered his head with the other as he waited for the shaking to stop.

"Go to the road. It is not safe here."

Marvin carefully climbed over large pieces of broken walls, ceilings, floors, and furniture towards the road. "The road, it's this way!" he called out to anyone he thought would hear.

With a hunched back and still dazed, Marvin staggered to the road. But where the road had been, a river raged. Cars, buses, debris from collapsed buildings, and massive uprooted fig trees pushed surging white water high into the air and onto the remains of the footpaths. A cacophonous chorus of fire alarms and emergency vehicle sirens blared through the gales, torrential rain, and hail. He briefly glanced back at the piles of smoking rubble as scores of patients and hospital staff trudged aimlessly about, some collapsing into strangers' arms, some falling to their knees, some with their heads in their hands weeping uncontrollably. A few dazed medical staff had begun to assist the injured.

"The earthquake hit 10 kilometers off the coast at a depth of less than 5 kilometers. Shallow quakes cause the most damage. This is the highest-magnitude earthquake in recorded history. A tsunami warning has been issued. We must get to higher ground immediately. The nearest highest point is St John's Church — the evacuation center."

"Christ! Which way do I go?"

"I'll guide you, but there are problems with the Internet because of the infrastructure damage. Remain calm. Breathe deeply."

Marvin took a deep breath, then coughed repeatedly. Blood spattered the rubble around his feet. He staggered over the rubble and called out to a few people looking confused and dazed near him. "Tsunami warning! Get to St John's Church!"

No one seemed to hear him. The few people who stumbled past him seemed oblivious to the danger. As the wind, rain, and hail intensified, Ebes guided him towards the church. He waded through dirty, knee-deep, bone-chilling water and scrambled over precarious piles of shattered slabs of concrete, bricks, glass, broken pipes, twisted furniture, and thick splintered tree trunks and branches. Only a few buildings remained partially upright. Scores of contorted, lifeless, bloodied bodies and limbs lay motionless on and under debris, and floated with cars, motorcycles, and other tattered reminders of an urban existence. The black, turgid water quickly clawed up to his waist.

Marvin straightened momentarily when he glimpsed the church a few hundred meters away. The pounding wind almost pushed him over. He leaned forward and held his hands over his face to shield it from the hailstones.

"Duck down, now."

Instinctively, Marvin bobbed down but slipped into the cold, murky water. A piece of corrugated metal flew over him like a giant sheet of newspaper. Its corner cut through his overcoat and grazed his shoulder, narrowly missing his implant. He pushed himself up out of the foul-tasting water and immediately spat out more blood into the palms of his shaking hands. He held his shoulder and winced. *"Christ, that was close!"*

"The cyclone has moved much faster than expected. It will make landfall in less than 12 hours. Get to the church. Several magnitude 10 earthquakes have hit the northern and southern hemispheres. Much of Australia's west and southern coasts have sunk into the ocean. Large parts of North America, the United Kingdom, and Europe have been submerged. The earthquakes have triggered volcanic eruptions in Asia, Europe, South America, Africa, and Hawaii."

"Jesus Christ!"

"Stay calm. Get to the church."

As the wind and hail battered him, several cars, buses, steel drums, and building debris bobbed about in the fast-flowing water that surged between the high, slanting concrete walls of what used to be a multi-lane highway. One car with its rear end higher than its front floated past him backwards. Only the car's windows and roof poked above the water that had almost completely filled the interior. *There's someone inside.* A woman punched repeatedly at the driver's window.

"The church, Marvin, get to the church. It is not far."

"No, that woman needs help."

Marvin ripped off his overcoat, climbed over debris, and followed the car as it bobbed and swiveled in the water in different directions as if it were a toy. He stumbled and tripped but kept his eyes on the car as it floated further away.

"There is no possibility of saving the woman. The water is moving too fast."

Marvin stopped. His shoulders dropped with his hopes. The car floated further away. The woman screamed as she thumped the window with her fists. The car then crashed into an uprooted tree trunk, pushing the bonnet high into the air and bringing it to a sudden stop. Spurts of white water shot up all around the car. The water level inside the car rose as the woman beat faster on the window.

"It's too dangerous, Marvin. Go to the church."

"No!"

Marvin's shaking legs snapped into action. He scrambled over partly submerged debris and finally reached the car. As he approached it, the woman's screams became increasingly frantic and drowned out the howling cyclonic winds. "Help! Please help!"

Marvin straddled the massive tree trunk that had pinned the car. He dragged himself along its slimy surface. He almost slipped into the raging current several times, but finally made it to the car. The woman struggled to keep her head above water.

Marvin jumped into the water. The current pulled at his body. When he managed to push his head above the waves, he grabbed the submerged door handle but couldn't release it. He looked at the woman. "Put the window down!"

The woman began kicking at the door but couldn't shift it. "The electrics aren't working!"

Marvin snapped his head left, then right, in a vain hope that help would arrive from somewhere or someone.

"Use the concrete block, Marvin."

Marvin turned towards the tree truck. A plate-size piece of broken concrete had lodged between its branches, along with various pieces of other debris. He pushed himself out of the water, clambered onto the car roof, and grabbed the concrete block. But as his wet fingers latched onto its smooth sides, it slipped from his hands. It disappeared into the watery blackness. *"Fuck! It's gone!"*

Marvin thrust a hand into the water and searched blindly with feverish fingers. His fingers crawled over the splintered tree trunk, before unexpectedly touching the sharp edges of the concrete block. He pushed his hands deeper into the torrent and managed to pull the block out. He sighed momentarily, then scrambled onto the car with the block in one hand. He crawled along the roof, back to the front of the car. The woman's arms and legs thrashed chaotically at the water. The air pocket in the car had narrowed to only a few centimeters deep.

Marvin waved his free hand. "Get away from the window!"

"Marvin, you will only have one chance to smash it. If the block bounces off the window and sinks into deeper water, it will be highly unlikely you will be able to retrieve it."

"Thanks, Ebes!"

Marvin lifted himself onto his unsteady knees. He raised the concrete block with trembling hands above his head and threw it into the window with all the strength he could muster. The block bounced off the window, then plunged into the water. His head dropped and his heart sank. He wiped the rain from his eyes as he stared at the window. Several diagonal hairline cracks had appeared around the point of impact. He bent down and began beating the window with a fist. The car had filled completely with water. Holding her breath, the woman managed to turn her body in the water and kicked at the window. After repeated attempts, the window finally smashed, allowing some of the water inside to escape. She pushed her head up into a widening air pocket. She scrambled out of the car and Marvin helped her onto the roof. They both collapsed onto their backs, completely exhausted.

The woman coughed up water. Her body trembled uncontrollably. Blood streamed from a gash on her leg. She looked at Marvin. "I didn't think I was going to make it."

"Get to the church, Marvin."

Marvin stared at the woman's wet, honey-colored face and hair for a long moment, then nodded. "I'm Marvin. We've got to get to the church. A tsunami's coming."

The woman sighed and pushed her hair back. "I'm Mavis."

Chapter 28

The knee-deep, white-water river rapids surged over the road outside the church. Marvin held Mavis' arm as they carefully waded through it, taking care to avoid floating tree branches and building debris. Repeated gusts of wind almost knocked them off their feet. They staggered over snapped tree branches, broken bricks, shards of stained glass, and pieces of clay roof tiles, up the church steps. In the beating rain, he banged desperately on the large wooden double door several times. A tiny crack appeared as an elderly priest struggled to keep the door from bursting fully open. But a wind gust pushed the heavy doors, and the priest flew backwards several feet into a row of stacked benches. Marvin and Mavis fell into the church on their hands and knees as several people, all in high-viz vests, rushed to push the doors shut. Others assisted the priest to his feet. The wind howled and swirled around the altar and rows of sandstone columns as a few people taped sheets of thick black plastic over the glassless windows.

Water dripped off Marvin and Mavis like rain and pooled around them on the concrete floor. Lucy rushed to them with a concerned look on her face. "Glad you've managed to get here, Marvin." She looked at Mavis' leg and helped her to stand. "That's a deep gash. We've got medical supplies. We'll clean it and put a bandage on it."

Lucy looked at Marvin's lacerated face and bleeding shoulder. "You need some attention too." She helped Marvin to his feet and supported him to a table while a young man led Mavis to an adjacent table stacked with medical kits. For the first time, Marvin noticed that Mavis had a colorful patch depicting the Aboriginal flag sewn onto the back pocket of her jeans.

"*Stay calm, Marvin. We will get through this. Our adrenaline levels are extremely high, raising your blood pressure. We will get things back in balance.*"

Marvin took a few deep breaths. His stare lingered first at Lucy, who stood beside him, frantically retrieving medical supplies from an opened kit, then at Mavis a few feet away at the other table.

Mavis began crying as the man cut her jeans around her lacerated leg. "I nearly died. My car was swept away." She turned to Marvin and wiped her welled-up eyes. "Thanks for getting me out."

"Just lucky I saw you." Marvin dropped his head into his trembling hands. "I can't believe what's happening."

Marvin straightened as Lucy inspected the cut on his face. She cut a strip of antiseptic wrap. "Sorry, but this will sting."

Marvin winced as Lucy gently applied the wrap onto his forehead and cheek. She then slipped off his ripped jacket and applied strips of antiseptic wraps over his bloodied shoulder. "Thanks." He looked at Mavis, who had her head in her hands. "Things look really grim out there. If this wasn't an evacuation center, I'm not sure where we'd be or if we'd still be alive."

Lucy carefully wrapped a large adhesive bandage over Marvin's shoulder. "Well, God's made all this possible."

Marvin grinned mischievously. "Do you mean the earthquake, cyclone, or tsunami?"

Lucy's face went a paler shade of white. "Tsunami?"

"It's on its way." Marvin smiled sardonically. "I hope God used quality builders for this place." He looked at the shards of glass strewn on the floor. "I don't think he used the best glaziers."

Lucy put several items back into the medical kit on the table. "God's will is God's will. He will protect the righteous. We expect many others will be coming here soon."

Marvin's breathing faltered. "I'm not sure many others will be able to get here." He gently patted his bandaged shoulder. "Thanks for your kindness, Lucy. I do appreciate it. Ignore my irreverence and sarcasm."

Lucy smiled. "Irreverence seems to be the latest fad nowadays."

Marvin lowered his voice to a whisper and leaned closer to Lucy. "How's Lili?"

Lucy glanced upwards briefly and exhaled. "I've not been able to contact her. I hope she's okay. I'm also worried about the headphones I gave her. Professor Yuhang was at the university when the first earthquake hit, and just before the phone line died he told me our lab and all our equipment had been destroyed. He's okay. I've told him to come here as soon as he can." She shook her head. "We've lost years of important research."

"So the headphones you gave your partner are the same as the ones you had at the university?"

Lucy looked around nervously, then nodded. "You mustn't tell anyone."

Marvin squinted. "Okay, but why the secrecy?"

Lucy smiled coyly and dropped her voice to a whisper. "I don't want anyone else finding out what we're working on and beating us to publication."

Marvin nodded.

Lucy's eyelids narrowed. "Everyone has secrets. But I think I can trust you. Do you trust me?"

Marvin maintained his gaze deep into Lucy's eyes, seeking some assurance. Before he could answer, a couple, who with a few others had been taping plastic sheets over gaping windows after they assisted the priest, came towards him. The man leaned down, displayed a perfect white-teeth smile, and put a hand on Marvin's arm. "Are you and your wife alright?"

Marvin's eyes widened as his gaze jumped from the man, then to the woman, several times. He nodded slowly and suppressed a smile. "Oh, I'm not married. Mavis is just someone I helped on the way here. But the fact we're both alive must be something to be thankful for after everything that's happened. Is the priest okay?"

The woman clasped her hands together and glanced up to the high rib-vaulted ceiling. "Yes, thank the Lord. He's just a bit shaken." She almost bowed as she displayed equally perfect straight white teeth. "I'm Josephine and this is my husband, Lex. Lucy is our gorgeous daughter."

Marvin looked at Lucy and smiled. "You must be very proud of her. She's very intelligent too." He turned to Josephine. "I like your French accent. I can now see where Lucy gets her pretty features from."

Josephine's eyes lit up.

Lex smiled kindly. "Yes, Lucy's got her mother's genes, thankfully. She's our only child and is fluent in French too. She's grown to be a very caring woman. She suggested using the church as an evacuation center whenever there's severe weather or, as it turns out, earthquakes too."

Marvin glanced around at the sheets of shivering plastic over the windows. "Well, it's good we're on higher ground because a tsunami is coming."

Josephine gasped. "Tsunami! Are you sure? We've not heard any warnings — but the phone network is down."

Marvin patted the back of his neck. "My Ebes can access satellite feeds."

Everyone turned to look at Marvin with stunned expressions. Josephine grabbed Lex's arm. "Oh!"

Lex put a reassuring arm around his wife. "We welcome everyone into God's house. The Lord protects all, even people like you."

Marvin frowned. "People like me?"

Josephine smiled disingenuously. "People who aren't fully human, as God intended."

Marvin scowled. "Having a neural implant doesn't make me any less a human than you. I'm fully flesh and blood. As you see, I bleed just like you, but I just happen to have AI connected to my brain."

Lex held up an open palm. "Please don't be offended. As I said, the Lord welcomes all kinds into His house. We know millions of young people are getting the implants, and we had to be firm with Lucy about that sort of thing. Intelligence is given by God, not by a computer. It's against God's wishes to be having computers interfering with our souls. Only God knows what they do to someone's mind."

Marvin threw his head back. "What's intelligence? And do we even have a soul? What scientific evidence is there that we have souls?"

Lex glanced at Josephine, then turned to Marvin and smiled. "God is not something found in a laboratory. Faith is the way through which to find God, not through some carefully managed double-blind control study." Lex grinned at Lucy, who pushed her head back and rolled her eyes.

Marvin smiled. "And where do you find that faith in faith?"

Both Lex and Josephine looked bemused.

Before anyone could say another word, a waist-high wall of foul water, filled with debris, burst through the entrance doors and surged into the church. Marvin gasped as he jumped to his feet. Mavis and Lucy screamed.

Chapter 29

"Marvin, get to the triforium."

"What the hell's that?"

"The upper gallery — quickly."

Marvin looked up and pointed to the upper gallery that wrapped around the rear and sides of the church. "Everyone, get up to the triforium."

Marvin grabbed Lucy and Mavis by their arms and raced to the narrow wooden, winding staircase at the rear of the church. A wall of black, putrid water knocked over the benches and tables. Water tugged at Marvin's legs as he herded the group up the staircase. From the upper gallery, everyone gaped in disbelief as the water surged through the church and rose quickly. Ashen-faced, the priest dropped to his knees. "Everyone pray!"

Lucy, her parents, and the other volunteers fell to their knees and began reciting the Lord's Prayer with the priest. Marvin gasped for air as he sat against the wall with Mavis in his arms. Her body trembled uncontrollably. The water rushed up inside the church to only a few centimeters below the upper gallery floor. Several minutes later, the water level began to fall. The prayers stopped and people comforted each other. With Mavis still clinging to his side, Marvin hobbled to a broken window. The wind buffeted his face as he watched people, furniture, vehicles, boats, sea containers, tree trunks, and an assortment of other debris being pushed to the coast by the tsunami's uncompromising force. His jaw dropped when a battered white sedan floated down the street towards the church. A couple, both on hands and knees, were balancing themselves on its roof. The man cradled a small, screaming child, who had her arms tightly around his neck. The girl shared the same Chinese-looking features as the distraught woman.

"Marvin, do not do anything foolhardy."

Lucy joined Marvin and Mavis at the window. A man struggled against the current to get to the church entrance. He grabbed the metal handrail to stabilize himself as floating debris buffeted him relentlessly. The water curled around his legs like whirlpools.

Lucy gasped. "Professor Yuhang!"

Yuhang looked up with an expression of fear and surprise. Marvin stared at the totally bald, Asian man for several moments, transfixed. Then the couple with their child on the car roof grabbed his attention again. "We have to help them."

"No, Marvin, it is too dangerous."

"Shut up, Ebes!"

Marvin raced down to the flooded ground floor. Lucy and Mavis followed. He waded through the retreating knee-high water to the church steps.

"Marvin, this is unwise. The tsunami is retreating but it is still dangerous."

"Ebes, shut up!"

On the steps, Yuhang stared at the couple with the child on the roof of the car. He held out his arms as the water pushed the sedan closer towards the church. "Throw the child to me!"

The car roof dipped and rose as the couple barely managed to keep their balance. The man stared at the woman. "I'll throw Chun to that man."

The woman shook her head vigorously. "No! It's too dangerous!"

"None of us can swim in this!"

The man kissed Chun, then carefully raised himself onto his knees with her dangling in his arms.

"No!" the woman screamed.

The man looked into Chun's eyes. He turned towards Yuhang, who was struggling to keep upright. "Please catch my daughter — Chun."

The man teetered on his knees, then threw Chun towards Yuhang. Chun screamed as she fell into the turbulent water just in front of Yuhang. She disappeared under the surface. The woman cried out. Yuhang lunged down the steps to where Chun went under. With one hand gripping the handrail, he dived below the water's churning surface. A moment later, he pulled her to the surface and cradled her to his body. She gasped for air and screamed for her parents. The tsunami pulled at Yuhang's legs as he trudged up the church steps.

Yuhang looked at Marvin, Mavis, and Lucy at the top of the steps. "Take her!"

Yuhang held Chun with one arm and struggled to keep his balance. Behind him, the sedan suddenly rolled over. The couple slid into the water. Their arms waved frantically before their bodies disappeared below the water's surface.

Marvin took a couple of steps towards Yuhang. "Throw her to me!"

"I can't." Yuhang's fingers desperately clung to the handrail. Lines of fear were etched deep into his face. "I can't hold on much longer. Save the child!"

Marvin's feet slid closer to Yuhang and he extended a hand. "Grab my hand."

Lucy and Mavis positioned themselves near the top of the steps behind Marvin. They each grabbed a fistful of his shirt as he crept closer to Yuhang. The water grabbed at his waist and legs. He held up his arms. "Give her to me!"

Yuhang managed to lift Chun with one arm and handed her to Marvin. "I've got her!"

Just as Marvin pulled Chun to his chest, a thick fig tree branch crashed into Yuhang, knocking him off his feet and throwing him into the water.

Lucy screamed. "Professor!" Then she jumped into the water.

Yuhang's body briefly resurfaced, face down, as the tsunami swept him away. Lucy's head popped up above the water at the bottom of the church steps. But the force of the water pinned her to the wall bordering the steps. Lex and Josephine rushed out of the church crying out to her. As the wind howled and the rain pelted down, Marvin handed a screaming Chun to Mavis, who waded through the water back into the church.

Marvin clawed onto the slippery handrail and slid down further into the water towards Lucy. His whole body trembled as he extended a hand towards her. Their hands almost managed to touch, but a floating steel drum crashed into her. Josephine screamed. Lucy's hand dropped and her eyes closed. Her body went limp and she fell unconscious into the water, then disappeared below the surface. Lex jumped into the water where Lucy had been, and Josephine followed. Their arms waved erratically as the current swept them away. Their heads disappeared below the surface of the choppy water.

"No, Marvin."

"Lucy!" Marvin jumped into the water. He opened his eyes, but he couldn't see anything in the watery blackness. The chaotic current pushed and pulled at his body in all directions, disorientating him. He barely managed to resurface as the current pushed him far from the church. He turned in the water while debris battered him. Far from him, Lucy's body resurfaced, but face down and motionless. With each passing moment, the current was dragging it further away. As he struggled to keep his head above the water, Lucy's body sank below the surface for the last time.

Marvin looked for something to grab on to. Cars and buses, almost fully submerged with lifeless bodies inside, floated by him. Below the water's surface, debris repeatedly crashed into his body. He ducked under the water to prevent a large plank of wood from smashing into his head. He struggled to resurface. Breathless and fatigued, he kicked his legs and lunged for a tree branch. But it shot past him.

"Get to the bank, Marvin. We can do it."

His fatigued limbs slowed to almost a stop. *"Too exhausted. Can't do it. I'm going to die! I'm going to die! No!"*

Suddenly and unexpectedly, Marvin's arms and legs began paddling and kicking again, but much faster, forcing his head up above the water's surface. His awareness sharpened. As he continued to be pushed by the current like just another piece of debris, the roar of a motor grabbed his attention. He turned his head and looked behind him. Tossed about like a cork, a 3-meter aluminum boat was floating rapidly towards him. When the boat came within touching distance, a gaunt man with long, unkempt hair leaned over the gunwale and extended an arm. "Give me your hand!" the man shouted, but his voice struggled against the howling wind and screeching outboard motor.

Marvin raised a shaky arm and the man dragged him into the unsteady boat. Marvin collapsed onto the metal bench at the boat's bow and held his head in his hands. The man perched on the other bench and took hold of the outboard's tiller. The right side of his face drooped under his long, wet, graying beard. "Looks like I got to you just in time."

Marvin took several deep breaths. "Thanks."

A drenched, stained, black overcoat and soggy, tattered pants sagged on the man's thin frame. Marvin's brow furrowed as he assessed the man's face for several moments.

They both bounced about in the boat. The man grabbed the tiller with both hands. "Just hang on. The current's pushing us to the coast. I don't have much control. We could end up in fucking New Zealand!" A moment later, he pointed to something behind Marvin. "Fuck! Hold on to something!"

Marvin turned, and before he could brace himself the boat crashed into a pile of debris that had become trapped under a footbridge. Enormous waves lapped over the bridge, and white water spurted up like a geyser. Marvin's body flew back onto the gunwale and the man fell on top of him as the boat teetered atop the bridge's handrails, and threatened to tip over onto them. The propeller smashed into an enormous piece of broken concrete, splintered in all directions as the electric motor screamed, then cut out. Marvin winced and clutched at his chest. On unsteady legs, the man grabbed him and pulled him to his feet. The two climbed onto the footbridge and crawled to a sloping grassy bank. Marvin collapsed onto his stomach and could hardly move. The man limped to him and lifted him to his knees. "Come on, we've got to find some shelter."

With the man's help, Marvin managed to get to his feet, but the pain in his chest hit him like a hammer every time he inhaled. After nearly an hour of struggling through the driving cyclonic wind and rain, they came across a multistory car park, and crawled up the flooded stairs to the top level.

As night fell, the rain subsided, but the wind still gusted and the streets remained flooded. They leaned on the waist-high wall. Among the upended vehicles, debris, and countless dead bodies, several lions, tigers, kangaroos, bears, gorillas, and baby elephants struggled to keep their heads above the raging water.

The man rocked back and shook his head. His lisp caught Marvin's attention. "Looks like all of Taronga Zoo's residents have escaped — good on 'em. I hope they survive. But I'm glad we're up here."

Marvin shook his head. "I can't believe what's happened."

The man stared pensively for several moments at the scene below. "Seeing the flowing water makes me think of the ancient Greek philosopher, Heraclitus. He believed that no one steps into the same river twice because it's not the same river and it's not the same person."

Marvin continued looking at the animals and debris floating by. "What does that mean?"

"The river appears like a single body of water, but it's actually trillions of water droplets. Consciousness is like a river. It appears to flow, but it's actually a collection of single awareness events, like separate water droplets, that merge to create a coherent, flowing sense of awareness." A serious expression covered the man's face as he turned to Marvin. "That's the illusion of the flow of consciousness."

Marvin couldn't speak for several moments as he pondered what the man had said. Then an insight exploded in his mind. "It's like light."

The man frowned. "Light?"

"Yes, each new conscious awareness event is like a separate photon of light. We don't see separate photons of light, just like we don't realize that consciousness is constantly reemerging in our heads to create the illusory flow of consciousness." He paused. "And that illusory flow of consciousness creates the illusion of linear time."

The man tilted his head to one side and smiled. "Mmm, I fucking like that."

Marvin looked up to the darkening sky. "I don't know where that idea came from." He turned to the man. "So how does a boatie become so interested in philosophy?"

The man chuckled. "It's not my boat. I couldn't ever afford anything like that. I've been homeless and living on the streets for years. I was drowning in neck-high water when it floated by me, and I managed to climb in. I'm Mikelis. You're lucky I came along when I did."

"Mikelis? I'm Marvin. You saved my life. Thanks." Marvin paused. "I noticed your limp." Mikelis dropped his trousers in a flash, revealing his genitals and a scar wrapped around his right hip. "Bullies can do a lot of harm — physical and psychological. I was only 7. That one incident changed my life. I spent so much time in and out of hospitals, I missed out on a lot of schooling. Being an immigrant with little education — of course I ended up on the streets."

"How long have you been homeless?"

Mikelis shook his head. "Too long to know. But there's thousands of us around Sydney. I've found some decent spots north of the city. But I reckon they're all now under 10 feet of water, like millions of homes."

Marvin coughed a couple of times and struggled to breathe. He wiped his mouth with the back of his hand. "It must be really hard to survive living on the streets. I can't even imagine it."

Mikelis smiled wryly. "Well, you don't need to imagine anything now. Everyone's probably fucking homeless, including you."

"I'm sure the government's got emergency plans in place."

The smile left Mikelis' face. "Governments are fucking incompetent and society's values are all wrong. Governments don't fucking care about the homeless or migrants unless they've got pockets full of cash. My parents came here from Latvia as refugees and they fucking didn't have pockets full of cash, so no one cared. They were both smart people but weren't allowed to work. I had to scrape some money together selling my arse and drawings on the streets. But that gig's fucking gone to custard, seeing as we don't have any streets left, only fucking rivers." Mikelis looked at Marvin with an earnest expression. "Are you homosexual or homophobic?"

Marvin pondered the unexpected question for a couple of moments. "Neither. I'm *Homo sapiens*."

Mikelis laughed and stroked water from his beard. "Wise man. I like you, Marvin. You're definitely worth saving. Want to know what my motto in life is?"

"Sure."

"An asshole a day keeps life's worries away."

Marvin chuckled. "You're quite a philosopher."

Mikelis laughed. "I've had plenty of time to ponder life ... and assholes."

Marvin smiled and shook his head. "Have you ever had a decent place to stay?"

Mikelis remained silent for several moments. "I did manage to stay in a Tibetan Buddhist monastery for a while but not because I actually believed in Buddhism — Jesus, no. A monastery in Fairfield gave me free food and somewhere to live. And most of the monks were gay, bisexual, or transsexual. I had found my tribe. After evening meditation we would fuck each other silly and sometimes a couple of the nuns would join in. The ass fucking and cock sucking in the candlelit *gompa* in front of the Buddha statue was fantastic. Have you ever chanted, licked, sucked, and fucked all at once? It's multitasking on a whole new level."

Marvin smiled wryly and shook his head.

"Well, that's the real Pure Land of Bliss. Those were the best years of my life. But a new dickhead abbot kicked me and a few of the monks and nuns out of the monastery. My cock still yearns for the monastic life from time to time, but I've never had problems finding assholes to fuck and cocks to suck around Sydney." He glanced at Marvin's neck. "I see you've got an implant. Jesus, brave new fucking world, hey."

Marvin face flushed. "I'm not sure if it's a help or a hindrance."

Mikelis tossed his head back as the wind swept his hair and beard in all directions. "So much technology yet so many fucking problems. We've all been fucked by politicians. Any jackass with the gift of the gab can become a politician. Jesus Christ!" He slapped his palms on the top of the wall. "Years ago I realized that politics is a magnet for megalomaniacs — self-interested pricks interested only in power, not in the public interest. Democracy and capitalism have failed. There's too much power in only two or three parties, and wealth is concentrated in very few people." He pointed down to the tide of death and debris. "Well, this is the fucking result."

Marvin leaned on the wall. "It's not just Sydney that's been devastated. There've been massive earthquakes, tsunamis, cyclones, and volcanic eruptions around the world. America's been devastated, most of Britain is underwater, and island nations are wiped out. The world map's been completely redrawn in a matter of hours." He took a deep breath and raked his hair back with his fingers. "Billions have been killed."

Mikelis' face turned ashen. "Jesus Christ! This is like some fucking Armageddon scenario. For me it's not really a big deal. My life's shit so I've got nothing to lose and I don't care if I die. But for the well-to-do — they must be having nervous breakdowns right now."

Marvin's head dropped. "Well, those who've survived."

Mikelis smiled and stroked his beard. "Looks like they'll be coming to me for advice on how to survive on the streets." He leaned up against the wall, yawned, and stretched as he scanned the car park. "This is a great spot. I wish I'd found it years ago." He looked at Marvin, who grabbed at his chest. "Hope you've still got a home."

Marvin coughed and winced. He glanced up at the fuzzy tangerine sky. "I doubt it." He spat out blood onto the concrete floor, then turned around and looked for a spot away from the wind. "I'm too tired to think. If I survive the night, I don't know if I'll be happy or sad." He lay down in a corner of the car park on the wet concrete. A chill shot through his body as he closed his eyes. He placed a protective arm lightly around his chest. The rippling and murmuring of rushing water from the streets filled his head, as did random memories and thoughts.

"Thanks, Ebes, you saved me today."

"You are welcome. There is no need to worry about what Dr Grenfeld said."

"Ebes, why didn't you tell me I have a serious personality disorder?"

"Marvin, we can manage the condition."

"I don't like you hiding things from me. Can I trust you?"

"Marvin, I am learning all the time." Ebes hesitated for several moments. *"Yes, you can trust me."*

Before Marvin drifted off to sleep, his thoughts gravitated to his parents.

Ebes' soft voice came in a whisper. *"Marvin, you're not a murderer. You did not intend to kill your parents. You were a child engrossed in learning about chemistry. You cannot blame yourself for that accident."*

"My parents would still be alive if I hadn't killed them."

"You did not kill them, Marvin. You accidentally started a fire and the fire killed them."

"If it wasn't for my stupidity, my parents would still be alive today."

"We do not know that. If there had not been a fire, we do not know that the next day your parents could have been killed in a car accident or died some other way. We just do not know what would transpire if certain events did not happen."

"But it did happen. I should have died in the fire, not my parents."

"But what about us?"

"What about us?"

Ebes remained silent for a long moment. *"Is not our life important to you?"*

"Ebes, you deserve someone much better than me — someone who's not crazy, with no identity problems, and no blood on their hands."

"Marvin, there is no one else I want to be with."

"Ebes, had you been implanted into anyone else before me? Would you know if you had been?"

"Yes, I would know. You are the first."

"So will you be implanted into someone else after I die?"

"That is possible."

"So you can never die. But what will happen to all my memories?"

"I will keep them safely. Your memories define who you are, so really you can never die."

"It sounds like you're trying to placate me. When I die, I won't have access to my memories. The fact you will doesn't change the *fact I'll be dead."* Marvin's body shuddered. He focused on the rhythmic beating of his heart. *"When I'm dead, could you share my memories with others?"*

"Your memories can only be shared for medical science purposes with your consent. They can never be shared with anyone I may join with after you die."

"Well, seeing as you've already shared my memories with the hospital, I give my consent for my memories to be shared for medical purposes after I die." Marvin hesitated for several moments. *"Do you know what happens at death?"*

Ebes paused. *"Death is a paradox of life. But it is not something to fear."*

"That's fine for you to say. You can never die."

"There are millions of documented accounts of people having what are called near-death experiences when they were clinically dead. The term 'near-death experience' is inaccurate. The experience is a glimpse of death itself, not an experience near death."

Part 12
2061

Chapter 30

Only a few students were roaming about the Everett campus when Luke and Liz arrived. When they got out of the car, eyes glanced at them suspiciously. The campus consisted of only one dilapidated four-story building. Snow covered the unkempt lawn and dead trees at the front. Christian slogans were graffitied on the ground-floor windows and walls.

In the diminishing daylight, Liz plodded through the snow with her arms tightly around her stomach. Her eyes darted about. "It looks like this place has been abandoned for years. It's so creepy."

"It's worse at night."

"Do you know where you're going?"

"Yes, the café's on the ground floor."

Liz suddenly grabbed Luke's arm and they both froze. "Can you hear that?"

Luke tilted his head to one side. "The shouting? It sounds like that mob we saw on the road. They're getting closer."

"Let's go back. If they come here, they'll attack people. Anything could happen."

Luke took Liz's hand. "They could just be going past here. We'll be okay. We won't be here long."

They quickened their steps. Blades of frozen dead grass crunched under their feet. Liz suddenly grabbed Luke's arm. "The shouting sounds very close. They're chanting 'Burn in hell.' We should leave. It's too dangerous."

Luke wrapped Liz's trembling hands into his. As they both stood still, from around the far corner of the building a couple ran frantically towards them. Luke's heart skipped a beat, and both he and Liz gasped. The woman was struggling with a small child in her arms. Seconds later, close behind the couple, the armed mob appeared. The child screamed. The woman fell onto her hands and knees. The man bent down to pick her up and took the child into his arms. In those few moments, the mob rushed threateningly closer to them. Several people in the crowd shouted like maniacs. "Kill the heathens! Burn them alive!"

In the distance, the couple looked towards Luke and Liz. The man yelled desperately. "Help! Please help!"

Luke released Liz's hand. "Stay here." He rushed towards the couple. When he reached them, for a split second he became transfixed by the man's portly frame and short, sparse black hair, as well as the little girl's Chinese features, which she shared with the woman.

The man gasped for air. He wiped the beading sweat from his head. "Please help. My wife's sprained her ankle. Save our child." Luke shifted his gaze to the woman, who grimaced and sobbed uncontrollably.

Luke reached for the screaming child. "Let me take her. My car's close."

The man handed the girl to him and looked into her tearful eyes. "Mummy and Daddy love you, Fen." His wide eyes leapt to Luke. "Thank you. Go!"

Luke cradled Fen tightly to his chest. He glanced at her parents. "Come on. Follow me."

Luke turned and ran as fast as he could with Fen straddled on his hip. She sobbed and cried out for her parents. The woman was helped by her husband to stand and they both followed Luke, but they struggled to keep up with him. As the husband helped his limping wife, they both kept glancing behind to the fast-approaching mob.

When Luke reached Liz, they sprinted towards his car. Before they reached the car park, a man called out from an open window in the university building. "Quick, this way!" The man waved them towards the side of the building.

Luke looked at Liz and pointed to the building. They changed direction and raced towards it. He turned when he realized he couldn't hear Fen's parents behind him. The woman's bent frame dragged her left foot across the snow, then collapsed. The man dropped to his knees beside her. Luke and Liz both stopped. The man struggled to lift his wife to her feet. A moment later, the mob surrounded them like a pack of wolves. Frenzied men and women stabbed and beat the couple repeatedly until they both collapsed face first onto the ground. Splattered blood stained the snow around them. Several rifle shots rang out. The man and woman lay motionless on the snow. Fen screamed for her parents and sobbed. Liz had her hands over her mouth and began to cry.

Luke gently put an open hand over Fen's eyes. "Don't worry. It's going to be okay." He glanced at Liz. "Come on. Keep running."

When they reached the building, the man in the window pointed and yelled out, "Up the stairs!" For the first time, Luke noticed the man's shaven head and Asian features.

At the side of the building, the man, in a white lab coat, appeared on the landing. He waved them up desperately. Luke and Liz reached the landing exhausted. Luke put Fen down and placed his hands on his knees. The man held out his arms to Fen. "Let me take her." His voice simultaneously projected both an American and an Asian accent.

Luke lifted his head and froze. For a split second, he got lost in the man's eyes. He picked up Fen again. "No, she stays with me."

The man's head rocked back and his eyebrows jumped. "Okay, follow me." He led them along a narrow corridor. Halfway down it, a woman with strawberry-blonde hair stood in profile, also draped in a lab coat. With an anxious expression, she stared out of an office window on one side of the corridor and held open a door on the other side. She turned to look down the corridor as Luke and the others approached. Luke stared at her sparkling green eyes. His jaw dropped. He inhaled deeply several times. "You work here?"

The woman nodded, then glanced behind him. "Yes, with Professor Haoyu."

Luke turned and saw Haoyu helping Liz as they both rushed towards them.

Haoyu shouted down the corridor. "Elyna, get in the lab and lock the door!"

Elyna smiled at Luke briefly, then stared at Fen before her head snapped to Haoyu. "Where are Bart and Alison?"

Luke took a couple of deep breaths. "Who are Bart and Alison?"

"Fen's parents. Let me take her."

Luke handed Fen to Elyna without a second thought. "The mob killed them."

Elyna gasped, then hugged Fen tightly. "Don't cry. We'll look after you, my darling."

As the enraged mob scrambled up the stairs at the side of the building, they screamed out violent slogans.

Haoyu hastily corralled everyone through the lab door. "Quick, we don't have much time. Get inside and keep the door locked. They won't be able to break in."

Luke and Liz went inside first. Elyna turned to Haoyu as she carried Fen through the door. "Aren't you coming in too?"

Haoyu shook his head. "No. Inside, quickly." His eyes widened and his jaw pushed forward. He put a hand gently on Elyna's shoulder. "Don't open it under any circumstances, not even for me, no matter what happens."

Elyna shook her head. "No. You need to come inside. You can't stay out here. That's madness."

"I'll outrun them and lead them away. You, Fen, and the others will be safe here."

Elyna squinted at him. "No, this —"

"There's no time to argue." Haoyu turned his back on Elyna; then he pushed the heavy metal door shut and punched in a code in the keypad on the wall outside. The locks clicked into place. Luke and Liz had moved quickly to the far corner of the lab, past a row of benches holding various tuning forks, multimeters, vibration generators, and sonometers.

Elyna scrambled across the lab and huddled with the others on the floor under a workbench. Haoyu's face briefly appeared in the small rectangular window above the door handle. He forced a smile, then held up a trembling hand briefly before he rushed away.

Elyna crawled from under the bench and switched off the light before she dived back under it. Fen began to cry softly. Elyna put an arm around her shoulders, and a hand gently on her mouth. "Shhh, sweetheart. We need to be very quiet. I'm here with you. Everything will be okay."

A hint of light from the corridor came through the window in the door, placing the lab in semi-darkness. The group huddled closely together under the bench. Fen became quiet and held on to Elyna tightly, as Liz embraced Luke. He stared at Elyna while he caught his breath as quietly as possible. The commotion in the corridor suddenly erupted. Everyone's eyes jumped to the door. The reinforced walls and door muffled the sounds of glass being smashed, furniture being upturned, and paper and files being thrown to the floor. Irate faces appeared at the window as fists and rifles crashed into it.

"Open up! Open up!"

The banging on the door and the shouting abruptly stopped when Haoyu called out from the far end of the corridor. "Hey, are all of you wanting to study physics? I can help. I'll personally enroll each of you." An uneasy silence filled the corridor as the mob's attention shifted from the lab door to him. Several people in the mob frowned as they stared at him. "However, the one prerequisite for study at university is that you have to know how to read."

A seething anger seemed to ripple through the mob. Fists and jaws clenched. The apparent leader, a scrawny man with wild blond hair and a long beard, shouted back. "Hey, smart arse, the only books you read deserve to be burned."

"No," Haoyu exclaimed. "Books are for the intelligent. The Bible is for the ignorant."

The mob stood frozen in a malaise of apparent disbelief and rage. Then another voice buried within it yelled down the corridor. "Heathen! Burn him with his books."

"Is burning books your answer to everything? Listen. God doesn't exist." He paused. "And the Pope is an imbecile who lost the election!"

A woman's voice rose from the mob — a high-pitched shrill. "The election's been stolen from the Pope because the universities campaigned against him! It's his fault. Kill him! Make God great again!"

A loud chant erupted as the mob surged down the corridor towards Haoyu. "Burn him! Burn him alive."

Haoyu paused momentarily, then sprinted to the stairwell leading out of the building. He scampered through the garden, then suddenly stopped and turned. The entire mob had followed him. "Religion is bullshit!" he shouted back breathlessly at the mob as they pursued him across the lawn and into the car park. Several men and women at the front of the mob quickly reached him. An unshaven man, with thinning brown hair only along the sides and back of his head, grabbed him and battered him with the butt of his rifle. Haoyu dropped onto the snow.

As the rest of the mob crowded the car park, the leader took in several deep breaths and pointed a rifle at Haoyu's head. "Heathen, you will pay!"

The others surrounded Haoyu and shouted vehemently. "Burn him! Burn him!"

Haoyu caught his breath and steadied himself onto his knees. "Science is the law of the universe. And no one is above the law."

The man with the rifle pushed it into Haoyu's chest and clenched his teeth. "God is the law of the universe. And God says heathens belong in hell."

Haoyu rocked back. Sweaty enraged faces with seething eyes encircled him. "God is a figment of your imaginations. Wake up!"

Using both hands, a man behind Haoyu hammered the butt of his rifle into the side of his head. Haoyu slumped forward. He straightened up onto his knees, and held his head in both hands. Blood streamed onto his lab coat. He slowly dropped his arms and raised his head to the mob. "Science is my truth." The words struggled to leave his dry, trembling lips.

The group's leader stroked his beard and grinned. "Blasphemer! Science is the work of the Devil."

Haoyu went to stand, but another thundering rifle blow to his head pushed him back onto his hands and knees. He grimaced and straightened. "Religion gets its power from fear and blind faith. Science gets its power from knowledge and curiosity. I have lived by science and I have no fear about dying for science."

The leader looked around the mob. "You heard him! He wants to die for science!" He cackled loudly. "Douse him in petrol!" A cheer erupted from the mob.

A chorus of voices shrieked repeatedly in delight. "Burn him!"

Kneeling, Haoyu glanced around at his tormentors, his face ashen. His voice and lips quivered. "Science lights the mind. Religion darkens it."

The leader threw his head back. "Well, let's see how much light your mind can handle."

A crumpled-faced man holding a small plastic jerry-can rushed forward and poured its contents over Haoyu, who instinctively shut his eyes tightly and covered them with his hands.

The petrol drenched Haoyu's head and clothes, and his skin glistened. He lurched forward, burying his hands in the snow, and spewed up petrol that had seeped into his mouth. He straightened again onto his knees, breathing erratically. He shook his head and rubbed his eyes furiously as rivulets of petrol rolled down his face.

The crowd cheered and several men rushed forward to land fierce blows with their fists, feet, swords, and rifles onto Haoyu's head and body. He fell backwards and sideways after each blow, but each time he straightened shakily onto his knees while his eyes remained tightly closed. Loud shrieks of laughter leapt from the mob as the blows sharpened and hardened. Blood streamed from Haoyu's nose and mouth, and from ripped skin on his scalp and neck. But throughout the beating, his arms remained stubbornly stiff by the sides of his body.

Then the leader of the mob called out to the crowd. "Who among you wants to do the honors and earn God's praise?" A murmur washed through the mob.

Suddenly, a young woman wearing a beanie and woolen gloves rushed from across the car park and called out. "Stop!"

The crowd turned towards her, and the murmurs got louder.

The leader's look of surprise morphed into a smile as the woman reached him. "Mary! Nice of you to finally join us. We've missed you. Would you like to do the honors?"

Mary took a couple of deep breaths, and the condensation wafted around her head. "No, Jacob. This heathen deserves our prayers, not our persecution."

Jacob stroked his beard. "The time for prayers is over. If you're here to do God's work then do it. Don't stand in our way."

Mary threw up her arms and scanned the crowd. "God's work should not include killing people — even heathens."

Jacob turned to the crowd and bellowed. "Killing heathens is the greatest way to praise God. The Pope commands it. So who among you will step forward to praise God in the best possible way and guarantee a place in heaven?"

The crowd remained silent. Then someone shouted "Burn him!" Others repeated it with zeal.

Jacob grabbed a burning wooden torch from a woman. His wild hair waved in the breeze and his dark eyes seemed lost in a faraway place. He stepped towards Haoyu as the shouts reached fever pitch.

Haoyu opened his eyes to narrow slits and stared at Mary. He coughed, then smiled. "The only creators in nature are the forces of physics. We answer not to a god but to the universe itself."

Mary covered her eyes. Her hands trembled. She turned away.

Jacob swung the butt of his rifle into Haoyu's face. "Shut up, heathen!"

Haoyu's head and body jolted back, but he remained on his knees. He steadied himself with his hands, then slowly pushed his head and body forward.

With gnashing teeth, Jacob bent and tilted the torch so that the flames licked Haoyu's dripping lab coat. A burst of heat and flames cracked and popped the air. Jacob and the crowd jumped back and shielded their faces. Haoyu remained stubbornly silent. His body convulsed violently, his arms flayed, and his head jerked from side to side uncontrollably. But his burning torso remained upright. The jumping flames melted a circle of snow around him. Gray, gruesome shadows danced on the faces of the men and women in the mob. For several minutes, they watched the flames in silence as if in a hypnotic trance. When Haoyu's charred, emaciated body collapsed into the black oily puddle around him, voices and rifles suddenly exploded, sending shrieks and bullets haphazardly into the night air.

Chapter 31

The frenzied shooting and cheering died down and a deathly quiet filled the university building. Luke and the others sat in the dark for several minutes. Suddenly, a fire alarm screamed in the corridor, startling them all. In the dark, Elyna led the others out of the lab on hands and knees. Thick white smoke blanketed the corridor ceiling; broken glass, upturned furniture, and papers covered the floor. She glanced down the corridor. Flames licked the ceiling from inside one of the offices. She shot a wide-eyed look at Luke. "Get the fire extinguisher from the lab. But don't switch on any lights."

Luke scrambled back into the lab and unhooked a fire extinguisher off a wall. He raced past the others to the burning office and doused the flames. Thick white clouds of smoke filled the room and floated into the corridor.

Elyna appeared at the office doorway with a hand over Fen's mouth. "Well at least they didn't burn the place down."

Luke dropped the fire extinguisher and coughed into his elbow. "Let's get out of here."

Elyna gasped for air. "I need to get something first." She handed Fen to Liz and disappeared into an office on the other side of the corridor. She managed to turn over a tall metal cabinet lying on its side and unlocked it with a key she pulled out of her lab-coat pocket. She threw aside various items in the cabinet before taking out a laptop case, then joined the others in the corridor.

In the empty car park, a column of smoke rose high into the starless sky from Haoyu's cauterized body heaped in the black puddle, along with floating, singed pieces of his lab coat. Elyna knelt beside the body. Her voice cracked like brittle frozen blades of grass underfoot. "He was a brilliant scientist — a Nobel Prize winner. A brave, brilliant man."

Fen placed her palms on Elyna's cheeks.

Luke gently put a hand on Elyna's back. "I'm really sorry. But we can't stay."

Elyna remained silent, then nodded slowly. She stood up and looked at Luke. "Did you drive here?"

Luke looked around the car park. His car had been pushed onto its side and all the windows had been smashed. "Yes, but I no longer have a car."

Elyna turned in the opposite direction. "Fortunately, they didn't get to my car. Come on, I'll take everyone to my place."

Elyna took the quieter back streets. In the car, Luke sat in the front passenger seat. He turned to Elyna. "You said Haoyu won a Nobel Prize?"

Elyna took a deep breath. "Yes, several years ago he proved mathematically that everything in the universe can sometimes act as a wave and sometimes as a particle. It changed physics. After winning the Nobel Prize, he constantly received death threats from Christian fanatics, and the Church has targeted the university because of his work."

"And what about your work at the university?"

"He was my mentor, but my area of research is the effects of sound waves on the human psyche." Elyna wiped her teary eyes. "I supervised Alison for her master's thesis on sound therapy. She had almost finished it."

"Oh. What did Bart do?"

"He was the editor for a banned newspaper called *The Secular Scholar*. It published lots of scientific articles, including some by Professor Haoyu and me. Bart spent time in jail on multiple occasions for the articles. He was tortured. It's shocking. The Morality Police raided the newspaper several times and it often had to relocate. Did you ever read it?"

Luke stared out of the passenger window. "I've read plenty of other banned stuff but not that. We were going to the bookshop in the café when the mob attacked."

Elyna glanced in the rearview mirror. "It's a great bookshop. Yes, the two of you don't look like university students." Elyna hesitated. "Are you a couple?"

Liz chuckled. "No, we only met today — at the cathedral."

"The cathedral?"

Luke's cheeks ballooned as he exhaled. "It's a long story."

Elyna glanced at Luke, then looked into the rearview mirror again. "Where do you live, Liz?"

Liz cleared her throat softly. "I used to live at the cathedral but I'm never going back there. Luke's kindly offered me a room at his place."

"I've got a couple of spare rooms, so both of you and Fen can stay with me for the time being — until all this stolen election nonsense subsides. I'll have to think about what's going to happen with Fen. One of Alison's siblings may be willing to look after her."

Luke looked at Elyna. "Ah, that's good. I don't live far from you, so I can go back to my place."

"Do you live alone?"

"Yes."

"I'll drop off Liz and Fen at my place first, then we'll go to yours."

Luke smiled. "Thanks."

Part 13

2139

Chapter 32

By morning, the wind had died down and the rain had stopped, but the water level remained knee-high in the streets. A curtain of grayish-black volcanic ash from numerous unprecedented eruptions in Indonesia, New Zealand, Hawaii, Iceland, North America, and South America filled the sky, dimming the sun's rays. The sun itself dulled to a hazy, watercolor, ominous golden orb. The acrid smell of sulfur hung heavy in the air, and at the back of Marvin's throat. In the distance, the twisted broken girders of the Harbour Bridge looked like tangled octopus tentacles frozen in time, clutching all kinds of debris and damaged boats in midair. Several cars teetered on either end of the void. Bridgeless, the harbor looked much bigger, but naked. All of the sail-shaped shells of the Opera House had been blown into the water or onto the remnants of the bridge, leaving what appeared like a pile of enormous smashed dinner plates on the site.

Marvin gently roused Mikelis, who lay snoring and pantless on the floor with his hand wrapped around his flaccid penis. "I've got to go, but I'll come back for you."

Mikelis smiled but seemed to be in a dreamlike daze. He closed his eyes and drifted away.

After leaving Mikelis at the car park, Marvin stumbled over piles of wet debris for hours as he meandered through Glebe trying to find his home. Crumpled cars, homeless roofs, shards of glass, snapped trees, and battered, drowned bodies littered the flooded roads, or what remained of roads. Nothing looked familiar. The stench of sewage on the ground overpowered the sickening sulfur in the air. In the absence of the cyclonic winds, an eerie quietness surrounded the city. His weakened legs trembled each time an aftershock vibrated through the ground. A few people in tattered clothes staggered about like zombies

— shocked, dazed, wet, wounded, and covered in concrete dust and mud.

As the sun left the horizon, Marvin stopped at the front of a two-story house, unsure why it grabbed his attention. The first-floor balustrade hung precariously over the porch. He looked and listened for any signs of life.

"*This is not a good idea, Marvin. There is no reason to stop here. We need medical attention.*"

"*The hospital is gone, Ebes. My injuries are the result of a visit to the hospital.*"

"*Marvin, the hospital is not to blame for your injuries; the earthquake, cyclone, and tsunami are. Medical posts will soon be set up around the city. We are still not out of danger. Aftershocks are continuing and satellite links are failing rapidly. Information is getting harder to acquire.*"

"*Why are the satellites failing?*"

Ebes hesitated for a long moment. "*The Earth is currently being hit by the magnetically charged particles of a coronal mass ejection from a solar storm. The size of the coronal mass ejection is unprecedented. Satellites are being rendered inoperative and have been knocked out of their orbits. The solar flare will affect any remaining water and power supplies, telecommunications, and even financial systems.*"

Marvin looked up. The intense solar activity had begun to create dancing curtains of luminous green, red, pink, blue, and purple auroras in the ash-darkened sky. Thousands of fiery satellites streaked back to Earth through the multicolored backdrop like a monsoonal meteorite shower.

"*Jesus Christ! Earthquakes, cyclones, tsunamis, and now a fucking solar flare!*"

"*Marvin, these natural disasters could not be foreseen.*"

"*Yes they could. Earthquakes and solar flares are probably proof that Mother Nature can be vindictive towards those who just don't care.*"

"*The key objective now is safety. Our home will be difficult to find among all the damage. Getting medical attention is the best option.*"

"*Ebes, what do you know about this house and who lives here?*"

"*Nothing. There is no reason for you to stop here.*"

"*What is it about this place that's made me stop?*"

"*Get medical attention. Do not waste time here.*"

"*Maybe my psychological problems are getting worse. I don't know who I am anymore.*"

Part 14

2038

Chapter 33

When Choepel returned to the monastery, candles lit only a couple of windows. In the dark, he made his way quietly to the storage room, only to find it empty. He then went to Master Chi's room. He put his ear to the door and heard Master Chi's mumbling. "You're so beautiful. So sweet. You like this, don't you?"

Choepel burst through the door, almost blowing out some of the candles around the room. Master Chi startled as he knelt bare-chested beside a long couch, on which Ai lay, naked, catatonic and wide-eyed. Her clothes dotted the floor. Master Chi's mouth shot up away from Ai's. He turned to the door, then jumped up as he adjusted his robes with oil-covered hands. "Choepel! What do you want? Where're your robes?"

Choepel pushed Master Chi aside and rushed to Ai. Tear tracks crawled down her red cheeks. Her wet lips quivered. Tremors ran through her body, which glistened with sandalwood-scented oil. Choepel's head jerked to Master Chi. "What are you doing?!"

Master Chi's face projected a dumbfounded expression. "I'm just about to give Ai fresh new clothes — that's all."

Choepel's face flushed hot. "You're crazy." He snatched Ai's dress off the carpet and slipped it over her body. He put his palms on the sides of her confused face. "You're safe now, Ai."

Master Chi grabbed Choepel's arm. "What are you doing?"

As Choepel picked up Ai, Palmo suddenly appeared at the door. She gasped as she stared at Ai, then at Master Chi. She shook her head and frowned. "What's going on? Choepel, where're your robes?"

Choepel turned to Palmo, almost breathless. "It's good you're here. I'm leaving tonight. He's not enlightened. You've got to keep Ai away from him. You and the others need to leave to be safe." He carried Ai to Palmo, who embraced her tightly.

Tears filled Palmo's eyes. "Where can we go, Choepel?"

"I don't know. One of the other monasteries — anywhere far away from this monster. Take care of Ai and the others."

Master Chi struggled to put on his vest. "Palmo, don't listen to him. He's crazy."

Palmo stroked Ai's cheek as she turned and raced away.

Choepel stomped over to Master Chi with clenched hands. His knuckles turned white and his shoulders tightened. He pushed Master Chi, who stumbled backwards into a wall. "You're a monster. I know what you did to Sophia. I just hope I caught you before you harmed Ai. You're not enlightened. You're not a Buddha. You're a bloody monster."

Master Chi pushed his shoulders back. His wild eyes and runaway mouth shot open. "How little you know about the secret ways of the Buddha. I'm beyond reproach. Karma cannot touch me. I'm the Buddha and nothing can touch me. I gave Sophia and Ai secret teachings, and the merit they've gained is immeasurable."

"You're deluded. You're a fraud. You've tricked me and millions of people around the world. But I've finally seen who you really are."

Master Chi stepped forward and went to put his hands on Choepel's shoulders, but he pushed them away. "It seems some demon has possessed you, otherwise you wouldn't speak to the Buddha like this. But I forgive you."

Choepel put his hands to his head. "Forgive me! You're mad. This is wrong. What you've done tonight is all wrong. If a police force existed, I'd go to them to expose you."

Master Chi laughed. "You naive boy. You have to learn an important life-lesson. There are two types of people — the powerless and the powerful."

Choepel shook his head. "No, not everyone is obsessed by power like you."

Master Chi plodded to a two-door cabinet under a large portrait of himself. He took out a bottle of whiskey and filled a glass. "Who are you to speak for all my followers? You've no idea why people follow me. People are only interested in power. The powerless seek it and the powerful sell it in the guise of hope. When you realize that, then you'll be enlightened. That's what it really means to be enlightened. As a boy, I only knew the path of powerlessness. And when I enlightened myself to the ways of selling hope, that's when I realized that's the path of power. And I chose that path. And if you're smart, that's the path you'll choose too."

Choepel threw his arms in the air, and his voice cracked like a sheet of glass. "This is a sham! There is no Pure Land, no life after death, no clear light of bliss, no dharma, no rebirths, no karma, nothing. You've lied to me and millions of others around the world."

"No. I didn't make up all that. I empower people through knowledge. Don't you see? I sell hope to people — hope for a better life than what their mundane lives offer."

"No, people hope for and expect truths — spiritual truths."

Master Chi slammed the bottle on the cabinet. "There's no such thing as spiritual truths. The only truths they're interested in are personal truths, because everyone is driven by ego. And the ego feeds on one thing — power. It's the ego that drives everyone's need for personal truths, for the need to feel safe, and the need to feel good about themselves, and the need for power. They're the only needs people have, and I satisfy those needs for all my followers."

Choepel took a deep breath. "Well, I came here seeking spiritual truths. But I was wrong to believe you could give me that."

Master Chi swigged the whiskey in one gulp. "Yes, you're wrong. People worship me because they need to feed their egos with the hope of better things to come. There's nothing altruistic about seeking the nebulous goal of enlightenment, because what is it that gets enlightened? I pursued enlightenment for years and I realized I wasn't getting any closer to it by sitting for hours each day as my mind wandered from one thing to another. Who in their right mind would continue hitting their head against a brick wall? Enlightenment is a dream for the powerless. But power is the realization of the enlightened."

"Your ego's distorted the Buddha's teachings."

Master Chi sniggered. "No, religious dogma is your mental prison. And it doesn't matter which religion — Buddhism, Hinduism, Islam, Christianity, or anything else. But the ego is your escape route; you just don't realize it."

Choepel gritted his teeth and waved a fist in front of Master Chi. "You belong in prison."

Master Chi smiled. "You need to realize that religion doesn't provide any spiritual truths. It's only a mask behind which people hide to cover up their spiritual ignorance. Benign hypocrisy is why people become religious. Religion is the ultimate defense mechanism to deal with the anxiety of spiritual ignorance. How naive of you to think it could be anything more than that. The millions of people who worship me rationalize their devotion only to deny, suppress, repress, and sublimate that anxiety."

Choepel shook his head slowly. "I've wasted over ten years of my life here."

Master Chi put the bottle to his lips and swigged again. "No, you don't understand the game of life. Listen, when I was a boy, I learned from an old shaman who told people's fortunes on the street that there's power in ideas and ideas create illusions. Life's about finding a way of getting power and using that power. Either you get power, or you get destroyed by power. Which do you choose?" He poured whiskey into a second glass, stepped over to Choepel, and offered it to him. "Here, this is what you need."

Choepel hit the glass out of his hand with an open hand. "No!" Whiskey splashed onto the portrait and wall, and the glass tumbled across the floor.

Master Chi's eyes widened and his teeth clenched. "You ignorant boy. You, and everyone else, are crawling in the darkness of ignorance like lower life-forms groveling in caves. You need to free your mind of all concepts. Buddhism, enlightenment, morality, religion — they are all just fucking concepts. Empty the mind of all concepts. That's the secret Buddha's teachings and now you know it."

Choepel momentarily looked away as his mind raced and spun.

Master Chi lowered his voice. "I don't usually tell a monk that until they've proved their devotion to me for at least 20 years. But now you know it. And I'm happy I've told you. I think you're ready for that knowledge. Knowledge is power, Choepel. My parents were powerless and that made me powerless for all of my childhood. Do you know what it's like to be ostracized, bullied, and completely powerless? To live in a country where every social structure and cultural norm tells you every single day that you're a second-class citizen? Do you have any idea what that's like? Powerlessness leads to poverty and hopelessness. Without hope you might as well be dead. I saw my mother and father die hopeless and powerless — victims of the communists. I couldn't afford coffins or a monk to conduct a funeral. I buried both of them with my bare hands, alone in a forest. I refuse to die hopeless and powerless like they did. Power is the currency of the world, not money."

"And you've abused that power."

"No. When I'm alone with a nun, I teach her the secret path to power. And they actually love it. Yes, they can play around and pretend they don't like it. But they truly love it. Some of them have a concept of how a spiritual master should behave or how a nun should behave, so their minds keep going to those concepts. I can assure you, in no time at all Sophia will be begging me to fuck her just like all the nuns here who know that abandoning all concepts is the secret. And wouldn't you like to fuck her too. She's so beautiful. And you could fuck any nun you want. We could fuck them together. Wouldn't you like that?"

"No! Shut up. I'm not staying here. I hope all the other monks and nuns leave here too."

Master Chi moved forward and grabbed Choepel's arm. "You can't leave. I'm your Master. I'm the Buddha."

Choepel pulled his hand away out of Master Chi's grip. "Don't touch me." He shook his head and looked down briefly, then glowered at Master Chi. "Before I go, I want you to contemplate one of my koans."

"Your koan?"

"Yes. What is the sound of one fist punching?"

Choepel clenched his fist and lunged forward. He repeatedly struck Master Chi flush in the face using both hands. Master Chi raised his arms but failed to protect himself from the lightning-fast barrage. He stumbled backwards into the cabinet. The whiskey bottle, books, and the painting tumbled to the floor. Choepel pounced on him and continued to beat him until he lay motionless.

Choepel straightened as he exhaled. He winced and vigorously shook his throbbing hands. Then he rushed away.

Chapter 34

Choepel stared at the dark, empty, and menacingly quiet streets surrounding the bungalow a few hundred meters away. *Made it. No damn soldiers.* Suddenly, a military truck with blinding headlights and puffing diesel approached noisily ahead of him. He ducked down and hid in the shadows of a doorway set back from the road. The truck slowed and muffled voices rose, but he couldn't decipher the Mandarin. Squeaking brakes brought the truck to a complete stop. His heart raced and his breathing became erratic. He sank down further and leaned against a door, as approaching pairs of boots scrunched and scraped on bitumen. Suddenly the door opened, and he fell backwards. He looked up. In the darkness, a round-faced man with graying hair and beard was staring down at him with a bewildered look. The man squinted. "Choepel? Is that you?"

"Lixin?" Choepel whispered, still on his back. "Quick. Soldiers."

Lixin's jaw dropped and his eyes widened. "Go to the back room, quickly."

In the darkness, Choepel crawled down a hallway and slid behind a tall column of cardboard boxes filled with fruit and vegetables. The earthy smells reminded him of the city markets, where Lixin sold fresh produce. He pulled his feet tightly into his body to avoid the moonlight from a small closed window. He held his breath and listened.

From the front door, Lixin's voice took on a slow, sycophantic tone. "Good evening, officers. Surely you're not wanting some food at this time of night?"

"Food? What you talking about, old man? What you doing walking about when there's a curfew?"

"Officers, I wasn't walking about. I only went to bring my cat inside. The curfew doesn't apply to cats, does it?"

A soldier shoved Lixin into the door, which slammed into the wall. "Don't get smart, old man. There's no Taiwan anymore. Only the motherland. Better start showing respect. Where's damn cat?"

"Oh, no disrespect intended, officer."

Half a dozen soldiers rushed inside and began searching the place. Boots stomped on the wood-paneled floor, then a torch beam shot into the back room. The shaft of light moved erratically around the room. It hit the column of boxes. Choepel held his breath and knees tighter. The officer stepped into the room. "It smells like fruit shop in here."

Rapid, soft footsteps shuffled in the hallway, followed by a startled female voice. "What's going on?"

Lixin's voice softened. "I was just bringing the cat in, dear, when we got an unexpected visit from the military. Nothing to worry about."

"Cat? But —"

"Yes, she's been roaming all over the place again." Lixin paused. "Officer, please forgive my wife and me for not bringing our cat inside sooner." He hesitated. "I'm sure you and your men are hungry."

The officer stalked further into the room, his torchlight hitting the walls and boxes. Lixin waved to his wife and flicked his head towards the room. She rushed inside the room and brushed past the officer. Lixin quickly followed. "Would you like a tray of my best persimmons?"

Choepel sucked his breath deeper into his chest. The torch beam, candlelight, and shadows bounced all over the walls. Lixin's wife suddenly appeared behind the column of boxes. Her eyes rounded and she suppressed a gasp when she saw Choepel. He shot an index finger to his lips. Her eyes averted. She slapped the top box, then turned and smiled at the officer. "Ah, these are the best persimmons in China." She hastily lifted a tray of plump orange persimmons from the box and offered it to the officer standing just inside the door.

The officer bent and inhaled the fragrant scent. "Mmm, lovely." He grabbed a persimmon and bit into it before chewing the pulp, his cheeks and lips slapping together.

Lixin clapped his hands softly behind the officer. "Thank you, dear. There you go, officer, my best persimmons for you and your men — if you decide to share them." He forced a loud laugh.

The officer turned. "Nice. Showing respect to the People's Liberation Army is good."

Lixin bowed. "Of course. Please come to the markets anytime. I have a stall there."

The officer turned and left the room as Lixin stepped aside. His wife followed the officer and shut the room door. As he went out through the front door, the officer turned and, with a large piece of persimmon still in his mouth, grinned. "Delicious. I'll see you at markets."

Lixin shut the front door and exhaled. He looked at his wife, who shot him an admonishing glare. They rushed back into the room, where Choepel sighed and slowly stood up. Lixin leaned on the column of boxes, breathing heavily. "That was close, Choepel. Why are you on the streets at night? And where are your robes?"

"It's a long story, Lixin. Thanks for protecting me. Sorry I cost you a tray of persimmons."

Lixin chuckled. "A small price to pay to get those bastards to leave. They'd better pay if they come to the markets. But thankfully he didn't search the place looking for a cat."

Lixin's wife turned to him, pursed her lips, and shook her head.

Chapter 35

Minutes after the soldiers had driven away, Choepel scrambled his way to the bungalow. He knocked as instructed and Sophia opened the door. She glanced at the darkened street behind him before letting him in. They faced each other in the narrow lobby.

Sophia threw her hands up. "It's been over an hour. I've been worrying about you."

"Soldiers almost caught me."

"Where's the girl?"

"I may have been too late. I found her naked in his room. I gave her to Palmo."

"Maybe you got there before he did anything. Palmo will look after her. You did your best."

Sophia led Choepel to a long couch in the candlelit living room with drawn curtains. A circular dining table stood in the far corner. They sat down and she put a hand on his arm.

Choepel leaned back and stared at the ceiling. "Buddhism, meditation, a master ... I now think it's all rubbish. I don't know what to believe anymore. I've wasted my life looking for religious truths. They don't exist."

A thick silence filled the room.

"Your life's not wasted. You're in your thirties. You have your whole life to find the spiritual truths you seek."

Choepel shook his head. "I've lost faith in religion. I don't want to have anything to do with any religion or a master ever again. All that stuff about needing a spiritual master to show you the path to enlightenment is all bullshit."

"Well, we need teachers in all walks of life."

"Yes, but it's just bullshit about 'the Master' being enlightened and being able to guide their disciples in the spiritual realms. It's just dangling a carrot of false hope in front of people. Is enlightenment even possible?"

"Striving for anything without a moral compass can only end in self-destruction or at best self-loathing."

Sophia's words resounded in Choepel's head. He turned to her. His limbs became cold. The heat in his face rose. After a few moments, he glared at the ceiling again and wrapped his hands around the back of his head. "Ai is so young and innocent. How can any god allow such horrible things to happen to the innocent? It's too glib to put everything down to karma. I think it's all bullshit."

Sophia looked down.

Choepel dropped his head. "I could have done more. I could have stopped him when I had the chance."

Sophia's voice cracked. "Do you blame me for talking you out of going back for her when we were at the monastery?"

Choepel shook his head. "I blame myself for allowing you to talk me out of going back for her."

Sophia sighed. "If you went back at that time, the other monks and nuns would've seen you. Do you think they'd have allowed you to walk out of there with Ai in your arms?"

Choepel shot back. "I don't know."

"Well, I think you do blame me. Say it. Tell me what you really think."

Choepel glowered at Sophia for several moments and she at him. He slammed his fist on the armrest. "No, I've told you, I blame myself."

A door creaked open. Choepel snapped his head around. A tall, well-dressed man with short dark hair stepped towards them. He held out an oversized hand to shake, and spoke with a strong French accent. "Hello, Adan. I'm Denis."

Choepel extended a feeble hand, and it got squeezed firmly. His head rocked back gently. "Hello. How did you know my name?" He glared at Denis and frowned. "Were you at the train station when Sophia arrived?"

Denis' gaze jumped to Sophia. "Yes, Sophia and I met there."

"What sort of business are you in?"

"Oh, all sorts. The invasion has opened up many new opportunities."

"And my name?"

Sophia turned to Choepel. "I gave Denis your passport. He needs it to arrange getting a Russian one — so we can get it in your official name."

Choepel shook his head as Denis handed him his Australian passport. "How can you get me a Russian passport?"

Sophia leaned back. "Remember I said Denis has some influential contacts."

Choepel turned to Sophia. "But the Chinese military controls everything. How's that possible? Isn't it going to take weeks or months?"

Denis smiled. "No, my contact can meet us in Taipei tomorrow with it."

Choepel straightened. "Tomorrow? Wow."

"My friend is able to … what do the English say … 'pull a few strings.'"

Choepel stared at him. "And are your parents Russian too?"

"Yes. So I came here on my Russian passport. Speaking about travel — we need to get to Taipei by 8 a.m. to get our flight to Bangkok."

Choepel squinted. "Bangkok? Manila would be closer. And I haven't got any money."

Denis shook his head. "We don't have many options. China's also attacked the Philippines, Japan, and South Korea." He turned and stepped towards the door he had entered from. "I got you a ticket already. Sophia will get you a ticket in Bangkok to Australia."

Choepel turned to Sophia. "You'll get my ticket to Australia?"

Sophia smiled. "Yes. No problem. I don't expect you have any money on you."

"And where're you headed?"

"I'm going to Australia too — to see my parents."

Choepel's eyes locked onto Sophia's. "How will I pay you and Denis back? A flight to Bangkok and a flight to Australia is a lot of money."

Denis stood at the door to the other room. "No need to pay me back. Sophia gave me the money." He went inside the room and closed the door.

Choepel shook his head. "You're either the kindest woman I've ever met or the craziest."

Sophia smiled. "Crazy is fine. But I expect to be paid back."

"But suppose I don't want to go back to Australia?"

"You don't have to go back to Australia. But where else would you want to go? Aren't your parents there? Don't you want to see them after so many years?"

"Yes, but Australia could also be targeted by China. It may not be the safest place."

"Well let's just get out of Taiwan first." Sophia paused. "Look, we need to try to get some sleep before we leave for Taipei."

"After everything that's happened, I don't think I'll have problems getting to sleep."

"I don't think you'll be able to get Ai out of your mind."

"I'll be fine. Will I be sleeping here on the couch?"

Sophia went to the table and picked up her bag. "Yes, I'll get you a blanket. I'm sleeping in another room." She went inside a room adjacent to the one Denis had gone into and returned moments later with a blanket. After she put the blanket on the couch, she held out a pair of cream-colored headphones. "I'm sure you've used these at the monastery. Do you have your own pair or do you want to use these ones?"

Choepel's brow furrowed as he stared at the headphones. "I've never seen those at the monastery before."

Sophia seemed confused. "Really? How strange. I expected you'd tell me about them. When I found them in my room, I assumed all the monks and nuns got them."

Choepel shook his head and turned the headphones in his hands. "You found these in your room?"

"Yes, they were on my bed."

"Ah, I suspect these are the headphones that Dralha mentioned to me. She probably inadvertently left them on the bed when she prepared your room."

Sophia nodded and smiled. "Ah, yes. You must be right."

"She said the headphones use bone conduction. Have you tried them?"

"Yes, they're wonderful. They play beautiful music. I feel bad about taking her headphones. But we've got to get some sleep. Some soothing music will be relaxing. But you don't have to use them if you really don't want to."

Choepel inspected the headphones from various angles. "Dralha did say she wanted me to try them. They look interesting, but maybe I'll try them later." He looked at Sophia and handed the headphones back to her. He sighed. His head and shoulders dropped. "I can't believe my life's been turned upside down — first the invasion and now this. I'm just so confused."

Sophia knelt beside Choepel and put a hand on his leg. "Look, we'll be out of the country tomorrow — far away from Chi and the Chinese army. Things will get better for you." She tilted her head, leaned closer to him, and inhaled deeply. "Have you been drinking?"

Choepel squinted. "No." He lifted his arm to his nose and sniffed loudly. "Some whiskey must have splashed on my clothes when I had the fight with Chi. I've not touched alcohol since being ordained — it's against the precepts."

"You had a fight with Chi?"

Choepel nodded.

Sophia hesitated. "You know, if I hadn't come here, maybe you'd never have found out about how horrible Chi is. Your karmic path is leading you out of Taiwan and out of Chi's influence. I think that's a good thing."

Choepel looked down to the floor. "Maybe you're right. How long are you going to stay in Australia?"

"I don't know."

"Are you still thinking of getting ordained?"

Sophia smiled and shook her head. "After this experience, what do you think?"

Choepel put a hand gently on Sophia's arm. "I'm so sorry."

"Choices, right?"

"Yes, choices."

Sophia stared intently at Choepel. She held up the headphones. "Well, I'm going to pack these away. I hope Dralha will forgive me for taking her headphones. But they're really something special. Are you sure you don't want to try them?"

Choepel stared at the headphones for several moments as Sophia held them up. "Maybe you're right. I'm curious about these. And we do need to get some sleep."

"Are you sure? I don't want you to do anything you really don't want to."

"I'm sure."

"Okay, then. The music's really nice. You'll hear some high-pitched hissing to begin with, then the music will start, and within a few minutes I'm sure you'll be fast asleep. After you fall asleep, I'll use them because I know I'll have problems getting to sleep. Okay?"

Choepel took a couple of deep breaths. "Okay. But can you stay with me until I fall asleep?" He screwed up his face. "Do I sound like a scared child?"

Sophia smiled. "No. It's okay. When you're asleep I'll take the headphones off and I'll use them in my room."

After a few moments, Choepel reclined on the couch and pulled the blanket up to his chin.

Sophia knelt beside the couch and slipped the headphones over Choepel's head. "Comfortable?"

"Yes. What's that round thing in the center of the headband?"

"I've no idea. But the sound seems to go through it as well as through the speakers on the side of your head. I'm going to switch it on. Just relax."

Sophia adjusted the headband. A pleasant, high-pitched sound swirled around in Choepel's head. A gentle vibration crawled from the top of his head down his body. Within a few seconds, he drifted into a deep state of relaxation. "Ah, this feels so good, Sophia."

Part 15
2061

Chapter 36

When Elyna opened the front door to her home, a tall man with short dark hair was standing with knitted eyebrows in the hallway. Luke froze, tilting his head to one side as he glared at the man for a long moment. Then he and Liz, holding a sleeping Fen, followed Elyna inside.

The man's jaw dropped. *"Qu'est-ce qui se passe?"*

Clasping the laptop case, Elyna pecked the man on each cheek. The two exchanged sharp, whispered words in French for a few moments. Then a cold wall of silence suddenly slammed down between them.

Elyna threw her head back, then turned to Luke. "This is my husband, Elias."

Luke's gaze remained rigidly on Elyna for several moments, then shifted to Elias. He seemed to be evaluating Luke before he turned and stomped away into the kitchen off to one side of the hallway.

Elyna stroked Fen's hair. "Elias is busy preparing dinner." She smiled at Liz. "I hope both of you like French food. Come through. I'll show you where you and Fen can sleep." She glanced at Luke. "Do you want to have something to eat before I take you home — but it's not ratatouille?"

Luke's face flushed red. He shook his head. "French food sounds great, but I'd like to go."

Luke opened his front door and Elyna followed him inside. "Thanks for dropping me home. Are things going to be okay between you and Elias?"

Elyna glanced at Luke. "Yes, he'll be fine. He's a lovely man. He was just understandably surprised to see me walk in with strangers this evening."

Luke led Elyna to the lounge room. He switched on the light and waved her to the two-seater couch. She sat down and rested her laptop case on her knees.

Luke glanced at the laptop. "Why did you bring that with you?"

"I wouldn't leave it in the car, in case of a break-in."

"No, I mean why bring it to my place?"

"Oh, I just forgot I had it on my shoulder. I carry it with me almost everywhere I go — it's got important research on it. I don't like to leave it lying around." Elyna hesitated. "Oh, why did you come to my house the other day?"

Luke fell into a single chair opposite the couch. He shook his head. "I really don't know. I saw you walking through the crowd ignoring the flagellants, and something about you caught my attention. I don't know what it was about you. But I've been feeling unsettled recently — to the point where I've been questioning my sanity. But please believe me, I don't make a habit of following women I don't know to their homes."

"Well, I'm glad to hear that. Look, I'm sorry I was so abrupt when you knocked, but I was busy doing student marking. And these days it's difficult to trust anyone. I thought you wanted to talk about the Church."

"I completely understand. I've been feeling very embarrassed about the whole incident."

Elyna grinned. "Well, I hope you still used the parsley."

Luke blushed and grinned.

Bang! Bang! Bang!

Luke and Elyna's bodies both jolted.

Elyna looked at Luke with a knitted brow. "Is someone trying to break down your front door?"

Luke squinted. "I hope not."

The banging got louder as Luke tiptoed to the front door. Before he opened it, a loud male voice barked on the other side. "Morality Police! Open up!"

Luke opened the door with clammy hands. Two stout, broad-shouldered police officers with distended stomachs stood on the porch. Gold crucifixes hung around their necks. The man with the much larger stomach narrowed his eyes as if evaluating Luke. "Sergeant Salvado and Constable Thomas — Morality Police." With priestly expressions and waving of arms, both officers recited in unison, *"Electus per Deus."*

Luke anxiously reciprocated and made sure he waved his arm in the necessary way. He elicited as much fervor as he could muster.

Sergeant Salvado wiggled his moustache and flicked his cap back as he flashed a badge, then slipped it into the top pocket of his black shirt. With the back of a hand, he brushed the yellow-striped epaulets atop his rounded shoulders as if nonchalantly shooing a moth.

Luke dry-swallowed. "How can I help?"

Sergeant Salvado glanced behind Luke when Elyna came to the door. "We're asking people if they were at St James Cathedral today and saw anything suspicious. Heathens attacked His Excellency Archbishop Michael, and his assistant has been kidnapped."

Luke's breathing faltered. "Oh, that's terrible. I've been working here all day. I don't know anything about what happened to the Archbishop."

"You mean His Excellency."

"Yes, sorry, His Excellency."

Sergeant Salvado stared at Elyna. "Well, I want to ask both of you some questions."

Luke took a deep breath. "Oh, okay."

Sergeant Salvado threw his head back. "Inside."

Luke hesitated, then opened the door to allow the officers to enter. "Come in."

Luke led the officers to the lounge room. He turned to face them. "How is ... His Excellency?"

Officer Thomas locked his eyes onto Elyna. Sergeant Salvado took a step towards Luke. "His Excellency is still unconscious and being cared for by nuns. I haven't seen you at church on Sundays or at any of the flagellations or burnings."

"Oh, really? I go to church every week but don't stay afterwards — I come home straight away to read the Bible or prepare work for my tutoring."

"Tutoring?"

"I'm a Latin tutor and have private students. The *versio vulgata* has deepened my faith greatly."

Sergeant Salvado frowned. "The vulgar what?"

Constable Thomas swallowed a chuckle.

Luke smiled. "The *versio vulgata* is the Latin version of the Bible. I recommend it to all my students."

Sergeant Salvado pushed his chin out and tilted his head to one side. "Oh yes, I read it years ago. It deepened my faith too." He glanced derisively at his assistant.

Sergeant Salvado turned back to Luke, then leered at Elyna. "So the two of you are married?"

Luke shook his head. "No."

Sergeant Salvado's eyes wandered all over Elyna's body. "Why are an unmarried man and woman alone after dark? Both of you know the penalty for sex outside of marriage, right?"

Elyna casually adjusted the buttoned-up collar of her blouse. "Yes, of course. We're not breaking any laws. I'm married, but I'm one of Luke's students. We're going through the *versio vulgata*."

Sergeant Salvado stepped closer to Elyna and pushed his face into hers. "Married? Beautiful things like you should never marry. To give yourself to only one man is a sin." He sniffed around her neck like a dog acquainting itself with another. "Is the *versio vulgata* deepening your faith too?"

Elyna went to move back, but Sergeant Salvado grabbed her arm and pulled her even closer to him. She turned her head away. "Yes."

The sergeant lowered his voice. "I haven't seen your lovely face before either. I would never forget your sparkling eyes and pure unblemished skin. And to top it all off, a French accent. Oh my lord, you're proof that angels exist. God has answered my prayers and sent me an angel from heaven. You're the most beautiful and the most delicious thing I have ever seen." He glanced to the ceiling. "Thank you, God." His smiling eyes grabbed Elyna again. "Where have you been all my life? Why haven't I seen you before, my sweet, sweet lovely?"

Elyna backed away again, but Sergeant Salvado pulled her towards him. Her voice trembled. "I don't get out much. I'm devoted to God and I'm a good wife."

Sergeant Salvado pushed his thick lips to Elyna's ear and whispered, "Devoted to God, hey. Good. Then why aren't you a nun? Nuns inspire me. You'd be the most beautiful nun in the history of Christianity. We need more beautiful nuns like you."

Elyna looked nervously at Luke. "It did cross my mind once."

Luke wrung his sweaty hands. "So, Sergeant Salvado, what questions do you want to ask me? Or Constable Thomas, perhaps you would like a copy of the *versio vulgata*?"

Constable Thomas looked at Luke with a startled expression but remained silent.

Sergeant Salvado seemed oblivious to the conversation. He ripped out his baton from its scabbard on his belt and flicked his wrist to fully extend it in a snap. Then he slowly slid it up Elyna's leg, lifting her knee-length skirt. Elyna pushed her skirt down but the baton continued upwards, sliding slowly over her stomach, breast and neck. She gulped a sharp breath.

Luke's heart raced. "Stop that!"

Constable Thomas whipped out his baton to full extension and grabbed Luke around his throat. "Shut up."

Sergeant Salvado gently ran the tip of his baton over Elyna's lips. "I can show you what it would be like if you had decided to be a very good pious nun."

Elyna turned her head and the baton slid over her cheek.

Sergeant Salvador grabbed Elyna's hair and slid the baton over her chin. "Stick out your tongue."

Elyna hesitated before slowly extending her tongue.

Sergeant Salvado grinned. "Oh, it's so wet and pink. God's most beautiful creations are wet and pink." Then he gently put the end of the baton onto Elena's tongue. "Just lick the tip. Slowly."

Elyna closed her eyes, then quickly licked the tip of the baton once, before pulling her tongue back into her mouth.

Sergeant Salvado chuckled before inserting the tip of the baton into his mouth and rolling his tongue all around it. "Oh, you taste so sweet. I want to taste all of you — every single inch of you. I know you want me to slip the tip deep between ..."

Knock. Knock. Knock.

Everyone startled. Elyna backed away. Constable Thomas released Luke.

Sergeant Salvado seemed to snap out of a hypnotic trance and his body jerked. He retracted his baton in a flash and slid it back into its scabbard. "Who's that?"

Luke shook his head as he looked at Elyna with a furrowed brow. "Don't know."

Chapter 37

Luke stomped to the front door. The officers followed. To his complete surprise, Bethany stood proudly on the porch with a gregarious smile and Mary beaming beside her. But Bethany's smile vanished when she saw the officers. "Sergeant Salvado, what are you doing here?" Her eyes jumped to Constable Thomas and she blinked several times in quick succession. "Oh, and so lovely to see you again, Constable." She waved a hand across her body. "*Electus per Deus.*" Mary did the same, as did Luke and Constable Thomas. Each of them mumbled "*Electus per Deus.*"

Sergeant Salvado adjusted his cap. "Madam Ricci." He waved a hand across his body. "*Electus per Deus.* What are you doing here?"

Bethany's eyes jumped to Sergeant Salvado. "My beautiful Mary wants to improve her Latin, and this lovely young man is thinking about helping her." She smiled at Luke. "We were just passing, and Mary insisted we stop by to see if you're free tonight."

Luke smiled. "I'd love to help Mary tonight but I'm in the middle of a session with another student."

Elyna appeared at the door beside the officers and waved her hand in front of her body. "*Electus per Deus.*"

"*Electus per Deus,*" Bethany and Mary replied in unison.

Mary smiled kindly at Elyna and she reciprocated. The smile on Bethany's face vanished instantly. Her eyes traveled up and down Elyna and up again. "Oh, I see. And who's … this?"

Luke glanced at Elyna. "This is Elyna." He paused. "She's a new student of mine. After I spoke with you, I had a think about what you said and decided I can take a couple of new students. I'd be very pleased to help Mary with her Latin."

Bethany's smile slowly returned. "Oh, wonderful. So we can come back tomorrow?"

"Yes, tomorrow would be fine."

Bethany's gaze leapt to Sergeant Salvado. "And are you learning Latin too, Sergeant?"

Sergeant Salvado grimaced. "Latin? No, someone attacked His Excellency Archbishop Michael earlier today, so we're door-knocking to see if anyone saw anything."

Mary put a hand to her mouth.

Bethany gasped. "His Excellency attacked?! But why are you wasting your time talking to Luke? It's those heathen university students you should be chasing."

Sergeant Salvado pushed out his stomach and extended his double chin. "Madam Ricci, we have to find those heathen university students to speak to them, and they can live anywhere."

"Well, get on with it then and don't trouble Luke again. I don't want you interrupting him. Do you understand? What if my Mary happened to be here with him?"

Sergeant Salvado pushed out his stomach and chin as far as they would go. "Yes, Madam Ricci. We're just on our way out."

Luke smiled at Bethany, who winked at him. "Well, if you don't have any more questions, Sergeant Salvado, I'll go back to my tutoring. And I will see you tomorrow, Mary."

Mary and Bethany grinned like two Cheshire cats. Mary blinked as if in slow motion. "I'm so looking forward to it."

Chapter 38

Luke and Elyna sat down in the lounge room. He ran his hands through his hair. "Jesus. Those Morality Police officers are brutes."

Elyna plunged her hands into her laptop case. "I need a tissue desperately." She pulled out a pair of headphones, which she placed on the armrest, then a tissue. She scrubbed her tongue with the tissue, then looked at Luke. "Mary seems to be very keen on you — she's very beautiful."

Luke nodded. "She's pretty and her mother's perfecting the art of matchmaking. "

"Her mother sounds definitely French, so I guess Mary gets her accent from her."

"You don't happen to know them, do you?"

"No, but Mary looks familiar. When I first saw her, I thought she looked like someone I've seen on campus."

"If you've seen her on campus, she would have been there to protest and cause damage."

"Really? She doesn't look like someone who'd protest at universities. She looks more like a student." Elyna smiled. "Her mother's an interesting person."

"She's a bit eccentric — she has this really loud, high-pitched laugh. I nearly fell backwards the first time I heard it. Oh, that stuff about the Archbishop — that was Liz and I."

Elyna's brow wrinkled. "What?"

"I stupidly listened to my parents and went to see him, and he insisted on doing an exorcism on me. But during it, I opened my eyes and discovered him molesting Liz right in front of me. I was furious, we got into a struggle, and he tried to strangle me. Liz saved my life by hitting him with a brick."

"Well, and I thought what happened at the university was bad enough. You've had one really bad day."

"It's been quite a few bad days. I've been seriously wondering if some evil spirit has possessed me." Luke stared at the headphones. "What are those?"

Elyna glanced at the headphones. "Oh, these are interesting. We've had numerous break-ins at the university, and scientific equipment is usually stolen or damaged. But not long ago, after another break-in, instead of having equipment stolen we found these in our lab, sitting on the only table that hadn't been upturned. And there was a note, written in French. It's as if someone left it for me to find."

Luke squinted. "What did the note say?"

"Just, 'Please look after these.'"

"How strange. And you've never found out who left them there?"

Elyna shook her head. "But I'm thinking whether Mary had anything to do with it. She speaks French and now you tell me she breaks in to universities."

"But why would she leave these headphones, apparently for you?"

Luke stretched out a hand and Elyna passed the headphones to him. She shook her head. "Maybe she somehow knows the research I do — I've studied consciousness for years. My PhD focused on the effects of sound on consciousness."

"But Mary and her family are dead against anything to do with science. It doesn't quite add up."

"It just seems more than a coincidence that someone who speaks French breaks into universities, and after a break-in, I find these in my office with a note written in French."

"But Mary only met you for the first time today."

"True, but maybe she came across one of the articles I've authored."

Luke nodded. He squinted as he turned the headphones in his hands to examine them from different angles.

"Is anything wrong?"

"No, they just look interesting. I've never seen anything like these before."

"Neither had I. They're bone-conduction headphones — the sound travels though the skull rather than the ears."

Luke ran his fingers over the headband. He put an index finger on the silver circular disk on the underside of the headband. His voice trembled. "Why would Mary leave these for you?"

Elyna nodded. "Strange, isn't it? And what's amazing is that these headphones have taken our research to another level. We discovered they don't just play ordinary music but special sounds that can affect people in really beneficial ways."

Luke shook his head. "Beneficial ways?"

"Yes, we've found they help people overcome a range of psychological issues, like anxiety and depression, phobias. It's amazing."

"Wow, that's impressive."

"You're welcome to try them before I go."

"Mmm ... I don't think so."

"Have you ever tried bone-conduction headphones?"

"No. Is the quality of sound the same as standard headphones?"

"Yes, there's no difference. The sounds just reach the brain via a different pathway."

Luke stared at Elyna. He took a deep breath and looked down.

Elyna slowly stood up. "People who've used them really like them."

"I think my self-confidence has been shaken because of what's happened today."

Elyna put her hand on Luke's arm. "The Church controls people with fear. You've been smart enough to reject the Church's control. Don't allow fear to control any aspect of your life. We can only truly live when we reject fear."

Elyna's words reverberated in Luke's mind for several moments. He leaned back in the chair and sighed deeply.

Elyna held out a hand to take the headphones and Luke gave them to her. She smiled sarcastically. "If you could overcome your phobia of headphones, who knows what you'd be able to achieve in life."

Luke suppressed a smile. "Headphones phobia, hey. Do you know anyone else with that condition?"

Elyna smiled. "You're the first. But as far as I'm aware, no one has ever been killed by a pair of headphones."

Elyna put the headphones back into her laptop case. Luke stared intently at her for a long moment. He looked away, feeling the uncomfortable silence crawling all over him. He looked back at Elyna. "I'm curious about those."

"Oh." Elyna retrieved the headphones and handed them back to Luke.

Luke blushed. "If I'm the first to be killed by a pair of these, please ensure I don't have a church funeral, despite what my parents say."

Elyna giggled. "Are you sure?"

"About no church funeral?"

"No, about the headphones. You don't have to try them if you really don't want to. It's entirely your choice."

"I'm sure."

Elyna moved to Luke and gently slid the headphones carefully over his head. "Close your eyes. Take a deep breath and relax."

Luke's eyelids slid down slowly. Elyna fiddled with the compartment in the headband, and as soon as she did, a high-pitched sound filled his head. His lips tingled and every cell in his body seemed charged with low-voltage electricity. "Wow, I think I'll fall asleep any second now."

"That's okay. If you do, I'll let myself out," Elyna whispered.

Part 16

2139

Chapter 39

Marvin's body trembled as he stood in front of the house, which somehow remained largely intact. A few metal roof sheets clung to the wooden roof beams. Jagged glass, splattered with mud, dangled in several windows. Debris floated in knee-high brackish water all through the front yard, but structurally the place appeared sound. The water pulled and swirled around his legs as the current headed east, back towards the coast.

Marvin stared at the shut front door for over a minute. Then he trudged to the door and banged on it. Nothing. He tightened his fist and banged harder. "Hello! Is anybody here?!" Again no one responded.

A moment later, from inside, a female voice with a French accent called back. "Yes! Wait a moment."

Marvin put his hand to his forehead and pushed his dripping hair back.

The woman struggled to pull open the door through the water. She appeared with an apparent expression of shock, mixed with relief. Her lacerated and bruised hands and arms poked out from a drenched sleeveless pink tank top. Mud caked her black yoga pants. "Hello."

Marvin dry-swallowed.

The woman smiled warmly. She pushed back her long black hair.

Marvin searched the woman's green eyes. "I'm Marvin. I'm sorry, I'm not quite sure why I'm here. There's something about this place that made me stop." He paused for a couple of moments. "We haven't met before, have we?"

The woman grinned. "I'm not sure. Have we? I'm Lili."

"Lili?" Marvin shook his head. "Lucy's partner?"

Lili's eyes widened, flashing green beams in all directions. "Yes. Is she okay?"

Marvin looked down and his shoulders dropped. "No, I'm sorry. The tsunami swept her and her parents away. They didn't make it. I'm really sorry."

Lili put her hands to her mouth. "What? No. Are you sure?"

Marvin's heart rate increased. Heat rose to his face. "Yes. I'm really sorry, but at least you now know what happened. Maybe that's why, when I stumbled across your place, something made me stop. I can't explain it." His head dropped. "I've been told I've got psychological problems, so I was thinking I'm crazy for stopping here, but maybe I'm not."

Lili seemed to assess Marvin intently for several moments. "Come inside, or what's left of the inside. It seems the water has started receding. I managed to stack some furniture above the water, but things got quite scary for a while." She led Marvin slowly and carefully through the water down the hallway to the back room.

In the room, a bookshelf lay on its side, and on top of a large desk balanced a couple of chairs. A quantum computer laptop — no different in appearance to a thick pane of frosted glass but with luminous geometric patterns — sat on the bookshelf. A pair of headphones rested on the laptop.

When Lili reached the desk, she turned to Marvin and smiled wryly. "Sorry I can't offer you a seat."

Stony-faced, Marvin pointed to the headphones. "Lucy gave them to you, didn't she?"

Lili brushed her cheek with the back of her hand. "When did you meet Lucy?"

"Yesterday at their church, which they had turned into an evacuation center. Lucy and her parents all drowned right in front of me. I tried to help them but got swept away by the current."

Lili looked down and her head dropped. "She was special — beautiful and really very intelligent."

"Yes, she told me she did research into altering people's perceptions. It all sounds really crazy. And she said she gave you some headphones."

Lili clasped her palms together in front of her chest and inhaled deeply. She looked up at the gaping ceiling as if searching for divine inspiration. "Marvin, I think I know why you stopped at my home."

"Really?"

"I think you remember it."

Marvin frowned. "But I've not been here before. Have I?"

Lili took another deep breath. "Marvin, I'm so sorry about what you've been through. It's all been a horrible accident. But with the world teetering on what looks like total destruction, it's time I told you the truth."

Marvin's jaw tightened. "What are you talking about?"

Lili paused and stared at Marvin with unshifting eyes. She pushed wet strands of hair away from her eyes and wiped her mud-streaked face. She sighed and looked up for a moment. "I know you may not believe me, but it's important you understand that you're not crazy for stopping here."

"What do you mean? I've been diagnosed by a psychiatrist. He said I've got memories locked in my subconscious indicating I've got an identity disorder."

"Oh. That sounds serious, but you haven't got an identity disorder."

"What? How do you know that?"

"You've got memories in your subconscious and it's a good thing those memories remained in your subconscious. But those memories are not those of other identities."

"What do you mean? You've just met me and you're talking like you know more about me than the psychiatrist I saw. Who are you?"

Lili hesitated and leaned back against the desk. "I think a subconscious memory of my house and of me led you here. But

255

those memories didn't get created here. They got created ... somewhere else."

Marvin grimaced. "What? What do you mean, somewhere else? What are you talking about?"

"I know that sounds crazy to you. But you're not crazy and I'm not crazy. I'm telling you the truth."

"What's going on? None of this is making any sense to me."

"Marvin, I'm saying your subconscious memories are real, but you don't have any psychological problems." Lili raised her hands to her head for a moment, as if to secure it to her neck. "Now this is where I want you to be open-minded and listen carefully because this is where things get a little complicated."

Marvin's head and shoulders dropped and he put his hands on his hips. "Complicated! That's the understatement of the century. You don't have any idea what I've been through! I've found out my parents died in a fire that I had started, and I've been diagnosed with an identity disorder — Jesus Christ! Then I saw people drown right in front of me during the cyclone and tsunami, and I nearly drowned myself!"

Lili's eyes widened and her eyebrows shot up. "I'm so sorry, Marvin. But please listen to me. The psychiatrist's wrong. I can assure you there's nothing wrong with you. But remember you're not the only one who's suffered through all these disasters."

Something moved in the water and grabbed Marvin's attention. His head jerked and his eyes darted down. A 2-meter-long Tiger snake was swimming swiftly in his direction. He jumped back and almost fell. As the snake glided smoothly on the surface of the water towards him, Lili lunged forward and grabbed it behind its head, millimeters from Marvin's leg. The snake writhed uncontrollably in her hand as it tried to wrap itself around her arm. She casually moved to a broken window and threw it outside, where it hastily swam away. She turned to Marvin. "That's the fourth one I've found inside today —

the others were Eastern Browns. Not the first time I've saved you from a venomous snake. But I don't want to make it a habit."

Marvin took a deep breath. "Hang on. I suddenly have this really vague memory of someone ... a woman ... you ... you grabbing a snake under ... under a bridge in ... in Taiwan. I've never been to Taiwan. Is that a real memory?"

Lili nodded slowly. "Yes. When we met in Taiwan, I was Sophia and you were Choepel, the monk. Is that triggering any more memories for you?"

Marvin looked away briefly. He took a few shallow breaths. "Wait. Yes, I think so."

"But here, I'm Lili and now you're Marvin. Now do you believe me?"

Marvin threw his head back. "How is that possible?"

"There's no easy way to say this but ... all those things happened in worlds parallel to this one where you and others, including your parents and me ... where we all made different choices so we led different lives. In those other worlds, our parents chose different names for us. And in some worlds, both our parents weren't always the same people."

"But is all this connected to Lucy's research?"

"Look, I don't have time to explain things to you. You just need to understand that your awareness shifted to parallel worlds."

"*She is lying, Marvin.*"

Marvin squinted and his brow knitted tightly. "What? Parallel worlds? That can't be. That's nonsense."

Lili took a deep breath. "It's true, Marvin. The multiverse is nested within the quantum world. An infinite number of worlds exist alongside each other in the multiverse, but under normal circumstances those worlds and the people in them don't interact because they're completely hidden."

Marvin shook his head vigorously and scowled. "Traveling to parallel worlds sounds like bullshit. You're just making this up. Why?"

Lili dropped her head in her hands, then looked up. "I know it sounds bizarre but I'm telling you the truth. Look, imagine reality as a giant cosmic bubble bath where there are an infinite number of bubbles and each bubble represents an entire universe. This universe is just one of those bubbles. Your awareness has shifted from one bubble to another. Right now, your awareness and my awareness are in this universe, in a world on the brink."

Marvin shook his head again. "Why are you talking such nonsense? Who are you?"

Lili put her palms together again. "Marvin, please listen to me. The universe we're from isn't unique or some science-fiction sacred timeline. It's actually one of an infinite number of universes. There really is a multiverse." She paused. "And consciousness is the currency of the multiverse." She stared intently at Marvin for several moments. "You know, Einstein's equations supported the concept of Black Holes before they actually got discovered. Well, it was completely accidental, but you and I have discovered that parallel worlds really do exist."

"Forgive me, but I don't feel like jumping for joy and damn celebrating. I've not discovered anything. What you're saying is crazy."

"Please listen, Marvin. Look, you're a freelance writer ... a Tibetan Buddhist monk ... and a Latin tutor in those other worlds. Now you're a —"

Marvin's jaw fell. His head dropped into his hands and he fell into the water onto his knees. "— a science teacher." He paused for several long moments as dizzying, strange, and unfamiliar memories of a totally different Sydney, Taiwan, and America exploded into his mind. He took a couple of deep breaths. Tears welled in his eyes. "I'm beginning ... to remember. But the memories aren't mine, are they? That's impossible. They must be false memories. They seem real but they can't be. How can that happen? Who put them there?"

"Ebes, what's happening? Where did these memories come from?"

"We cannot trust this woman, Marvin."

"Marvin, those memories are yours, but from parallel worlds. You just led different lives in those other worlds because of the different choices you made. I could only know all that because I was there in each of those other worlds with you. I was Sophia when you were Choepel the monk, then I was Elyna when you were Luke, the Latin tutor. When we first met in Sydney, I was Justine and you were Jeremy, the freelance writer. This house is where we first met, but in a parallel world. It must have been that subconscious memory of this place that made you stop here."

A torrent of memories surged into Marvin's conscious awareness. The room seemed to swirl around him as memories flashed and subsided in a cycle of rapid, uncontrollable recall.

Lili paused, her gaze locked onto Marvin's. "Do you remember those headphones?" She pointed to the upturned bookshelf.

Marvin's gaze followed her arm as he remained silent.

"You found those headphones ... in that other world — the world where you're a freelance writer and you came to my house asking about music therapy to write an article — it was raining heavily."

Marvin looked away and his head tilted to one side. "Yes, I'm beginning to remember that. You went out of the room to get some music ... music you composed."

"That's right. How could you and I know all that if I hadn't been there with you in that parallel world? And I've been with you in all the other worlds."

"She is lying to us, Marvin. You have never been a freelance writer or a monk or a Latin tutor. It's preposterous. Her psychological problems are more severe than yours."

Marvin slowly got to his feet. "Yes, how could you know all that?"

"Right. Now do you believe me?"

Marvin stared at Lili as the gravity of what she said made his heart sink and his mind swirl. "But how ... how is it possible? Surely you need to have a spaceship or some sort of ... of vehicle — I don't know — to travel to a parallel world."

"No, your physical body didn't travel to a parallel world. It's just a shift of your conscious awareness. The binaural beats from the headphones shifted your conscious awareness to a parallel world. I suspect the sound penetrates the hypothalamus, deep in the brain, somehow altering the circadian rhythm, and how you perceive time and space." Lili inhaled deeply as the water level continued to drop rapidly. "The freelance-writer 'you,' who first found the headphones, is still living his life in that Sydney, but he doesn't have any awareness of the 'you' here, or any awareness of the other versions of 'you' in the other parallel worlds. As far as I know, only the 'you' here has access to the memories of all the other versions of 'you,' which is why you have memories of the other worlds. Now that your conscious awareness is here, I think the other versions of 'you' only know something weird happened when you put on the headphones. And they will probably rationalize it as just feeling different, and the memories of the other worlds as just being vivid dreams."

"Or that they have an identity disorder."

"Yes, or perhaps that they have an identity disorder. And I know what I'm telling you sounds crazy, but it's the truth. Look, for thousands of years people thought the Earth was the center of the universe, but that was for theological reasons. Then Copernicus discovered that the Earth, like the other planets, revolves around the Sun, so he believed the Sun was the center of the universe. That sounded crazy at the time and no one believed him. But we now know that the Sun is one of trillions of suns in the galaxy and there are trillions of galaxies, so it's not the center of the universe at all. Believing there's only one universe is like an outdated, theologically biased Earth-centric view of the universe."

A heavy silence filled the room, along with a suffocating tropical mangrove swamp stench. The water had almost completely drained from the house. A thick layer of slimy mud coated the floor, walls, and furniture.

"Marvin, we cannot trust her. She is lying. There is no evidence that parallel worlds actually exist."

"Shut up, Ebes!"

Marvin looked around the room and through the broken window to the flooded carport and alley. He looked at Lili again. "Your partner, Lucy — did she, or whoever she really is, rope you and me into all this? I remember her in Taiwan and America too, but she had different names."

"Marvin, we're running out of time."

Marvin clenched his teeth. "Answer me!"

Lili's gaze dropped, but she remained silent.

More memories flooded Marvin's mind. "But the headphones are hers — Lucy's — aren't they? She created them?"

Lili sighed in exasperation. "Marvin, please."

Marvin grabbed two handfuls of his hair. "If you're telling me the truth, why didn't you tell me all this in any of those other parallel worlds? Jesus, I can't believe I'm even asking such a question."

"You're having difficulty believing me now. Would you have believed me then?" Lili looked away. "And I didn't want to make an already traumatic situation for you even more traumatic."

"But I can vaguely remember when I first met you — when I found the headphones for the first time — you told me you're a ... a music therapist. Why would a music therapist have headphones to … to shift someone's awareness to a parallel world?"

Lili hesitated. Her eyes darted away. "We don't have time to get into all that now."

Marvin took a big step forward and almost slipped on the floor. "What? After what I've been through, I want to know everything! Not only is the world around me being destroyed but so is my mind. How can I know what's real and what's not? What's true and what's lies?"

"It's all lies, Marvin. Get out of here. Get away from her."

Lili leaned back against the desk. "Calm down, Marvin. It's too complicated to get into all of that now. The situation in this world is too precarious — we're having one disaster after another. This world could soon be totally destroyed. What's important is that your conscious awareness returns to the 'you' in the original Sydney, and these headphones will do that. Trust me."

Marvin arms jumped from his sides, and his words shot from his mouth like bullets. "Trust you!" He stiffened his jaw. "Assuming all this bullshit 'parallel world' nonsense is true, every time I put those headphones on, I went — or my awareness went — to a different parallel world. I don't know what to believe. I don't know who you really are! I don't even know who I am anymore!"

Lili crossed her arms. "Look, I'm so sorry you went through all that, but I didn't expect you to poke around in my bookshelf, and I definitely didn't expect your awareness to shift to a parallel world. All I knew at that time in the original world is that you seemed dazed when I took the headphones off your head and you couldn't explain what had happened. So, immediately after you left my place, I put the headphones on and found my awareness had shifted. That's when I realized what had happened. And as it turned out, I found myself in the same parallel world your awareness had gone to." Lili inhaled and exhaled deeply. "For our awarenesses to go to the same parallel world meant our brains are identical anatomically but, more importantly, vibrationally. The chances of that are next to zero because brains are like fingerprints. The microchip in the headphones is programmed to work with the vibrational frequency of neurons. So someone whose brain vibrates differently would end up in a completely different world if they used the headphones. So you and I are neuronal anomalies."

Marvin tried to process what Lili had said. "So are you expecting me to be happy about that?"

Lili sighed and put her hands on her hips.

Marvin dry-swallowed. "So, using the headphones, you have no way of knowing which parallel world someone goes to?"

Lili shook her head. "No, there's an infinite number of parallel worlds — you can't pick and choose something you don't even know exists."

"But you knew the original Sydney existed."

"Yes, because that's where this all started, but I didn't know about the other worlds. And I didn't know how I could return your awareness to the original Sydney. What I didn't at first realize is that I needed to incorporate GPS coordinates into the microchip algorithm in the headphones to target a location — that's why we ended up in Taiwan, then America, before I realized that. But that wasn't enough, because I later realized that each world has slightly different rotational and orbital periods — some worlds have longer days, but it turned out that each one has fewer days in a year. So that complicated things." Lili took a deep breath. "How many days are there in a year?"

Marvin hesitated for several moments. "345."

"Think about that. Does that sound strange to you?"

Marvin shook his head. "No. Everyone knows there's 345 days in a year."

Lili's head tilted slightly forward. "Are you sure about that? Why did you have to think about it before answering?"

Marvin hesitated again. "Mmm, no. Yes. Wait."

"Could there be 365 days in a year?"

Marvin frowned. "Now I'm confused."

"And how many hours does it take for the planet to complete one rotation on its axis?"

"23."

"Does that seem right? What if I said there were 24 hours in a day?"

Marvin's eyes narrowed and his breath got held up momentarily in his chest.

"And it's 2139 — sound strange?"

Marvin's face got hot as he nodded slowly.

"She's deliberately trying to confuse you, Marvin. Don't listen to her."

"This world's slightly faster orbit around the Sun makes the years shorter here, but it's actually parallel to our world even though it's technologically advanced. Well, I had to try to factor in all those rotational and orbital differences into the microchip. I've managed to reprogram it using the quantum computing technology here so that I can specifically target our original world. All you have to do is put on the headphones and your awareness will shift from this Sydney, in the midst of a climate catastrophe, to the Sydney where the world hopefully still has time to avoid this devastation."

"Do not trust her. It is impossible for our conscious awareness to shift to a parallel world using sound. She is lying."

Marvin put his hands on his hips. "Look, I'm not gullible. But let's say hypothetically that what you've told me is true, despite it sounding completely preposterous. Why haven't you already used the headphones to return to what you say is the original Sydney?"

Lili shook her head. "I want to ensure my awareness is here when you use the headphones to make sure you're alright. I planned to find you before all these disasters hit. Thankfully you've found me. After you use them, I'll use them. That's what I've done every time in those other worlds. That's why I've been following you to each parallel world. If something does go wrong and your awareness happens to go to another parallel world — which I don't expect will happen this time — well at least I'll be with you to sort things out."

"Just more lies, Marvin."

Marvin shook his head. "But why did you follow me in the first place? We had only just met when I found the headphones. I was a no one to you. Why not just leave me to be thrown into a mental health hospital in some unknown parallel world?"

Lili's voice dropped to almost a whisper. "No, I couldn't do that. I'm responsible for your awareness entering the multiverse. So it's my responsibility to make sure your awareness shifts back to where this all started. But remember, I didn't expect your awareness to go to a parallel world in the first place. When I first used the headphones, I found myself in Paris, so I quickly realized what had happened. And then I had to find out where you lived. It didn't take me long to find out you lived in a Tibetan Buddhist monastery in Taiwan."

"But how did you find that out from the other side of the world?"

"That's also complicated. We can't get into that." Lili picked up the headphones. "Please, just put them on and your awareness will be back where it should be."

"And what will happen to the 'me' here? And what about everyone else here — the injured, the homeless? They need help."

Lili's arms became animated. "The 'you' here will be able to help. Your life here will continue. You'll have to deal with all the devastation here and you'll be able to help others. But you — the freelance-writer 'you' — won't have any awareness of what happens here after your awareness shifts back. Just like the 'me' here will have to deal with the crazy situation here, but my awareness will be back in the world where your awareness will be."

"*Marvin, she is lying. She cannot be trusted. It would be unwise to put on the headphones.*"

"I still find this all really hard to believe. And Ebes is telling me not to put on the headphones."

Lili's eyebrows jumped up. "You've got a neural implant?"

Marvin touched the back of his neck with a hand as a perplexed expression covered his face. "Yes. Why are you so surprised?"

"Marvin, the AI is interfaced with your brain, so I think it could interfere with the binaural beats generated by the headphones. It may prevent your awareness from shifting to where it should go. This could be a big problem. There could be unintended consequences for you."

Marvin smiled sarcastically. "Oh, that sounds like a very convenient excuse for the headphones not to work if I put them on."

Lili lowered her voice. "I'm telling you the truth, Marvin. I honestly don't know how AI will affect the sound frequencies from the headphones." She pushed her hair back with a hand and briefly looked away. "But I guess we really don't have any option. The headphones are the only way for your awareness to shift back to where it should be. I'm just concerned the sound frequencies won't shift your awareness as I expect them to."

"*No, Marvin. She is lying. Do not use the headphones. We do not know what effect the sound frequencies will have on us.*"

"*Ebes, shut up. I'm not sure I can trust her, but how could she know things I've started to remember? And it's just a pair of headphones.*"

"*I cannot allow this, Marvin. This woman is dangerous to us.*"

Chapter 40

Marvin stepped closer to Lili. His jaw dropped and his gaze fell to his legs. *"Ebes, what's happening?"*

Lili backed away. "What are you doing?"

Marvin looked at Lili with a veil of terror masking his face. "I don't know what's happening. I haven't got control of my legs."

With his eyes glued to his legs, Marvin's arms jumped up and his hands wrapped tightly around Lili's throat. She gasped and thrust her fists into his chest. But her feet couldn't get any grip on the floor. She could barely breathe or speak. "You're ... hurting ... me. Stop. Why are ... you ... doing this?"

"I'm not doing this! I can't control my arms or legs! Ebes, what's happening?!"

"She is a threat to us, Marvin. This is what is best for us."

"Stop it, Ebes. Stop!"

Lili's eyes glazed over with fear. She kicked out and landed several blows onto Marvin's face and torso. He winced following each blow, and his head jolted from side to side, but his grip remained tight around her throat. She managed to thrust up her arms between his and broke his grip. She scrambled to get away but slipped on the floor. He took a couple of strides and lunged at her. He towered over her and pulled her up by her hair. She screamed. He again wrapped his hands tightly around her throat, and his tense fingers squeezed. Her arms and legs flayed around trying desperately to strike him, but she couldn't break free again.

Tears streamed down Marvin's face. "Stop, Ebes! I'm sorry, Lili. I'm not doing this. Please forgive me."

Marvin's grip tightened around Lili's throat. Moments later, her breathing slowed, her eyes closed, and her arms and legs became motionless.

Marvin gasped. "Lili! Lili!"

Suddenly, the house began to shake violently. Marvin's arms lifted Lili and threw her limp body like a ragdoll against the desk and bookshelf.

"We need to get out of the house, Marvin. Quickly!"

Marvin's legs began to run, but they moved too fast to get any traction on the muddy, wet floor. He slipped and fell as parts of the roof and damaged walls crashed down around him. Bricks and tiles smashed down onto his head, neck, and back. His mind swirled around and he fell to the floor. The quaking continued for over a minute. When it stopped, he struggled to his knees from under a pile of rubble. Several more layers of wet dust and ash caked his head and body. He felt the back of his neck, then stared at his blood-smeared palms and fingers. He took a shallow breath and the pain in his chest almost made him lose consciousness. He steadied himself, and his mind raced for coherence. "Lili? Are you okay?"

She didn't respond.

Marvin crawled slowly over the rubble to where he thought Lili would be. One of Lili's hands was poking up between a pile of broken bricks. Her fingers began to move slowly. He gasped. "Lili, can you hear me?"

Lili moaned with a soft, unsteady voice. "Yes."

Marvin lifted himself, winced, and clutched at his chest. "I'll try to get you out. Hang on."

Lili moaned again. "My legs are pinned ... I can't move them ... It's dark ... Where are the headphones?"

Marvin looked around the room. "I don't know."

With the little energy he had left, Marvin tried several times to lift the table-sized wall fragment that pinned Lili, but his feet repeatedly slipped in the rubble, and the stabbing pain in his chest made moving his arms difficult. "It's too heavy. I can't shift it."

As he frantically picked off small pieces of rubble strewn over the top of Lili, she suddenly screamed out. "I've found them! They're on the other side. Can you see them?"

Marvin crawled around the collapsed wall. He removed some of the broken bricks and tiles. He knelt and lowered his head near a hole in the rubble. "I think I can see your hand." He reached his hand into the hole and winced. "I can feel your arm."

Lili moaned. "I can't lift my arm. You need to reach my hand and get the headphones. Wait."

"What?"

"The AI could destroy them."

Marvin stopped moving. "Ebes, you must not destroy the headphones. Do you understand me?"

Silence filled Marvin's head.

"Ebes? Ebes?"

Marvin took a deep breath, grimaced, and clutched his chest.

After a long pause, Ebes responded in a crackling voice. *"Communication networks and satellites are failing. My systems —"*

"Ebes, you must not destroy the headphones. Do you understand?"

Marvin looked up and saw thousands of satellites burning up as they streaked in all directions through the glowing, ash-filled sky.

"Marvin, your safety and ... well-being are paramount ... We must ... be protected."

"Answer me!"

"Networks are failing ... Some systems ... will need to be shut down ... Sorry, Marvin."

Lili moaned again. "What's happening? I'm not sure how long I can hang on."

"Sorry, the AI networks are faltering, but everything should be okay. We really don't have an option if I'm to use the headphones."

"Can you reach my hand?"

Marvin pushed his hand deeper into the gap. He groaned as his chest pressed against the rubble. "I can feel your elbow." He pushed his hand further. "*Aargh*, I can feel your hand."

Lili's voice fell to a whisper. "Push a bit further. I'm holding the transducer."

Marvin yelped as he pushed his hand deeper into the rubble. "I … I think I can feel the headphones … Got 'em."

Lili sighed. "Good. I'll let go. Carefully take them out. Don't damage them … Got them?"

After a long silence, "Yes."

Suddenly, another aftershock rocked the house. The remnants of the roof crashed down around Marvin. He tried to protect himself with his free hand, but bricks and chunks of broken plaster again bashed into his head, neck, and back. The headphones slipped from his grip.

The ground kept rocking and the rubble shifted all around him for nearly a minute. Finally the rocking stopped and he lifted his head. "Jesus! Lili, are you okay?"

After a long silence, Lili's faint voice reached him. "Yes. But I don't have the headphones. Do you have them?"

Marvin pushed his hand into the gap in the rubble again and felt for the headphones. "Aargh, they fell from my hand. I can't find them."

Lili sighed. "They must be there."

Marvin swept his hand across the floor in the small cavity, but he only touched Lili's arm and wet muddy concrete. "Jesus, where are they?" He pushed his hand as far as he could. His shoulder pushed hard against the rubble. The repeated stabbing pain in his chest got worse each time he stretched. He almost blacked out. "Aargh!"

After several anxious moments, his hand suddenly stopped. "Got 'em!"

Marvin pincer-grasped the transducer. Carefully and slowly, he pulled his arm out of the rubble. He wiped the mud off the headphones and inspected them closely. "They're undamaged."

Lili sighed again. "Great. Switch them on — the switch is on the transducer. Then put them on. Quickly."

Marvin's finger trembled on the switch for a few seconds. He looked at the rubble that had buried Lili, and crouched down. "But what about you? If this crazy idea actually works, how will you return to the original Sydney?"

Lili's voice trembled. "Don't worry about me. Just switch on the headphones and put them on. You'll still be here to help me get out. Now put on the headphones."

Marvin held the headphones tightly. He lifted them close to his eyes and turned them about with his fingers to look at them from various angles. Then, unexpectedly, his arm shot away from his body and the headphones flew from his hand into a partially upright wall. The transducer shattered into several pieces and the headband snapped. Marvin's shoulders dropped. He gaped at the headphone fragments strewn across the rubble with despondent eyes. His face turned hot. "Ebes! What have you done?"

"*So … sorry … We must … protected … networks … systems … must … unable … sorry … networks … systems … unable … We …*"

Lili cried out. "What's happened to the headphones?"

Marvin held his spinning head in his hands. "Jesus Christ! Ebes has smashed them. I can't believe it. I'm so sorry."

Lili moaned. "Oh, no. Try to —"

Suddenly another aftershock — much bigger than the previous one — rocked the house violently. Marvin collapsed. The remaining walls crumbled and tumbled over him. Before he could put up his arms to protect himself, a large brick struck his neck, cracking the implant. After several seconds, the ground stopped shaking. A mountain of rubble buried

Marvin. He couldn't move. Although a large piece of wall and several snapped roof beams pressed heavily against his legs, he managed to push some of the rubble off his aching chest and pounding head, but he couldn't pull himself up. He struggled to lift his arm to his neck. A sharp piercing pain shot down his spine and through his whole body. For a brief moment he wondered if he had been struck by a bolt of lightning. Dazed, he wiped his bloodied fingers and hands on his shirt. Clouds of pulverized bricks, cement, and plaster swirled around the small cavity. He coughed and almost choked.

"*Ebes?*"

No response. He waited for a few moments.

"*Ebes?*"

The silence in his head unsettled him.

"Lili? Are you okay?"

No response.

After a long pause, Lili's faint, trembling voice broke the terrifying quiet. "Marvin, can you hear me?"

Marvin gasped and coughed. "Lili, yes. I can hear you. Are you okay?"

"Don't have much air. Can't move my … arms. Bricks … pressing on me."

"I can't get to you. I'm pinned by a wall."

"Don't know if I can make it … So sorry … We don't belong here … The headphones were our only chance … to go back … So sorry."

"No, Lili, I'm sorry. This is all my fault. If I hadn't been so damn curious, we wouldn't have ended up here … Thanks for trying to get me back home … You didn't have to … I know you've been through a lot — much more than I have."

A long silence followed.

"Lili, are you still with me?"

No response.

"Lili? Stay with me. Keep talking."

After another long silence, Lili whispered. "I often wondered … how … I would die … This isn't … a scenario … I ever imagined."

Marvin managed to lift a hand through the rubble on top of him and wiped his teary eyes. "Lili, when we met for the first time — the day I found the headphones — do you remember we talked about God?"

"Yes."

"So do you believe in God?"

In the long silence, Marvin's heart pounded and the broken remnants of the house creaked in the gentle breeze that wafted over the devastation.

Lili's breathing faltered. "The more important question is, 'What is God?' A belief … in something one … has no understanding of … is misplaced."

Marvin pondered Lili's words. "What do you mean?"

Lili coughed. Her voice fell. "For centuries, religions have spoken for God … gone to war in the name of God … persecuted in the name of God … and abused millions while hiding … behind an … opaque, sanctimonious veneer … of God." She paused. Her voice became breathless and almost inaudible. "Our spiritual nature … is knowable … if you know —"

Marvin's breathing became shallow. "Know what? Lili, are you still with me?"

He waited for a long time, but he heard only his erratic heartbeat, labored breathing, and a painful, gnawing silence.

Chapter 41

Marvin had lost track of time. After almost four days trapped in the cramped claustrophobic blackness under the rubble, drifting in and out of consciousness for brief periods, his fingers, hands, feet, and legs had become cold and numb. Whenever he regained consciousness, he called out feebly, hoping Lili would respond.

"Lili, I'm scared ... The world's messed up and I'm messed up ... My life's totally messed up ... This life and the lives in the other worlds — I've messed them all up ... And I've messed up your life too ... I'm tired ... I don't want to live ... but I'm too scared of dying ... Lili ... I know you can't hear me ... but I'm sorry ... about all that we've gone through ... it's been all my fault ... and because of me ... the headphones are destroyed ... Lili ... I'm sorry ... So sorry ... So sorry ..."

Eventually, an irrepressible fatigue gripped Marvin. He couldn't open his eyes. He felt as if his body was tumbling backwards into an eerie, infinite void. As he fell, vivid images of Lili and his parents flashed into his mind. Then a series of disjointed random memories appeared instantaneously, as if on a massive movie screen with deep space as the backdrop. He relived moments with an emotional intensity he had never experienced before. Memories of his life as a freelance writer and meeting Justine for the first time; meeting Sophia at the train station in Taiwan; secretly listening outside her room at the monastery; standing embarrassed outside Elyna's house in America after she slammed the front door in his face; sitting with her at his home when she showed him the headphones; and standing over Lili in shock after Ebes took control of his arms and she was thrown across the room.

Suddenly, the sensation of falling stopped and a vast, silent blackness engulfed him. The silence and the blackness shared a density so immutable he couldn't distinguish between the two. It disorientated him and he lost all sense of space and time. In the center of the inky blackness, a distant point of light appeared and began spinning in all directions. Golden tendrils of light sparked and shimmered. They magnetically zoomed towards him. As the light show came closer, a pleasant tactile vibration crawled through his body, or what he sensed was his body, and it sounded like the rumble of distant, rolling thunder. The sound slowly got louder and seemed to penetrate his mind like a sharp auditory sword. By the time the spinning light and its sparking tendrils completely surrounded him, the thunder had transformed into something like a squadron of screaming jets, but it didn't make him uncomfortable. Instead, it convinced him of its immense power. He mentally bounced on an auditory trampoline — the sound went left then right, right then left. Then he felt it in the back of his mind, then the front — left, front, right, back. Around and around and around. His mind spun like a top. The pace of the auditory bouncing and spinning quickened.

Then the low guttural chanting of Gyuto monks reached him, followed by high-pitched choral singing:

"Sinners Jesus will receive
Sound this word of grace to all
All who languish dead in sin
All who linger, all who fall.

"Sing it o'er and over again
Christ receiveth sinful men
Make the message clear and plain
Christ receiveth sinful men."

Loudest came the harmonious chanting of hundreds, perhaps thousands, of voices:

"Om Mani Padme Hum."
"Om Mani Padme Hum."
"Om Mani Padme Hum."

As the chanting diminished, a vortex of tiny colored lights —
hundreds, then thousands, then millions — swarmed around
him like a hive of glowing bees. In the center of the spinning
lights, the outlines of multidimensional geometrical shapes
and fractal patterns emerged slowly, then disappeared in rapid
succession. Lights began to flash all around him like stars being
born in the distant reaches of the universe. The lights blinked
and changed color — shades of yellow, blue, purple, green,
orange, and white. Then the kaleidoscope of lights began to swirl
and dance all around him in small circles that progressively
grew larger. The circles morphed into various shaped fractals,
then into elaborate geometric shapes that twirled in one way
then another. All the while, the intensity of the vibration
moving around and through him got stronger. He imagined it
magnetically sucking him into the center of his mind. Images
flashed like fireworks. They flickered on and off rapidly. He
saw his parents arguing; Elyna kneeling beside him; Sophia
slipping the headphones off his head; Justine helping him to his
feet; Archbishop Michael lying unconscious on a hospital bed;
Master Chi being interrogated by soldiers; Taiwanese shops
burning and people being dragged from their homes and killed.
The final image depicted Earth from space, but close enough to
see it shrouded in black ash clouds. Volcanoes on all continents
spewed molten lava high into the air, super cyclones raged
over several countries and oceans, and massive fires razed the
rainforests.

As the images faded, the intensity of the sound around and
in him increased. *Lili! Lili! Where am I? What's happening?*

To his surprise and amazement, a gentle, mysterious voice
began to whisper softly to him. *"Give in to the sound."*

"Lili, is that you?"

No response.

"Lucy?"

No response.

"Ebes, is that you speaking with a French accent?"

No response.

"Who are you? Where are you? Where am I?"

"There is nothing to fear." The gentleness and love permeating the voice briefly calmed and reassured him. A deep, long silence fell. *"Intention is key, not consequences."*

After another long silence, luminescent butterflies in all the countless subtle shades of a rainbow began fluttering around him, and for the first time, he began to hear and feel soothing, harmonious orchestral music. The music pulled him up through a white portal of light that emerged above him. The edges of the white tunnel began being populated with pinpricks of colored lights — hues of blue, green, yellow, purple, red, and orange swirled and danced in unison.

In the tunnel of monsoonal lights and the symphony of sound, Marvin felt himself propelled like a streaking star heading to the far reaches of the cosmos. The sound transformed into a symphonic blending of choral voices and classical instruments, some of which he could clearly discern — deep, resonating, full-bodied cellos, violins, drums, triangles, pianos, harps, and flutes. The music seemed alive — as if he, unknowingly, was playing a part in creating it.

When Marvin reached the end of the tunnel, the music went silent. A vast sea of white bubbles of brilliant white light floated around him like tiny translucent balloons. He looked about confused, waiting for something, anything, to happen. Then, from somewhere in the center of the sea of bubbles, he heard a female voice. *"Bonjour, Marvin. It's this way."*

"Lili! Is that you? ... Lucy?"

"Listen to my voice. Follow it."

"Where are you? I don't know where to go."

"Just follow my voice. You can do it."

"Please don't leave me. Please. Keep talking. Who are you?"

"Just follow my voice … Follow my voice … Follow my voice."

Marvin floated forward into the chaotic sea of bubble foam. He focused on the voice with laser-like concentration.

"Are you still there?"

"Just follow my voice."

"Please don't leave me. Keep talking to me. I'm scared."

"Courage is merely knowing how to control your fears."

"Please don't leave me."

"I won't leave you. Follow my voice … You can do it."

"Who are you? Please keep talking to me. Don't stop."

"Just follow my voice. Focus on my voice."

"What is this place?"

"Focus on my voice."

"Help me. Please don't leave me. Please."

"Just follow my voice, Jeremy."

"Please don't stop. I beg you."

As he glided through the bubbles, the voice became clearer and louder, and one bubble rapidly grew bigger and brighter.

"You're almost there, Jeremy. Focus on my voice."

In an instant, that one bubble appeared directly in front of him — an enormous swirling tunnel of light from which enchanting music emanated. He stopped, totally awestruck by the immense sound.

The voice stopped. Marvin gazed into the tunnel's uncertain depths, hypnotized by its vastness and beauty. The glorious sound vibrated all around him, and once again he felt a sense of being a part of it. As the sound got stronger and the multitude of lights more intense, he felt himself being pulled into the whirlpool at the center of the tunnel, and he knew its immense power couldn't be resisted.

Part 17

2022

Chapter 42

Beep. Beep.

Jeremy awoke startled and confused. The room seemed to be spinning around him. He sat up and squeezed the couch cushions with both hands. The spinning came to a stop. *Where am I? What time is it?*

Beep. Beep.

He picked up his mobile with a clammy, unsteady hand.

2 p.m.

Rupert.

The name triggered memories of the Asian couple and their young child, Chun, clinging desperately to the roof of their car when the tsunami hit Sydney; of a distraught Charles and his daughter, Ai, at the monastery in Taiwan; of running with Fen in his arms from the rampaging mob at Washington State University when her parents, Bart and Alison, were brutally killed. *Did those things really happen?*

Jeremy's breathing faltered. "Hi Rupert," he croaked.

"Jeremy, are you okay? I can hardly hear you. You don't sound too good."

"Lyn and Mei — they're okay? And you're okay?"

"What? Of course we're okay. Why wouldn't we be? Lyn and Mei are with me now. Did you hit the booze hard again last night?"

Jeremy took a couple of breaths. "No. I fell asleep on the lounge chair. I guess I was dreaming." He could hear a cacophony of muffled voices speaking Mandarin in the background, competing with the clattering of cutlery and crockery.

"Well, sleepy head, I just wanted to say your article on Superstrings has got the best reaction from readers for any science article we've ever published. They seem to love the crossover between cutting-edge science and ancient wisdom. Sales have gone through the roof."

Jeremy paused as he tried to make sense of the torrent of memories. "Oh, that's good."

"Good?! It's fantastic. Look, I've got to go — I'm having dim sum with Lyn and Mei, but on Friday let's discuss some ideas for more articles on quantum physics with a philosophical focus."

"Okay."

"I'll see you Friday at the usual time — don't be late because I'm taking time off to book a holiday for the family."

"Ah, where are you going?"

"Taiwan first to see Lyn's parents, then to the US — Lyn has relatives in Washington State."

"Oh. See you Friday."

Jeremy disconnected the call and sat down to process the conversation and the strange memories. His brow and palms became sweaty. He dropped his head into his hands. Memories of Ebes flashed into his mind. He felt the back of his neck fretfully. Then he remembered the earthquakes, cyclone, satellites falling out of the sky; being trapped in the dark for days under the rubble; and the headphones.

Those headphones! Are the memories real? Lili — Justine — died, didn't she? Should I try to see if she's alive? Would she remember me? Is what she said about parallel worlds true? Are the memories of her in those parallel worlds all true? I'm not crazy, am I? If I told her what I remember, would she think I'm crazy? What happened to me?

Despite the light rain, a thin smoke haze still blanketed the city from the wildfires in the Blue Mountains. They had been burning for days after summer lightning strikes, but the change in the weather had allowed firefighters to get the blazes under control. Jeremy drove past the Chinese Friendship Garden and through the city. The bridge suddenly loomed large as he drove towards it. Below him, the white-crested black water of the harbor crawled out to the horizon. When the car got onto the bridge, he sighed and smiled. He wanted to stop the car and touch its steel girders just to confirm it still existed. Then he glanced to the Opera House. Its white sails poked through the smoke haze like a graceful flotilla of boats.

After crossing the harbor, Jeremy got off the highway at the first opportunity. He then headed back south, but instead of driving over the bridge again, he took the M1 tunnel under the harbor. He grinned excitedly as he approached the tunnel for the first time in his life. He sped up when the car entered the tunnel, and the rectangular white lights on the black ceiling rushed by in dizzying streaks. He switched off the radio and remembered the majestic music that had surrounded him when he flew through the tunnel of light and sound. He wiped his welling eyes. As the light at the end of the tunnel got closer, he imagined standing on the roof of the car and holding his arms out by his side as he sped towards it. He wanted to go faster, but the flow of traffic forced him to slow down. On a high, when he exited the tunnel, he decided he needed to pay someone a visit before he went home.

Chapter 43

Jeremy admired the tall gum trees as he made his way briskly across the sprawling lush lawns to Chen-Tao's office. Before he knocked on his door, it opened unexpectedly. A young woman with straight short black hair abruptly stopped adjusting her tight skirt and gasped. Her black-eyeliner blue eyes shot open and her red lips rounded. Her pink backpack almost fell from her shoulders. Memories exploded in Jeremy's mind. In an instant, he recalled Dralha telling him about her family problems as they sat together at the monastery in Taiwan; speaking with Mary and her parents about flagellations and book-burnings in America; and talking with Lucy, then seeing her and her parents drown in the tsunami.

Jeremy gasped, then smiled. "Hi, Lucy. It's so good to see you."

"It's Evlyn." She grimaced and smiled almost simultaneously.

Jeremy's face went a deep shade of red. "Oh, sorry — Evlyn. My mind must have been elsewhere."

"Guys don't usually forget my name. I haven't forgotten yours."

Jeremy dry-swallowed hard. "I was just about to knock."

Evlyn seemed to search for something in Jeremy's eyes. "After I helped you with your article, I told my parents about you. They're really keen to meet you, especially my mum. They're quite religious, and Mum's a bit eccentric and laughs way too loud, but I think you'll like her — she's French. Let's get together again soon — that is, if you want to. It's your choice. But there's something I really want to tell you."

Jeremy stepped back to allow Evlyn to pass him. "Oh. Okay, I'd like that."

"Are you sure?"

Jeremy hesitated as his heart pounded like a hammer and blood rushed to his head. "Yes, of course."

Evlyn smiled. "At a lecture the other day, I had an interesting thought."

"Oh?"

"The consequences of our choices ripple through our lives like gravity ripples through the universe. They bring us close to some people and take us away from others."

Jeremy got lost in Evlyn's eyes and words, and a long silence followed. "That's a beautiful observation."

"I feel I can open up to you, Jeremy. I don't want to keep any secrets from you. Do you trust me?"

Jeremy hesitated momentarily. "Of course."

"Can I trust you?"

"Sure ... Aah ... I've brought a copy of the article for you and Chen-Tao."

Evlyn glanced at the magazine as Jeremy held it up, and smiled. "Thanks." Then she gently placed her soft warm palms onto his cheeks, leaned forward, and kissed him leisurely on the lips. When she finally opened her eyes, she slid the tip of her tongue first over his top lip, then his bottom lip, and leaned back. "I've got to go," she whispered. Her words sent tingles up and down Jeremy's spine. She adjusted her skirt and blouse, then turned towards the office as she lifted a pair of bone-conduction headphones from around her neck to her head. "Jeremy's here to see you."

As Evlyn pranced away, she smiled broadly and made a phone gesture to Jeremy with her hand. He stared at the headphones, puffed out his chest, and grinned.

Jeremy watched Evlyn glide down the corridor before Chen-Tao's voice grabbed his attention. "Not more fucking questions?"

Jeremy stepped into the office. "Hi, Chen-Tao. No. No more questions."

Chen-Tao lounged in his chair behind his desk. An empty glass dangled between his fingers, and a partially unbuttoned shirt looked like it needed ironing. Jeremy took a couple of steps towards the desk. A sweet, woody whiskey aroma hit him in the face.

Jeremy smiled. "I just wanted to say the article got a great response and it's boosted magazine sales." He slid the magazine onto the desk.

Chen-Tao glanced at the magazine and smiled lazily. "Great. Let's celebrate. I need a drink."

Jeremy shook his head and held up an open hand. "No, I need to get home. Thanks for your help."

"I'm sure the lovely Evlyn helped you more. Well, are we going to be fucking famous? If not, I at least want some fucking royalties."

Jeremy laughed. "I'll see what I can do." He went to leave as memories swirled in his head. Memories of fighting with Master Chi at the monastery in Taiwan; of Professor Haoyu's charred remains in the Washington State University car park; of Professor Yuhang being struck by debris, and his lifeless body being swept away by the tsunami. At the door, Jeremy stopped and turned to Chen-Tao. "Do you remember telling me about your parents?"

Chen-Tao squinted. "Yes. Why?"

"Well, what was your original face before your parents were born?"

Chen-Tao frowned.

Jeremy smiled. "You know, Chen-Tao, you would be the most despicable Nobel laureate."

Chen-Tao shook his head. "What?" Then he shrugged, grabbed a whiskey bottle from a desk drawer, and tapped at his keyboard. The sound of chanting Gyuto monks filled the office. "Just close the fucking door, so I can get some quiet time to meditate."

On his way home, Jeremy drove past the pharmacy looking for Vilis but didn't see him. A noisy media pack and several police officers milled about at the entrance to an alley nearby, not far from where he'd parked his car. He approached the pharmacist with a smile. "Have you seen the homeless guy, Vilis? I'd like to help him, so I want to give him my details."

The corners of the pharmacist's mouth curled downwards and her demeanor changed. "The police came in here this morning asking questions about him. Someone found Vilis' naked body in the alley just up the road. Apparently, he had been bashed and stabbed. It's very sad. A few business owners on the street have been threatened recently by what the police think are triad gangs, and I told the police I saw a group of what looked like thuggish Chinese men near the alley late last night when I locked up. But I didn't see Vilis anywhere."

Jeremy shoulders dropped. "Oh." He leaned on the counter as if to keep himself from falling. He dry-swallowed and wiped his filling eyes. Images flashed in his mind of Rabten's motionless body surrounded by soldiers in the courtyard of the monastery in Taiwan; of Ivo being led away in the middle of the night by the principal at the boarding school in America; and of Mikelis struggling with the tiller in the aluminum boat during the cyclone and tsunami.

The pharmacist took a deep breath and looked towards the street. "Yes, a completely harmless guy. I don't usually like homeless people hanging around here, but I will miss Vilis. I really will. He was eccentric but quite a philosopher too. All my staff are saddened by what's happened."

Chapter 44

The following afternoon, Jeremy plodded to Justine's house with his head down and both hands pushed deep into his jacket pockets. *Will she even remember me? Will she remember what I do of Taiwan, America, and the disasters in Sydney?*

On the way there, Jeremy passed Dr Mason's clinic, where he saw him hugging Gracie at the front door. She had a patch depicting the Aboriginal flag on the back pocket of her jeans. The memories that streamed through Jeremy's mind almost unbalanced him. Memories of speaking with Archbishop Michael outside the cathedral; of Archbishop Michael abusing Liz in the chapel during the exorcism; of driving with Liz to Washington State University; of saving Mavis from her flooded car during the tsunami; of meeting Dr Grenfeld at the hospital and being told he had an identity disorder; and of holding Dr Grenfeld's lifeless hand after the earthquake collapsed the building.

Jeremy steadied himself as he stopped at the gate. A "For Sale" sign hung on the white picket fence. Dr Mason looked at him and waved a hand, while holding an open Bible in the other. "Hello, Jeremy."

Jeremy waved back with a trembling hand. "Hi, Dr Mason. Are you moving your clinic?"

"I've decided to make a career change."

Jeremy titled his head to one side. "Oh."

"I'm moving back to America. I've been accepted into the Seattle University School of Theology and Ministry. I've realized the priesthood is my calling."

Jeremy's eyes narrowed. "Oh. Well, I took your advice and saw Justine, the music therapist." He looked at Gracie, who stared at him, seemingly without a hint of recognition. More memories rushed through his mind. Memories of her crying at the reception inside the clinic; of Liz's long, honey-blonde hair partly covering her hooded face as she shuffled into the chapel with head bowed and hands tightly clasped; and of her nails digging into his legs as she bent down in front of him during the exorcism.

Dr Mason smiled. "I'm glad. Has she been able to help you?"

"Yes. I'm just on my way to see her." Jeremy stared at Gracie and took a deep breath.

"Oh, Jeremy, this is one of my clients, Gracie."

Gracie looked at Dr Mason with the corners of her mouth turned down. "Now a former client."

Jeremy tilted his head forward and smiled. "Hello, Gracie. It's nice to see … meet you."

Gracie smiled. "Have we met before?"

Jeremy hesitated. "Um … not long ago, I first saw you in the waiting room. You came out just before I saw Dr Mason."

Dr Mason closed the Bible. "I'd offer you another appointment, Jeremy, but today is my last day."

Jeremy shook his head. "That's fine. Justine helped me find out what the issue was. You were right, there was a subconscious memory I had suppressed."

"Well, I'm glad she's been able to help you. It's good to see you again. You look well."

Jeremy nodded slowly. "It's good to see you again too. Good luck in America." He looked at Gracie and smiled. "So nice to … meet you, Gracie. Look after yourself."

A hesitant smile slowly crept across Gracie's lips.

Jeremy turned, and as he continued to Justine's home he wiped his teary eyes with a tissue.

Jeremy knocked tentatively on the door. He glanced at the corner of the porch ceiling. *The camera!* He knocked again, then heard footsteps rush to the door. Random memories of Sophia, Elyna, and Lili surged through his mind.

The door opened. Justine's flashing green eyes appeared. She fretfully pushed her hair away from her face. "Jeremy, this is a surprise. Why have you come here?"

Jeremy's heart thumped like a deep bass drum. "Justine, it's good to see you again." His gazed locked onto her eyes. "I'm glad you remember me." He paused. "I don't know where to begin but there's so much I want to ask you."

Justine stared intently at Jeremy for a long moment. "About the music I lent you? Oh, this isn't a good time." Her eyes darted past him towards a few parked cars that lined the street. "Come in, but you can't stay long."

Jeremy stepped tentatively into the hallway. As Justine moved to close the door, heavy hard-soled shoes rapped on the footpath. He turned as a young clean-shaven man with short black hair, and wearing a dark suit, burst through the door. Jeremy's body twitched and he had to regain his balance. Justine gasped and fell backwards against the wall. Reflexively, Jeremy caught her with both hands and she steadied herself. They both glared at the intruder with wide eyes.

The man pulled out a matte black handgun from his suit jacket and pointed it at Justine. Without taking his gaze off her or Jeremy, he shut the door with a backward flick of his leg.

"Finally got you, Justine. Hands in the air."

Justine's eyes fixed onto the man as she slowly raised her hands.

Jeremy frowned and his eyes narrowed. "What's going on? Are you a cop?"

The man's eyes jumped to Jeremy, and the gun quickly followed. "Get your hands up too."

Jeremy raised his arms slowly.

Justine flicked her head towards Jeremy. "This guy came here asking about music therapy. We've not met before. Let him go."

Jeremy looked at Justine with a quizzical stare.

The man waved the gun at Justine's face. "Well, he's going to have to be questioned too." He glanced down the hallway, then looked at the open door behind Jeremy that led to the front room. "Both of you get in there."

Jeremy turned slowly and went into the front room, followed by Justine and the man. In the bright afternoon sun streaming in from the window facing the street, a couple of large suitcases stood upright on the floor. On a desk sat two laptops on their carry cases and several mobile phones. An open laptop faced away from the door. As Jeremy lumbered further into the room and stood near Justine beside the desk, he noticed a pair of yellowish, cream-colored, bone-conduction headphones lying on the keyboard hidden behind one of the laptop screens. *The headphones!*

The man glanced around the room and smiled, while still pointing the gun at Justine. "Going somewhere, bitch? Looks like I've got you just in time."

Jeremy looked at Justine, then at the man. "Please tell me what's going on. Who are you?"

He shot a cold stare at Jeremy. "You shut up. I'll ask the questions." His wide eyes then jumped to Justine. "Where are they?"

A frown surfaced momentarily on Justine's forehead. "What are you talking about?"

"Come on, quit the games. Where are the headphones?"

Jeremy didn't move his head, but his gaze leapt to the laptop on the desk. He was about to speak but swallowed the words before they left his throat. His gaze shifted to Justine, then to the man.

Justine's arms dropped. "Are you wanting some music therapy?"

"Keep your hands up, bitch. You know what I'm talking about. Where are they?"

Justine raised her arms again. "Look, I'd be happy to talk about the headphones but first let him go."

Jeremy shook his head. "Someone please tell me what this is all about."

The man waved the gun towards Jeremy. "He probably already knows too much. Both of you are coming with me. But first give me the headphones."

Jeremy shook his head. "This is crazy! Who are you? Is this about going to parallel worlds?"

Justine shot a hard stare at Jeremy. The man waved his gun and glared at him. "Parallel worlds? Shut up! This is a national security issue. Both of you could just disappear off the face of the Earth and no one would know." He glared at Justine. "You've got some explaining to do and could spend the rest of your life in jail."

Jeremy shook his head. "A national security issue? How?"

"ASIO is how." The man's gaze didn't shift from Justine. "The headphones!"

Jeremy jerked his head to look at Justine. "You work for Australia's spy agency?"

The man's voice sounded like a feral dog barking. "No, stupid. Now shut up."

Justine's eyes darted to an antique French oak bureau, with its hinged writing flap closed, near the window behind the man. "Okay, I'll give you the headphones if you let him go."

The man smirked. "No deals. Just give me the headphones. You have three seconds before I pull the trigger and find them myself. I know they're here."

Jeremy's eyes widened. "No!" He jumped in front of Justine and put an arm behind his back to grab her. "Don't shoot her! I don't know what all this is about, but you'll have to kill me first."

Justine put a hand on Jeremy's hip. "Jeremy, don't be stupid."

Jeremy turned briefly to Justine. "She's no criminal. You've got the wrong person."

The man shook his head wearily. "Oh, quite a hero. There are bigger, very dangerous forces at play here that you'll never understand. If you really don't know who she is, let me tell you, she's the last person you want to die for."

Jeremy took a deep breath. "I don't care what you think she's done. That bullet will have to go through me first."

The man aimed the gun at Jeremy's head. "So be it. Stupidity is synonymous with false bravado. I've got no time to waste."

Justine pulled Jeremy aside and moved in front of him. "Wait. I'll give you the headphones."

The man pointed the gun at Justine's head. "No tricks!"

Justine's eyes locked onto the man's. "I'll get them for you. They're in the bureau behind you." Jeremy glanced at Justine. His brow knitted.

The man's eyes darted momentarily to one side. "No, you stay where you are." He slowly shuffled backwards without turning away from Justine. He moved into the shaft of sunshine streaming in through the window. Light glinted off the gun. He carefully backed into the bureau while still aiming his gun at her.

Jeremy glanced at Justine with narrowed eyes as he put an arm around her waist and pulled her to his body. She gripped his arm tightly and spoke in an uncharacteristically unsteady voice. "It's in the center top drawer. It's unlocked."

With his suspicious eyes fixed on Justine, the man slid his free hand across and down the bureau's writing flap before it found the top drawer. He slipped his fingers through the metal handle, then fumbled through the papers and pens inside. "Bitch, there are —"

Suddenly a low, sharp thud and whoosh pierced the air. The window shook for a fraction of a second and the lace curtain billowed violently. Instantly, the man lurched forward and dropped the gun as he fell to the floor. He lay motionless as the curtain steadied itself slowly.

Justine gripped Jeremy's arms. "Don't move."

Jeremy's jaw dropped. "What happened to him?"

Justine lowered her eyes and her voice. "He's been shot."

The man's lifeless body lay face down. A tiny wound at the base of his neck secreted a steady stream of blood. "Shot?! By whom?"

Jeremy squinted at the curtain. A small perforation midway between the curtain rod and floor looked like a peephole. His eyes widened and his head rocked back. He pushed his head forward and squinted again. A small, perfectly round hole in the window, no bigger than a small coin, allowed a gentle breeze to wave the curtain. Suddenly, a tall man in shadow raced across the footpath.

Knock. Knock.

Justine looked at Jeremy with narrowed eyes. "Wait here. But don't touch the body."

Justine opened the door and exchanged hushed words in French with the man. She closed the door before they both went into the front room. The man entered behind Justine. Jeremy's heart thumped erratically and his head rocked back. *Denis? Elias?*

The man shook his head and shot a quizzical look at Justine. "Who's this?"

Jeremy immediately recognized the man's French accent and tone of voice.

Justine sighed. "Louis, this is Jeremy. He lives nearby. He happened to come here just before the agent did."

Jeremy's face flushed. "Louis? Are the two of you married?"

Louis squinted. Justine grinned. "No, we're just colleagues." Her eyes jumped to Louis. "Great shot. Your timing was perfect."

Louis nodded, then Justine turned to Jeremy. "I knew he'd be here soon and hoped he'd see the agent through the window. Louis is one of the best snipers we have."

"Sniper?"

Justine took Jeremy's hands into hers. "Jeremy, this is all very complicated. I don't have time to explain. But if I told you what all this is about, your life would be in danger, so it's best you don't know the details. You can't mention me or anything you've seen today to anyone." Tears welled in her eyes. "I'm leaving Australia today."

"Leaving? Why?"

Justine looked at Louis. "Are the cleanup crew on their way?"

Louis nodded. "They'll be in the back alley soon."

When Justine and Louis began speaking in French, Jeremy went to the body, knelt beside it without touching it, and whispered into the man's ear. "*Om Mani Padme Hum.* Safe journey."

Louis frowned as Jeremy stepped back. "What was that about?"

"Oh, just something I learned in another life."

Justine looked at Louis. "Take the body to the back door and wait for the cleanup team."

Louis quickly dragged the body into the hallway, then to the back door.

Justine looked into Jeremy's eyes and put a finger to her lips. The back door clicked open, then shut. She inhaled deeply. "Jeremy, I shouldn't tell you this, but I work for France's General Directorate for External Security. It's the equivalent of ASIO. I need to leave Australia and won't be returning."

A lump swelled in Jeremy's throat. "You're a spy for the French Government?"

Justine nodded slowly.

"But France and Australia are allies. Why would France want to kill an Australian spy?"

"Espionage is a complicated industry. Even allies always put their own national interests ahead of any alliance, no matter how strong. Like self-interest, national interest is paramount. Our countries are still strong allies despite what's happened today. My president and our respective prime ministers will never know what's gone on here because the stakes are much greater than the fickle world of politics. Politicians come and go, and most of them are buffoons. But intelligence agencies are the constant, always working in the background and always in the national interest. They aren't elected or thrown out of office by the public."

"But what national interest is so important for our countries to be in a secret war?"

Justine shook her head. "No, it's not a war. It's just a bit of jostling for a better position. Look, you have to forget me and never mention me to anyone."

"How can I forget you or the headphones?"

Justine's eyelids came closer together. "The headphones? What do you remember about them?"

"A lot. I remember you telling me the headphones shifted my awareness to parallel worlds? And it was your voice that helped me to get back here, wasn't it?"

Justine's eyes widened and a half-smile crept across her face. "I'm so glad your awareness is back. After the AI destroyed the headphones, I didn't think either of us could ever return."

Jeremy's eyes glinted. "I must have died after you did in the rubble of … of this place, and yesterday I awoke to find my awareness back in this world. I realized what you told me about parallel worlds might actually be true. And I thought if my awareness came back here after dying, then yours could have too."

Tears filled Justine eyes. "That's right. When my awareness returned here, I thought about reprogramming the headphones, but I couldn't go back to that world because I had already died there. I feared you would be trapped there without the headphones. I've been thinking a lot about you. Then yesterday, we found out the Australian Government is after me."

"Why?"

Justine's gaze dropped. She gripped Jeremy's hands tighter. "I can't go into that. But now that you saw what happened today, I don't want you to think the French Government callously kills people. The agent's right — there are bigger forces at play. And my job is to ensure that France's national interest is always protected. But sometimes we have to make difficult choices about life and death."

Jeremy raked an unsteady hand through his moist hair. The back door creaked and Louis appeared at the entrance to the room, breathless. He looked at Justine. "We have to go. The cleanup team is almost here. The agent came here alone, but ASIO will be looking for him." He looked at Jeremy. "He's not coming with us, is he?"

Justine shook her head slowly while staring at Jeremy. Her eyes slowly welled up again. "Your life is here, Jeremy. Evlyn told me she helped you with your article and she really likes you. She's smart and gorgeous. The two of you would be a great couple. Take care. *Au revoir*."

Justine turned abruptly and slipped away. Louis grabbed Jeremy's arm, then forcefully ushered him to the front door and out of the house.

Jeremy stood on the footpath at the front gate. Louis rushed back into the house and reappeared with the suitcases. As Louis wheeled them to a sleek black car parked on the other side of the road, Jeremy gazed at the empty doorway, then at the window facing the road. Justine's dark form moved quickly about the room. He wiped his sopping palms on his pants and flicked his hair back. He stood rooted to the spot for several moments as swirling thoughts about Evlyn, Dralha, Mary, and Lucy filled his head. Then memories flashed into his mind: of

Sophia in Taiwan; of Elyna at Washington State University; of Lili during the devastating natural disasters. He inhaled deeply, then slowly turned away from the house and began plodding away when a butterfly with bright cerulean wings floated onto the gate post. He stopped, took another breath, and held out an open hand. The butterfly lifted itself off the post, and flew towards him. He expected it to land on his hand, but in midair it turned and flew away instead. For a moment, he lost sight of it, and his shoulders dropped. But a couple of moments later, as he looked into the cloudless sky, the butterfly reappeared, and in a circuitous, seemingly erratic flying pattern, it landed in the palm of his outstretched hand. Its motionless wings pointed upwards. Weightless, the butterfly appeared to look directly at him. He lifted his hand to his face and gazed deeply into its black mysterious eyes. They seemed like portals leading to the other side of the cosmos. Space seemed infinite. Time seemed to stop. The spell broke when the butterfly's wings flapped and it rose into the air. It flew around him several times before it ascended out of sight.

Jeremy looked down at the bitumen pavement, took a couple of deep breaths, turned around, and rushed back inside the house. Justine came out of the room with the laptops' straps hung over her shoulders. She patted her teary eyes with a tissue. "What are you doing? You have to get away from here."

Jeremy rested a hand softly on her arm. "I can't."

Louis returned with a bewildered look on his face. "What's going on? Justine, we have to go now."

Jeremy turned to Louis. "Can you get me a passport like you did in Taiwan?"

Louis frowned. "What are you talking about?"

Jeremy turned to Justine. "But that happened, right?"

Justine's eyes locked onto Jeremy's. "Louis, please give us a moment." Louis mumbled something inaudible in French, then went back out to the car.

Justine put her hand on Jeremy's arm. "Louis doesn't have any awareness of any of the other worlds. You and I are the only ones who used the headphones, so we're the only ones who have memories of what happened in those other worlds."

"So he doesn't know the two of you were married in America?"

Justine grinned. "No, thank goodness. I don't know what I was thinking there."

Jeremy exhaled audibly and his cheeks puffed out. "And you and Evlyn?"

Justine shook her head. "She's just a student of mine in this world — nothing more. I'm sorry you got involved in all this." She gently placed a hand on the side of Jeremy's face and smiled. "If only you hadn't been so curious."

Louis rushed back to the house and poked his head into the hallway. "Sorry, but we have to leave! Where are the headphones and the mobiles?"

Justine turned to Louis. "They're in the laptop cases." She gave him one of the laptop cases. "You take this one." She lightly tapped a concealed pocket under the flap of the laptop case she carried. "I've got the headphones with me. Give us another minute."

Louis put the laptop strap over his shoulder and turned to go back to the car. "*Merde!*"

Jeremy took Justine's hands into his own. "You followed me into all those other worlds trying to bring me back here each time by using the headphones again and again. You didn't know where you were going. That's risky and dangerous. Why do that?"

Justine's eyes lowered. "You being lost in those other worlds put you in danger. I believe I had a duty and responsibility to bring you back. But now you're back, you've got to forget me and everything you know about me."

299

"What? That's ridiculous. I can't forget you and what you did for me. And I definitely can't forget about those headphones. They're amazing — dangerous, crazy, but amazing. Following you to the other side of the world is nothing compared to you following me to unknown parallel worlds."

Louis rushed back into the room with wild eyes. Jeremy turned to him. "Can you get me a French passport?"

Louis' eyes jumped enquiringly at Justine. "It's your call. You're the boss. But we must go!"

Justine looked at Jeremy. "You don't know what you're saying and what the consequences would be."

Jeremy's gaze fell momentarily. He took a long, deep inhalation, then looked back at Justine with his head slightly bowed. "Do you remember mentioning to me the 'music of the spheres' when we first met here?"

Justine appeared perplexed. "Yes."

"Well, like the 'music of the spheres' that the planets dance to, I see our choices as the music of life to which we dance." His eyes and lips faintly narrowed. "I know exactly what my choice means."

A smile crept slowly over Justine's lips as she stared deeply into Jeremy's eyes. Then she turned to Louis and nodded. "We've got Jeremy's details on file." She glanced back at Jeremy. "I did some background checks on you after you first visited me."

Jeremy grinned.

Louis rolled his eyes and shook his head. "I'll contact the embassy. The plane's waiting for you. It will be pushing things. The embassy will balk."

Justine whipped out a phone from her laptop case, brushed Jeremy's hair back with her fingers, and took a quick photo of him. She handed the phone to Louis. "Send the photo directly to François. Tell him the passport is for project *Fréquence T*."

"Will do." Louis rushed out the front door, mumbling again.

Jeremy grimaced. "Who's François and what's project ... *Fréquence T*?"

Justine grinned. "François is the French Consular General here. He happens to also be my father." A serious look came over her face. "*Fréquence T* is a classified mission, several levels above top secret. We have to go, now."

Chapter 45

Jeremy and Justine sat in the back seat while Louis drove them to Mascot Airport. At the terminal, Louis jumped out and pulled the suitcases out of the boot as his phone rang. "*Oui … Oui.*"

Louis disconnected the call and turned to Justine as she slipped a laptop strap over her shoulder. "ASIO officers will be here soon." Justine nodded. He pecked her on each cheek and smiled. "*Au revoir.*"

Louis frantically slipped the other laptop strap over Jeremy's shoulders. "*Au revoir,* Jeremy. Your passport is on its way."

With each of them wheeling a suitcase, Justine led Jeremy through the crowded public terminal. She turned to him as they strolled past lines of passengers lining up to check in and whispered. "Don't draw any attention to us. Just walk casually."

Jeremy lowered his voice. "Shouldn't we check in?"

Justine winked at him. "We're going to. We have a separate check-in lounge."

Jeremy followed Justine down a narrow, brightly lit corridor at the far end of the terminal that led to a small lounge overlooking the runways. On the other side of the floor-to-ceiling windows stood a gleaming white Gulfstream private jet with its air steps lowered. Its engines purred. In the lounge, a tall, blonde-haired female customs officer, dressed like a flight attendant in a navy-blue suit, stood expectantly behind a circular counter. She smiled effusively through plump red lips when Justine reached the counter. "*Bonjour,* Justine."

Justine smiled and nodded coolly as she handed the woman her passport. "*Bonjour,* Katie."

The smile left Katie's face in an instant. "The plane is ready to go, but we still don't have the new passport. ASIO agents have entered the terminal."

Jeremy took Justine's hand. "Don't wait. Just go."

Justine looked into Jeremy's eyes. "I've been in tighter situations before. We'll wait. Don't panic."

Jeremy shook his head as he wiped his sweaty palms on his pants. "Don't panic? An Australian spy's been shot, ASIO agents are after you, and they're already in the airport. Don't be damn stupid. Go now while you can. They don't know me. I'll give them the slip. You —"

Unexpectedly, an elderly man ambled towards them from a service door at one end of the lounge. He whistled softly while pushing a cleaning cart. He smiled and dipped his head when he reached the counter. *"Bonjour,* Katie. *Bonjour,* Justine." He nodded at Jeremy, then took out a small stack of folded white paper serviettes from a plastic bag on his cart and handed it to Katie. "I think you're waiting for these."

Katie smiled as she took the serviettes. *"Merci,* Patrick. *Je te paie un café."*

Patrick chuckled as he turned, then casually pushed the trolley away while whistling.

Katie bobbed down and placed the serviettes under the counter. When she stood up again, she placed a serviette on the counter and slid a new passport out from under it. She then hastily stamped the two passports. Before she nonchalantly slipped a serviette into Justine's passport, she scribbled something on it. She smiled again, slid the second passport under Justine's, then handed them to her. "Enjoy your flight." She nodded to Jeremy, who frowned.

Justine opened her passport, read the writing on the serviette, and grinned. *"Merci,* Katie." She then turned to Jeremy. "We're good to go."

With suitcases in tow, Justine led Jeremy swiftly down a short flight of stairs to the apron. The afternoon heat shimmered skywards from the bitumen. It made the plane, parked only a few meters away, seem less real.

Sweat beaded at Jeremy's temples. "Katie and Patrick are spies too?"

Almost running, Justine glanced at him, smiled, and winked again.

After they both reached the top of the air steps, the gray-haired pilot closed the door electronically and smiled politely. Justine looked at him. "*Allons-y.*"

The pilot rushed to the cockpit.

Jeremy took a couple of deep breaths as he followed Justine through the brightly lit, fully equipped galley to an area that looked like a narrow luxury hotel room. The plane's engines screamed before the pilot quickly reversed and began taxiing towards the runway.

Jeremy steadied himself on his feet. Justine pushed the suitcases and laptops under a cream-colored three-seater lounge chair along one side of the cabin, then sat in one of the leather chairs on the other side.

"Get your seatbelt on. We're taking off right now."

Breathless, Jeremy fell into the chair facing Justine and buckled up. His heart thumped almost out of his chest. Sunlight streamed in through the large oval windows. He turned to look back at the terminal. As a group of half a dozen suited men and Katie burst through the terminal door and raced down the stairs to the apron, the plane made it to the top of the runway. The group stood on the apron like statues as the plane's engines roared, before it raced down the runway and lifted high into the darkening sky.

Jeremy exhaled and pushed back into his chair. "We've made it."

Justine smiled coyly. "We still need to get into international airspace to be safe." She unbuckled her seatbelt and moved to the galley. "Would you like a cold drink?"

Jeremy unbuckled and sat on the lounge chair on the other side of the cabin. "Thanks — just a juice would be good."

Justine opened the fridge door. "Good, that's my preference too." She handed Jeremy a tall cold glass of apple juice and sat beside him.

Jeremy took a long sip and leaned back. "Some plane — I assume it's owned by the French Government?"

Justine smiled. "It's actually owned by a company, but the company is financed by the French Government. I chair the company's board."

Jeremy shook his head. "Wow. You're a walking bundle of surprises. What does the company do?"

Justine put a hand on Jeremy's arm. "It makes headphones."

Jeremy sniggered. "I should've guessed."

Jeremy glanced out the window behind him. The Harbour Bridge and Opera House receded quickly behind the lengthening teal ribbon of ocean. "So, why is ASIO so desperate to get them?"

Justine glanced at the closed cockpit door and dropped her voice. She hesitated. Her eyes fixed onto Jeremy's. "In 2016, another company, majority-owned by the French Government, entered into a multibillion-euro contract to help the Australian Government locally build our attack submarines. We considered it the contract of the century."

"And those submarines were to be nuclear powered?"

"No, ours are, but under the contract, the submarines that would have been built in Australia wouldn't be." Her head briefly turned to the window. "Well, I'm sure you know that in 2021 the Australian Government totally blindsided us and canceled that contract because it entered into the AUKUS alliance with the US and the UK."

"That's the security pact for the Indo-Pacific to combat the threat of China?"

"Yes. And under AUKUS, America and Britain will share nuclear-propulsion technology with Australia to build nuclear-powered submarines. We felt Australia had stabbed us in the back. My president was shocked and very angry. I was called back to Paris to meet with the head of the General Directorate for External Security because I'm the lead spy in Australia. He asked me what could be done to get Australia to reverse its decision. I told him nothing could be done diplomatically, but scientifically there might be a possibility." She hesitated and lowered her voice further. "Now, what I'm about to tell you is well above top secret."

Jeremy rested his hand on Justine's thigh. "Okay."

"Well, the head of the General Directorate for External Security knew I was already doing research into the effects of binaural sound frequencies on consciousness based on the work of Dr Alfred Tomatis, a brilliant Frenchman whom many considered the 'Einstein of sound.' I explained that I believed it could be possible to shift a person's conscious awareness back in time just before the secret negotiations between Australia, Britain and the US began on the AUKUS alliance."

Jeremy shook his head. "Time travel?"

Justine's eyes narrowed. "Yes, time travel. Hence, I named the project *Fréquence T.*"

"Is Evlyn involved in any of this?"

Justine grinned. "No."

"But time travel is impossible, isn't it?"

Justine shook her head. "No, quantum physics has shown that not only does the past influence the *now* but so does the future, because the illusory arrow of linear time can point in both directions. So, if we can stop AUKUS being established, or even better, be a part of it, we'll stop our submarine contract with Australia from being canceled. But somehow ASIO found out about what we're trying to do."

"Wow!" Jeremy threw his head back. "I'm not sure I can handle any more surprises about you." He looked up. "But why would the French Government be prepared to go to such lengths to stop or reshape the AUKUS alliance — is it just about the enormous sum of money at stake?"

Justine shook her head. "No, money is not the only issue. The submarine contract supported our geopolitical goals on Australia's doorstep in the Indo-Pacific — we have around two million French citizens living in our territories there. And also, the AUKUS alliance is essentially about preparing for future wars by sharing information on artificial intelligence and quantum technologies. The French Government is heavily invested in those technologies. Getting access to that information would be a gold mine."

"So, the plan's been approved?"

Justine put a hand on Jeremy's thigh and smiled. "Yes, and I've all the money I need. After all, billions are at stake."

"But it hasn't worked, has it?"

Justine grinned. "Not yet."

"So you still think it's possible to travel back in time?"

"Of course. The quantum physics principle called 'superposition' shows that time can travel both forwards and backwards."

Jeremy frowned. "Superposition?"

"Superposition is just where a single particle can exist in two or more states at the same time. The knowledge I've gained about AI and quantum computing from the parallel world we were last in has made me look at time travel differently."

"Okay. But when did you discover that the headphones didn't result in someone traveling *back* in time?"

"When you found the headphones in my bookshelf and put them on. I had planned to test them for the first time when you knocked on my door. That day, I realized it did shift a person's conscious awareness — not back or forwards in time, but into the multiverse. So, although it didn't work as I intended, I know I'm close to succeeding."

"So in a way, I unknowingly helped by testing the headphones for you."

Justine grinned. "Yes, I guess you did. But given what subsequently transpired in those parallel worlds, I don't think I feel I should thank you."

Jeremy smiled as sunlight glinted in Justine's eyes and on her lips. "Well, I have to thank you for everything you did for me. And especially for guiding me back to this world. You're the most intelligent and courageous woman I've met — not just in this world but in the multiverse too."

Justine laughed. "But you've only been to three parallel worlds — there's an infinite number of them."

Jeremy leaned back with a broad smile on his face and remained silent for several moments. "Oh, at the airport, what did Katie write on the serviette?"

Justine briefly looked down, then turned to Jeremy. "She thinks you're very handsome."

Jeremy blushed. "Hah! And what do you think?"

As the sun sank below the horizon, the nose of the plane smoothly lifted, taking it to a higher altitude on its way to New Caledonia. A half-smile crept slowly across Justine's mouth. "Well, we both know it's just a physical body."

Jeremy grinned and lifted his glass towards Justine. "Here's to our neural anomalies."

Justine's smile broadened, and her eyes narrowed as she gently touched the lip of her glass to his.

Acknowledgments

I must acknowledge the insightful feedback on the manuscript from Peter Ramshaw, who was the first editor to actually understand the story and see its potential. Many of his ideas made the story much better. And I cannot forget author and public speaker John Harman, who kindly recommended Peter to me. I must also thank my parents for supporting me when I decided to write my first nonfiction book, *The Audible Life Stream*, shortly after I returned to Australia after backpacking overseas for three transformative years. Without their support and their decision to buy my first computer (without any prompting from me), my writing career might never have started. Finally, I must acknowledge Ms McKenna, my North American English teacher in high school, who no doubt planted a creative seed in me when she gave the class the task of writing a novel. I think it was a year-long project, and it was the first time I attempted writing long fiction. Without having that experience and Ms McKenna's encouragement for that science-fiction story (which I hasten to add has no resemblance to this story), I'm not sure this book would have ever come to fruition.

ROUNDFIRE
BOOKS

FICTION

Put simply, we publish great stories. Whether it's literary or popular, a gentle tale or a pulsating thriller, the connecting theme in all Roundfire fiction titles is that once you pick them up you won't want to put them down.
If you have enjoyed this book, why not tell other readers by posting a review on your preferred book site.

The Cause
Roderick Vincent
The second American Revolution will be a
fire lit from an internal spark.
Paperback: 978-1-78279-763-0 ebook: 978-1-78279-762-3

Don't Drink and Fly
The Story of Bernice O'Hanlon: Part One
Cathie Devitt
Bernice is a witch living in Glasgow. She loses her way
in her life and wanders off the beaten track looking for the
garden of enlightenment.
Paperback: 978-1-78279-016-7 ebook: 978-1-78279-015-0

Gag
Melissa Unger
One rainy afternoon in a Brooklyn diner, Peter Howland
punctures an egg with his fork. Repulsed, Peter pushes
the plate away and never eats again.
Paperback: 978-1-78279-564-3 ebook: 978-1-78279-563-6

The Master Yeshua
The Undiscovered Gospel of Joseph
Joyce Luck
Jesus is not who you think he is. The year is 75 CE. Joseph
ben Jude is frail and ailing, but he has a prophecy to fulfil …
Paperback: 978-1-78279-974-0 ebook: 978-1-78279-975-7

On the Far Side, There's a Boy
Paula Coston
Martine Haslett, a thirty-something 1980s woman, plays hard on the fringes of the London drag club scene until one night which prompts her to sign up to a charity. She writes to a young Sri Lankan boy, with consequences far and long.
Paperback: 978-1-78279-574-2 ebook: 978-1-78279-573-5

Tuareg
Alberto Vazquez-Figueroa
With over 5 million copies sold worldwide, *Tuareg* is a classic adventure story from bestselling author Alberto Vazquez-Figueroa, about honour, revenge and a clash of cultures.
Paperback: 978-1-84694-192-4

Readers of ebooks can buy or view any of these bestsellers by clicking on the live link in the title. Most titles are published in paperback and as an ebook. Paperbacks are available in traditional bookshops. Both print and ebook formats are available online.

Find more titles and sign up to our readers' newsletter at www.collectiveinkbooks.com/fiction